one
of the
good
guys

ARAMINTA HALL

one of the good guys

GILLIAN FLYNN BOOKS

A **zando** IMPRINT

NEW YORK

zando

Copyright © 2024 by Araminta Hall

Gillian Flynn Books is an imprint of Zando.
zandoprojects.com

First Edition: January 2024

Text design by Aubrey Khan, Neuwirth & Associates, Inc.
Cover design by Julianna Lee
Cover photograph © Peter Cade | Getty Images

The publisher does not have control over and is not responsible for author or other third-party websites (or their content).

Library of Congress Control Number: 2023933798

978-1-63893-155-3 (Hardcover)
978-1-63893-095-2 (ebook)

10 9 8 7 6 5 4 3 2 1
Manufactured in the United States of America

To Oscar, Violet, & Edith

one
of the
good
guys

INSTAGRAM

 WALK FOR WOMEN @walkforwomen
And we're off!

Setting off today from Land's End and aiming to reach Margate sometime in mid-January. Our plan is to walk the whole South Coast, averaging around ten miles a day. We're carrying everything we need for the month on our backs and wild camping along the way. Please come out and support us if you can. Let's get our voices heard!

Because if we don't start talking about it, nothing's going to change. And things have to change.

In the past twelve months, four of our friends have had their drinks spiked in a nightclub, nine have been called whores for refusing advances from drunk men, eighteen have been touched inappropriately, thirty-four have been catcalled in the street, forty-one have received unrequested sexually explicit photos in their DMs, fifty-three have had abusive or sexual comments posted on their social media feeds by men they don't know, and absolutely every woman we know has felt unsafe or uncomfortable in at least one situation when she was out alone. One friend has had to report an ex-boyfriend to the police for harassment because he couldn't accept that she didn't want to be with him, and, tragically, in a terrible manifestation of all these threats, one friend was raped by a man she went home with after a night out.

We're raising money for Safe Space UK, a charity that helps women put their lives back together after experiencing acts of violence or coercion because we recognize that, even with all the things that have happened to us and to our friends, we're still the lucky ones. We're not one of the 1,500 women murdered each year in the UK, around two a week killed in their own homes by their partners. And we don't have to navigate our days around a violent man or try to keep our sanity as someone manipulates how we think. But way too many women do. Because for all those who die, there are thousands of others living in fear all day, every day.

Please follow our progress here, on Twitter, and locationtracker.com, or donate on our JustGiving page @walkforwomen.

Peace, Moll & Pheebs

[ID: Two women wearing backpacks]

(likes 56)

MANINTHEWILD

stupid bitches. Hope you get raped on your stupid walk.

(likes 3)

one

I moved to get away, which is probably the reason anyone makes a significant life change. And my need to get away wasn't particularly special either. Very simply, I was trying to outrun the pain that had engulfed me since my marriage fell apart and my heart felt like it had been removed from my body and stamped on, so it was nothing more than a few interconnected tissues.

My new home was on a remote stretch of coast in the South of England and it's no exaggeration to say that I felt an almost instant sensation of calm when I stepped out of my rental van on that first day in early October, the air still warm with the last of the summer, golden sun lingering in the fields, and birds chirping in the branches overhead. I stretched my arms out wide and gulped down a few deep breaths, imagining the air's passage through my blood like I'd learned when online yoga sessions had been the only thing to get me out of bed in the morning.

That first week I hardly ventured farther than my garden gate, which meant I didn't speak to anyone because my cottage sits entirely on its own at the end of a river that leads down to the sea. It's near The Wildlife Hut, where my new job was based, so I caught glimpses of people passing along the lane, but nothing more. I had meant to pop over and say hi to Holly, my new boss, but it took much longer than I'd anticipated to get the cottage straight. I'm not the sort of person who's happy to drop things where they fall or leave a ring around the bath or let the bin overflow, so I was never going to keep my possessions molding in boxes. I was always the tidy one in our marriage—emptying the dishwasher, sweeping dust from the shelves, picking dirty clothes off the floor, hanging up wet towels left on the bed.

The evening before I was due to start my new job, I walked down to the beach as a reward for all my hard work. I'd caught tantalizing glimpses of the countryside as I went about my domestic jobs, the high majestic hills and the glinting curve of river. And I don't mind admitting that it filled me with a real sense of pride, the realization that I'd made a change for my own benefit after years of never putting myself first. The sun was just dipping down as I left my cottage, casting the sky in a beautiful hue of pinky purple, a flock of geese silhouetted against it in a raggedy V, the air fresh with the sharp tang of salt. I reached the beach in about fifteen minutes and sat on the warm shingles, filling my lungs with the cleansing air.

I'd be lying if I said I wasn't feeling scared or sad sitting there. I couldn't not. I'd just left behind everyone and everything I knew to start again, which is a terrifying prospect even when it's what you want. Or maybe, in my case, it would be more accurate to say what I needed. Before I left London, people had started to feel overwhelmingly messy and the idea of being alone for a bit, of reconnecting with myself, felt pretty imperative. But the landscape was ridiculously romantic, and that evening I found it impossible not to associate it with Mel and feel her absence like a missing limb. I let myself wallow, which is something I'd promised myself I would stop doing after the move. But my wife is a conundrum that I'm not sure I'm ever going to be able to solve. I have, quite simply, never been as sad or lonely as she made me feel at the end, although I find that thought hard to reconcile with all the things I know were great about our relationship, and all the ways I loved her.

We met on a dating app, swiping left and right until we matched. And even though that sounds soulless, we both knew immediately that we'd found our person. In fact, on our very first date we both deleted the app in front of each other. Maybe we rushed into it? It's something I worry about quite a bit, as we were both thirty-six and shared a sense that time was ticking. Five months later we'd moved in together and six months after that we were married. We didn't start trying for a baby right away because Mel had just started a new business, but we talked about our family from the beginning, so I never imagined it wouldn't happen.

She went off the pill about eighteen months after our wedding. Mel's business was pretty successful by then, so we agreed that I would be the main caregiver when the baby came. I would lie awake at night fantasizing about pushing our child's stroller through the park, mashing bananas for first tastes, holding chubby hands for first steps, marveling over first words. I saw myself recording those moments and sending them to Mel, who'd glance at the buzzing messages in the middle of her meetings and smile.

In those early, heady days of trying, we talked endlessly about selling our flat, which we both loved but was too small for a family. I'd spent months renovating it when we moved in and it really was beautiful, but it was up four flights of stairs and had just a balcony for outside space. We looked online at houses with gardens, and I thought about the swing set I'd build and the barbecues I'd cook on weekends.

But we couldn't get pregnant and all too quickly we were both about to turn forty, so we decided to try IVF. Mel insisted on going private, because the NHS waiting times were awful in our postcode. It's not an easy procedure and Mel was a superstar, but still the first and second rounds failed. After the first failure, I started doing lots of research and, from everything I read, it soon became obvious that we both needed to slow down to give it the best chance of working—which sparked the idea about moving to the country. The more I thought about it, the more vital it seemed. London had already started to seem so busy and polluted and fast that I couldn't imagine bringing up our children there, with all its failing schools and drug gangs.

I was also worried about Mel, who seemed constantly stressed and pulled in so many different directions with her business. I didn't want her to have to live like that, or to sacrifice her relationship with our children just so we could live in a house that cost as much as an entire street in other parts of the country. Material wealth has never mattered to me, and I had lots of ideas for businesses we could start instead that wouldn't make us rich but would give us more time together. Mel seemed interested, she even seemed keen, but nothing ever changed. In fact, if anything, she sped up after the second failure, always working or going out with clients, always letting the stress get to her, always exhausted.

The months before we started the third round were pretty dire, and I felt about as alone as I ever have. It was a bit like being back at school, when I'd been at a remove from all the other boys who seemed to understand the rules of life in ways I didn't and who clearly disliked me for not wanting to scream and rampage. I tried everything I could think of to make things easier for Mel, but she withdrew further and further, never properly communicating with me. I wish she'd articulated how she was feeling during that time, but she's too proud and puts up a front like a suit of armor. Not that I blame her for that. Being a successful woman and building your own business means you have to be twice as hard as any man, which is ridiculous but true.

I only wish she hadn't lumped me in with all that and remembered I wasn't the enemy. She was so mean to me in the end, so spiteful and hurtful, I sometimes thought she had confused me with someone else. Sometimes my heart feels so broken I have to stand very still or I'll disintegrate into the million pieces she made of me. Sometimes, I almost feel scared of her, like she would do me harm if she could.

The first few weeks after moving passed in a blur, mainly spent getting used to my new job as a wildlife ranger, which was so different from my old desk-based office job and took up pretty much all my attention. I never fit into the alpha male office culture thing. The banter, as people like to call it. The nudges and winks and raised eyebrows. By the end I was so desperate to leave, I could feel the office on my skin even when I wasn't there, like slime. Being outside all day was the tonic I needed. The landscape and grandeur of the sea were totally awe-inspiring, both changing so continually, every iteration like a painting by an old master. I started to feel more connected to the land than I'd even dared to anticipate and awoke every day actually looking forward to going into work, which was a unique sensation for me.

As a reward for getting through the past couple of years, I started doing something that was just for me. I started swimming in the sea every morning before dawn, even as the calendar turned and autumn, then winter, set in. It was something I'd been researching for a while before I moved, and I was particularly interested in the benefits it gave to the nervous system. Still, actually doing it came as a surprise because it's not easy, forcing your body into cold, wild water. But my god, I'm glad I found the strength because it feels amazing being in the sea at that time of day, encased by the freezing, antioxidant waves when I wouldn't have even thought myself capable of it a year ago. It gives you a real clarity of mind, cold like that. And, of course, the mental strength from overcoming fear is incredible.

There is only one man-made structure on our coastline, an old coast-guard cottage that sits on the edge of the cliff, right above my nearest beach, about a fifteen-minute walk from my house. I'd known about the cottage before I moved because I'd studied the ordinance survey map and it had caught my eye, so I'd googled it and read its romantic backstory about a faded profession and crumbling cliff. But until I saw it in the flesh, I hadn't appreciated how precariously on the edge it was and I certainly hadn't considered that anyone lived in it.

A few weeks into my new life, I was on the path that leads right past its gate and looked over at the rickety clapboard structure, its white paint peeling and its small windows dancing in the light from the low sun and was surprised to see a woman in the front garden. She was bending over a pot, wearing wellies on her feet and a thick cardigan over a long cotton dress imprinted with little flowers. The sight was so wholesome and bucolic it brought me up short. In moving I'd sworn off all forms of materialism, but if they bottled and sold the swelling feeling of contentment I got as I stood at that gate, I'd be first in line with my cash. I only let myself linger for a moment, though, walking on before she saw me. I'd already noticed how walkers often stopped and took photographs there, which seemed like an invasion of privacy I had no intention of being part of now that I knew it was someone's home.

But after that, wherever I was on the hills or beach, I found myself always aware of the cottage, like a beat in my blood. Often I'd see smoke trailing from the chimney and get a rush of coziness, thinking about the woman who lived there going about her day. I couldn't help quickly glancing in whenever I passed, and sometimes I'd catch sight of her, puttering in the garden or reading in the sitting room. Over the weeks I never saw a sign of anyone else there, which made me think that she lived alone.

I reckon mid-December was when I started to think about this new life as my actual life, rather than some elaborate role-play. And around that time I got a late-afternoon call reporting a sheep trapped in some barbed wire. I trudged over to the coordinates I'd been sent and sure enough there was a ewe, her thick coat completely entangled. She'd clearly wrapped herself tighter against the wire in her distress, and now she was sagging limply, making sad plaintiff moans into the dusky air. She tensed when I approached, but I was gentle, handling her body with such care that she soon came to trust me. I eased her away from the spikes, managing to only nick her skin once, a drop of bright blood blooming on her dirty white coat. By the time I got her free, she was calm and even seemed grateful. I stroked her funny sharp face and she pushed against my hand, making me smile.

"Off you go, now," I said, nudging her rump, but still she hesitated for a few moments before running off to her flock.

As we were approaching winter, the darkness had fallen completely by then, so I lost sight of the sheep pretty quickly. I love that time of year when the night is king. It feels so cozy and exciting, like there's magic in the air and anything's possible. And in the country the darkness is so much more absolute than it is in a big city. But, that evening, a flash of light caught my eye down the hill, which I knew must be the glow from the coast-guard cottage.

Since it was easier and safer to get home via the path that ran by the cottage, rather than cut across the field to the beach, I glanced into the lighted sitting room window as I passed and was met with an absurdly charming and homey scene. Fairy lights glinted along the mantelpiece and the fire glowed orange in the hearth. The chairs and sofa sagged with comfort, and the walls emanated a golden warmth. Small lamps sat on wonky tables and a mirror reflected the lights so they seemed to bounce and move. A large shrouded canvas on a wooden easel sat in the corner of the room, which made me smile. Painting seemed like a perfect hobby for the woman, perhaps it was even how she earned a living, selling the odd piece at quaint local galleries and craft fairs.

The woman came into the room and I shrank back into the night. She went over to a table by the fireplace and fiddled around with a speaker until I heard the beat of music filtering through the glass. She was wearing a russet-colored dress with buttons down the front, with bright yellow tights and thick socks. Her hair was piled on top of her head and the wavy tendrils that had escaped made her face look like it had a frame. Her cheeks were rosy from the heat and her lips were moving as though she was singing along to the tune. She started to dance, throwing her hands above her head with abandon, which made her dress catch on her hips. The sturdiness of her body sparked such joy in me; it was so soft and undulating, so different from Mel's sharp lines.

Mainly, though, I was impressed by how comfortable she seemed in her own skin, how grounded and solid. It had been a long time since I'd seen a woman look like that, and it made me feel sad about the pressures we put on women and girls nowadays to shrink themselves down and conform to male ideals. If I ever have a daughter, that's one thing I'll be sure to teach her—not to get distracted, and to let her body find its own shape.

I had to look away for a moment to stop myself from tearing up. Because, even though I had sort of settled into this new life, looking at the woman made me realize that I was lonely. It wasn't that I wanted another relationship, but I did miss the companionship of marriage. That lovely ease of coming home and knowing someone was going to be there, that conversations were waiting to be had, that suppers would be shared. Not, of course, that Mel and I had done much of that in the last year or so before the breakup.

I forced myself to walk on because even though the countryside was deserted and there was no one to witness me watching, the moment was private. Besides, I would have hated for the woman to catch sight of me and feel scared. Mel loves those shows in which beautiful women end up ugly dead. Sometimes she'd ask me to sit with her, curled up warm and cozy on the sofa, but I didn't see how anyone could enjoy watching shit like that when you can turn on the news to see it all being played out in real life.

I carried on my descent to the beach along the coastal path, the space beside me like a huge empty void. I am fascinated by the coastline and can't imagine a day when that feeling will ever leave me. Because it isn't what I expected. Before I moved, I hadn't appreciated how the land does literally just stop, and not even in a neat way, but in a jagged mess, as if even nature is as confused by how to end things as the rest of us. The path is about three feet away from the edge and marked by a loose line of string, along which there are a few macabre notices proclaiming danger. Erosion is very bad on this section of coast and the cliffs are very high, veering down toward either rocky beaches when the tide is out or wild seas when it's in. It's really stupid to step over the barrier onto the part of the cliff that will be the next to fall, but that evening, I felt drawn to the edge in a way that's hard to explain. I knew I was being insane because it's actually part of my job to stop the teenagers who come here from sitting on the edge to take ridiculous photographs. But, in the end, I couldn't resist and stepped across, feeling more invigorated with every step, until I was standing with my feet clipping the nothing at the edge of the world.

The night was bitterly cold and the salt-saturated wind was whipping off the sea and churning the clouds so the moon was hazy. I could hear the waves slamming into the bottom of the cliff, so I knew the beach was temporarily swallowed. My heart was high in my throat as I looked out into the blackness, broken only occasionally by the white tips of waves. It should have been an invigorating moment, but the loneliness I'd just felt was nagging at my back, threatening to follow me home. I took a deep breath and forced myself to focus on the positives, and, when I did that, I was able to see that although Mel was still a shard of glass in my heart, it didn't feel as ripped and raw as it had a few months earlier. I was in fact physically healthier all round: my breath ran smoother, my eyes were clearer, my digestion calm, and long-forgotten muscles were starting to push through my skin.

I thought about the woman dancing in her cozy home, and it made me smile. Perhaps her happiness could be infectious? Next time I saw her out on the cliffs I decided I would nod, maybe say hello. I liked the idea of being part of the community, becoming a local. Not that I wanted a *Cheers* "everybody knows your name" level of intimacy, but I wouldn't mind feeling properly part of something after a lifetime of feeling as if I were on the margins.

The woman seemed so completely part of the landscape I felt sure she'd always been there, perhaps even descended from a line of coast guards, brought up in the cottage with the whole of nature always on her doorstep. Perhaps she'd learned to swim with the seals and picked wildflowers and eaten the blackberries on the path to the farm. I began to wonder if it was possible that, having spent so much time surrounded by nature, she knew a secret denied to the rest of us. A secret that could help me become the person I so desperately wanted to be. Maybe, if I got to know her, I could ask her how she lived so serenely. I doubted the first thing she did in the morning was scan her brain for signs of cracks and I longed to reach that state of equilibrium.

I hadn't known anything about the Christmas party until I came into work the next morning to find Holly pinning up a list of jobs on the notice board. Her usual high color was even brighter than normal as she told me excitedly that it was my job to collect the kegs of beer donated by the local pub every year. Holly's job was to get some holly, which it also was every year.

"It's fun," she said, which made me realize my embarrassment must be showing. "A local band plays and we make the Hut look all festive. Everyone who's mad enough to live round here is invited."

"I'm not sure," I said. "Although of course, I'll pick up the beer."

She pushed me on the arm. "Come on, Cole. You've been here three months and I've never even seen you in the pub. It'd do you good to meet a few of the locals. We don't bite, you know."

I could tell that I had to go and reasoned that it would probably be very different to the Christmas parties I so hated at my old job, which were usually lost in white powder and rounds of shots chased with endless days of regret.

"Also, when you're out and about over the next few days, can you check the barriers all have the appropriate warning signs on them?" Holly said. "Those Walk for Women girls are due to pass quite soon and word is they're attracting a few fans."

I was lost. "Walk for Women girls?"

Holly laughed, "Really, Cole? Come on. Don't tell me you haven't heard about them. They're all over socials."

"I don't have social media."

Holly's eyes widened in the way I'd become used to. "Wow, okay. Well, these two girls are walking the South Coast to raise money for some sort of domestic abuse charity, I think it is. And in some places people have been coming out and cheering them on along the route."

"Right, okay. And they're going to pass by here?" My neck felt tight, so I stretched it from left to right.

"Yeah. In the next few days. To be fair, they're more likely to get a reception somewhere a bit more populated. But better safe than sorry and all that."

As soon as Holly had gone, I googled Walk for Women and, within seconds, found links to various articles and posts which told me that Molly Patterson and Phoebe Canton, both aged twenty-three, were indeed walking the South Coast to raise money for a domestic abuse charity called Safe Space UK.

On one post they'd written,

Our mothers and grandmothers did such a fantastic job of changing things, but they made the mistake of trying to start a conversation with the men in power. But that was never going to work because why would they want to give up their privilege. We have to do this for ourselves now, in a different way. It's up to us to make as much noise as possible to get this conversation on the national agenda.

Their posts made me feel sad, like that hollowness you can get after a bad argument. Of course, I didn't disagree with what they were saying, you'd have to be a Neanderthal to do that, but they reminded me that we live in such a polarized society. I know it's a terrible cliché to say "not all men," but also, genuinely, not all men. In that moment I missed my wife and wanted everything to be less complicated.

Stupid though it sounds now, it never even occurred to me that the woman from the cottage might be at the Christmas party. I'd seen her a few times in the week leading up to the event, through her windows, and once on the beach, where we'd sort of nodded at each other.

When I arrived, she was talking to Holly, who waved me over. I felt oddly nervous as I slowly made my way through the throng of people, squeezing between sweaty bodies. The woman was wearing a pair of worn jeans and a bright shirt that tied up in a bow on her shoulder. Her hair was pulled tight against her head, and there were large golden hoops hanging from her ears. She'd also painted her lips a bright red, which unnerved me. I mean each to their own, but I've never been a fan of makeup. I once said to Mel that I thought she looked better without it, which I meant as a genuine compliment, but it didn't go over well. She threw her hairbrush at me, and I had to lie to everyone and say I'd walked into a door.

"Cole," Holly slurred. "You've got to meet Lennie. She's new here as well."

"Hi," the woman said, holding out her hand. "Nice to meet a fellow newbie." She had a harsh accent, with letters that faded from the ends of words. It sounded like it had originated in London and reminded me that people are rarely what they seem.

"Anyway," Holly said, "I'm going to the bar for a refill." She smiled as she walked away but might as well have winked.

I leaned in a bit closer and smelled musky roses wafting off the woman. "Sorry, I don't think I got your name."

"Lennie," she said.

"Lennie?" I repeated.

She smiled like she was used to that reaction. "Well, technically Leonora. But that was just my mother's delusions of grandeur. It doesn't, you know, suit me, or her for that matter. You're Cole, right?"

My brain felt tight, which is usually a sign that a bad headache is building, and I should go to bed. "My mother as well. 'You Do Something to Me' was her favorite song."

Lennie bobbed her head. "Excellent taste. So, Cole, how long have you been living here?"

"Since October. And you?"

"Oh, I beat you by a month, got here in September. I've seen you out and about, where do you live?"

"I've seen you, too." I felt strangely embarrassed by the way I had invented a version of her that wasn't really her, even though it's what we all do all the time. "Right next to the Hut. I'm one of the wildlife rangers so the cottage came with the job." I realized I had to return the question or it would look odd. "How about you?"

"I'm in that mad old coast-guard cottage right on the edge of the cliff." She waved vaguely toward the direction of the sea. "I'm sure you've seen it."

"Of course. I walk past it all the time for work."

As I was speaking, I got this strange sense that neither of us were saying what we meant. That our words were just sounds with no meaning. I used to get that all the time at work, incredulous that no one ever threw water in their boss's face or stripped naked and ran around the office.

"Well, you should come in and say hi next time." She smiled over her glass. "I didn't expect it to feel so bloody lonely. Which is stupid because, I mean, I could hardly have chosen a more isolated spot."

"Why did you then? Choose it, I mean?"

She laughed. "Oh, well, I turned forty at the beginning of the year and had one of those cringey 'what's it all about' crises. Got it in my head that I needed to lock myself away for a while. Regroup, I guess you'd say. How about you?"

I felt my stomach turn the way it used to in London and imagined an ulcer nestling in my gut. "Much the same."

"So, is it a sabbatical for you, then?"

"No, not at all. A total life change."

She raised an eyebrow. "Oh, right. Where have you moved from?"

"London."

"Me too. And you've done it on your own?"

"That's right."

"Well, that's two things we have in common, then." She clinked my glass with hers. "Here's to being brave and following our hearts."

The thought of following my heart relaxed me. "How long are you here for?"

Lennie, Leonora, shifted her weight to her other hip. "Well, I have to be back in London for work in June. And I've taken the cottage for a year. But we'll see how long I can keep the bogeyman at bay."

"What do you mean?"

She did a funny shiver. "Oh, just, at night, it could be the setting for a horror film, that cottage. You know, right on the edge of a cliff, with no one around for miles. No one to hear you scream." But then she smiled. "Sorry, I'm being melodramatic. I'm enjoying it, really."

It seemed like an odd thing to say because I'd never thought of the cottage as scary, simply beautiful. Although that thought made me feel a little ashamed because obviously it would be different for a woman living alone there. She was jigging a bit to the music so, to change the subject, I said, "Do you want to dance?"

She dipped her head. "Goodness, I haven't been asked to dance in about twenty years, but, yes, that would be nice."

"Oh no," I said too quickly. "I don't mean with me. I just meant you look like you want to dance, and I don't want to stop you."

"Oh, right." She spoke in that tone Mel would use when I said something she thought was mean. A mixture of hurt and regret that made my balls feel like they were shrinking. It was hard to tell what would produce that reaction, the goal posts ever changing. And then I just felt exhausted by the fact that I was standing in a dark room making small talk. It seemed like such a mountain to climb to get to know someone else as intimately as I had Mel.

"Sorry, that was rude of me," I said. "It's just I never dance. I hate it. Of course, I'd dance with you if I did." My face felt hot, and I was glad of the thickness of my beard and the darkness of the lights.

But she laughed away my worries. "No sweat. I'm not easily offended. But you should dance, you know, it's one of the few things absolutely guaranteed to make me feel better."

I smiled because it was the sort of thing Mel would have said. She was constantly offering advice for things I could try, like drink more water or take up running or practice positive visualization, stuff like that. I'd always thought it was sweet of her to care so much but, since the breakup, I'd begun to wonder. It had occurred to me that she could have been trying to change me because she was so fundamentally disappointed in me. She always said that she didn't mind being more successful workwise, but I wonder how true that was. On dark nights I sometimes cringed at the thought that maybe I embarrassed her. I wish I'd started talking to her about giving up all the corporate bullshit and moving to the country years ago. If we'd done it when we first met, I think we could have made a good go of it together, which makes me feel very sad. I worry that she'll wake up one day and realize that all her rushing has meant life has passed her by. The band encircling my head tightened. I was too aware of the heat and noise and my shoulders were starting to clench.

"I think I'm going to make a move," I said.

"But not on the dance floor," Lennie laughed. "But seriously, it's only just gone nine. Don't go yet."

"I have to get up early."

One of the things I'd promised myself before moving down was that I'd get enough sleep and, also, that I'd give myself a break. I'm a natural introvert, whereas Mel is a real social animal, which had taken a lot out of me over the years. One of the good outcomes about being on my own was that I was going to take things at my own pace and be happier with a smaller, more sedate life.

My sight was already starting to zigzag when I stepped out into the cold night air, the precursor to a terrible headache that would make me feel as woozy as if I were drunk. When I get a really bad one, I can even black out—whole sections of time lost or half-reflected in these weird hazy memories that feel more like dreams. It's a terrifying sensation when I come round, my brain scrambling for clues that never fully emerge. It's why I try to put myself to bed as soon as I get the first symptoms, so I can account for myself when I wake up.

A couple of years ago Mel made me go to the doctor about them, but he just prescribed some really strong painkillers and asked if I wanted to think about antidepressants, which I actually found more depressing than the headaches. I hate the way we're always encouraged to think of a chemical, rather than a lifestyle, solution. When I said no, he said I should at least think about taking a holiday, although at that time I found holidays almost as stressful as work. Mel used to plan our holidays, and by plan, I mean color-code notes on what to do, what to see, and where to eat. Naturally, nothing ever worked out exactly and there was always one moment in the two weeks that she'd end up screaming at me in front of a picturesque view.

I put myself to bed as soon as I got in, but sleep eluded me, so I had to lie in the dark watching the swirls telescoping my vision until it was nothing more than a pinprick. But there was a tiny loosening in my neck muscles that told me it wasn't going to be a sledgehammer one. Although, as I let myself relax slightly, the real pain started, which is probably a metaphor for something.

I must have drifted off to sleep eventually, because I was awoken by a weak sun nudging its way into my room through the badly drawn curtains, which meant it was much later than I usually woke up. I contemplated still going for my swim, but the light seemed too exposing, and I had a terrible vision of someone calling the coast guard if they saw me in the water, which would have been so humiliating. It was Sunday, so I didn't have to go into work, but knew I had to get out or I'd feel restless all day.

I showered and got dressed with the cold weather in mind, then went downstairs and made tea and porridge, which I ate looking out onto my little garden, with its outhouse tucked in the far corner. My plan is to become fully self-sufficient, only eating produce I've pulled out of the earth with my own hands. I'd also bought a trap, as eventually I hope to only eat meat that I've killed myself, something that my outhouse is all set up for. But I had yet to christen my knives, because up until that morning, I'd only ever caught a couple of rats, which I'd let go, as it felt like a step too far to actually eat them. Still, I dutifully checked the trap before I set off on my walk, only to find it resolutely empty. I know it's bullshit, but it made me think that, just for once, I wouldn't mind being an advert man, as I call them, a man who looks ripped and smells good and achieves the things he sets out to do.

I wasn't making for the coast-guard cottage, it's just that once I'd walked along the beach a bit and thrown a few stones into the water I had the option of either retracing my steps, which seemed a little pointless, or walking up past the cottage, across to the Long Barn and back down to mine. And the day was cold but bright, which is my favorite weather, making the scenic walk extra tempting. A few other walkers were taking the path up, so I fell into step behind them, looking out at the white cliffs, smart against the blue of the sky and sea.

My name was called as I passed the cottage gate. Lennie was barely dressed for the weather, a coat thrown over some pajamas and her feet stuffed into fluffy boots, with a laptop clutched to her chest.

"Ah, you've caught me," she said.

"Doing what?" I wondered for a mad moment if she'd stolen the laptop. But then I saw her hair was a mess and she had dark globs of mascara under both eyes, so I guessed that must be what she meant.

"It's pathetic," she said, holding her laptop up. "Too many bloody years in London. I locked it in my car boot last night because I was frightened about it being stolen."

"Oh, right." I'd lived in London for almost twenty years but never locked anything in the boot of my car. But then another thought struck me. "Did you walk home alone?"

"Well, no one was exactly going my way." She laughed.

I used to hate it when Mel came home on her own late at night. I linked our Uber apps so I'd get an alert whenever she ordered one, and would track its electronic progress across the city, sweating whenever it took a strange route. I felt terrible that I hadn't thought of the fact that Lennie would have had a horrible fifteen-minute walk home the night before.

"I'm so sorry I didn't think to ask you last night. I should have walked you home."

Lennie smiled. "That's sweet of you, although no reason why you should've done." She took a few steps toward me so we were standing on either side of the gate. Her voice wavered slightly. "Although, if I'm honest, it was really horrible. I was so scared at one point I thought my legs were going to give out. There were just so many noises, you know. And then, when I got home, it was like I couldn't shake the fear. I've been awake most of the night convinced someone was trying to break in."

"Oh, that's awful," I said. "I'm so sorry. Shit, I should have walked you."

"I was being silly, really. I mean, it would be pretty ridiculous if a murderer were waiting along the river path for someone to pass. They'd be waiting a bloody long time." She laughed. "Anyway, do you fancy a cuppa?"

I hadn't swum and my headache was still nestled sickly behind my right eye, as it often is the day after a bad attack, which can feel almost prophetic. "Actually, I've got a banging headache, I need to get some fresh air."

She laughed again. "That ale is lethal."

I nodded, but I hadn't even finished one pint as, truthfully, I've never been a heavy drinker. Mel used to say it was one of the things she loved about me, after years of dating men who saw getting drunk as a competition, although in the end it was definitely one of the things that irritated her when I refused to share the wine she liked at the end of the day.

"Anyway, another time," I said, shoving my hands deep into my pockets.

"Sure," she said. "I'm going to see some friends in Dorset tomorrow for Christmas, but I'm back on the twenty-seventh. Why don't we go for a drink in that dead time before the new year?"

"Oh," I said.

"Unless you're going away?"

I shook my head. "Oh, no, not at all."

"Sorry, I'm being pushy." She looked down at the ground. "I'm not some mad stalker type, but I've felt pretty lonely down here and it would be nice to have a friend nearby."

I liked the sound of a friend, as they were in short supply in my life. "Look, sorry, I didn't mean to come across rude. It's just, I'm recently off the back of a very painful breakup."

She reddened. "Oh no, I wasn't suggesting a *date* date."

It was my turn to redden then. "Oh no, I know. I meant, I'm sorry if I'm acting a bit weird."

She reached forward and patted my arm. "Listen, it's fine. I totally get it."

My arm felt warm under her hand, and it made me realize that no one had touched me, even accidentally, for a couple of months. "If I'm honest, it's been a pretty brutal year. I actually still don't really understand lots of things that happened, and it's made me question stuff." I'd started speaking before I'd thought about what I was going to say. To stop myself I looked behind Lennie at the horizon, the gray sea meeting the gray sky, worried I was going to cry.

"I'm so sorry for your pain," she said, which made me focus on her again, on her kind eyes.

"Look, I'm being silly. I'd really like to go for a drink with you. I just wanted, you know, to let you know where I am."

"Well, that's super sweet of you, Cole." She fished a phone out of her coat pocket. "Give me your digits and I'll call when I get back."

She bit her bottom lip in a strangely alluring way as I handed back her phone. "I hope you have a very merry Christmas. See you on the other side."

Christmas wasn't great, if I'm honest. Although that was hardly a surprise. I doubt many people have a good first Christmas after a painful breakup and mine was no different. Everything seemed duller without Mel, and I felt exhausted from the moment I woke up. When we were together, we spent every Christmas with her parents in Devon, a studiedly jolly affair in their overheated house, where fairy lights were left on for days at a time and there was more food than we could have ever possibly eaten. Mel has a brother and a sister, both married with two children. They'd alternate years at home with years at their partners' parents', which obviously wasn't something we could do. I don't know which years felt more uncomfortable, either the noise of the children or the sound of silence amplifying everything we didn't have. I would have loved to occasionally spend Christmas alone, just the two of us, but Mel liked going there and I understood that.

I woke, as everyone else must have done, to the news that a man in Cambridge had murdered his estranged wife and children the night before. He'd dressed up as Santa Claus and tricked the youngest daughter into opening the door. But once inside he'd stabbed them all and then himself in a frenzied attack. There's nothing to be done with information like that so I went down to the beach like usual. My anger at the man gave me a false sense of warmth on my walk, but the temperature was actually just below freezing, so when I first dove in I thought my heart was going to stop. It was a bad start and the farther out I got, the more I could feel my fear creeping up from the depths.

Mermaids are my most frequent terror, which probably sounds stupid, but my mother had a series of pictures of Barnum's mermaids displayed on her study wall when I was growing up. They were grotesque, like mutant fishes stretched into human form, a terrible parody of what mermaids are meant to be. I clearly remember the first time she told me what they were. I must have been about thirteen and the information felt like a gut punch because they're not at all beautiful. But when I said that, my mother basically told me not to trust the male imagination, which I recognized as criticism even at that age. (I wouldn't, by the way, recommend being brought up by a psychiatrist if you want a trauma-free adulthood.) Naturally, I became totally fascinated by the mermaids and found myself sneaking into her study to look at the pictures most days, which might explain why I feel their icy hands around my ankles in the early morning sea and am sometimes sure they're going to pull me under.

There comes a point during all my swims in which the pain of the cold starts to feel dangerous, so I turn for the shore. I bolster myself with a glance up at the coast-guard cottage. But when I saw it on Christmas morning, knowing it was empty made me feel unexpectedly sad, so I lost my rhythm and swallowed a gulp of seawater. The tide was also stronger than I'd realized, the sea sucking outward, so my arms and legs tired quickly. I wondered if I was going to make it back, which filled my head with images of my own bloated corpse washed up on a distant shore. No one would have reported me missing for days, and it was hard to work out what I was doing in the pitch-black freezing sea on Christmas morning.

I drank a cup of tea and ran a hot bath as soon as I got in but must have warmed up too quickly because when I got out my brain was buzzing and my limbs felt like they were made of string, so I had to lie down on the bed for a while before I could get dressed. Breakfast didn't make me feel a whole lot better and then I felt even worse when I checked the trap and it was still empty.

I did all the cooking while Mel and I were together and, if I do say so myself, am pretty good. But it had seemed so depressing to cook Christmas dinner for one that I'd cycled forty minutes to the nearest co-op the day before and bought a packet of fresh pasta and sauce, plus a chocolate cake. When I'd paid, the elderly woman cashier smiled in such a pitying way that I'd nearly run out of the shop without my food. And, as I chewed my way through the bland, synthetic tastes, I wished I had because I couldn't work out what I'd been thinking.

I considered firing up Netflix on my laptop after lunch but was worried that Mel would have changed the password, which would have depressed me further. Besides, I'd promised myself that I'd try to expand my mind now that I lived alone, which meant I shouldn't be indulging in made-up stories. I'd bought a series of nonfiction books just before leaving London, but they were still languishing accusingly in a bag in the corner of my bedroom. And truthfully, the thought of losing two hours to a Bond film, even with its appalling misogyny and glamorization of violence, seemed pretty appealing at that moment.

I opened a bottle of prosecco around three, which was another ill-advised purchase that made me wonder what the hell my psyche had been playing at the day before. I've never liked its sweetness and all it did was remind me of Mel, as it's her go-to drink. I rung her almost automatically, the numbers like muscle memory in my fingers. Then it annoyed me that I felt surprised when she answered. Although all she said was, "Cole," in a way that made me feel like a naughty schoolboy.

I felt immediately foolish and briefly considered hanging up, but that would have been pointless, so I ended up lamely saying, "Happy Christmas."

"Have you just rung to say that?"

The sharpness of her tone flustered me. "Where are you?"

"Obviously at Mum and Dad's." Her words conjured up the scene as if it were in front of me—the excess of food and drink that would be thrown in the bin, the fire and central heating blaring, every light twinkling in an explosion of electricity, the dogs fat and unwalked, the mountain of presents so deep that many would be lost or broken before the day was out. And then it was impossible not to also see the pain that had gone into creating the day—all the low-wage workers staying late in supermarkets, all the third-world children stitching together garments, all the plastic and paper left out for pollution-spewing rubbish vans to take to incinerators and burn into tiny fibers that would find their way into the lungs of children too poor to be housed anywhere else.

"Is everyone there?" I asked, even though we both knew the answer.

"Yup."

It seemed strange that I hadn't even lit my fire and I was suddenly aware of the silence surrounding me. I could hear a low hum punctuated by the odd childish shriek from her end and presumed she'd stepped out of the room to answer my call. I knew that when she went back in they'd all talk about me for a while. Maybe even pity me.

I tried to laugh, but it came out wrong, like a sneeze. "In fact, I was thinking about our New Year's holiday last year and how glad I am not to be in the heat."

She puffed her breath, which made me realize I'd said the wrong thing. "If you remember rightly, we went on that holiday because we'd had such a shit year."

"Yes, of course I remember." I immediately thought of Dr. Leggart's office and blood-stained sheets and Mel crying in the bathroom while my insides curdled.

"Not on some whim of mine." Her voice had a dangerous edge to it, like she was near to tears.

"I didn't mean . . ." I tried, although I knew I'd already committed one of those impossible to predict verbal sins that she punished me for so thoroughly.

"I'll be there in a second," Mel called, and I could tell she'd leaned away from the phone.

"Who's that?"

"Just Mum, they want to cut the Christmas cake."

But then I heard Mel's mum close to the phone saying, "Come on, Melanie, please."

"Can I say hello to her?"

Mel snorted. "I don't think that would be a good idea."

"Why?"

She lowered her voice. "I've told her things, Cole. Let's just say you wouldn't want to hear what she's got to say to you."

I wondered for a brief second if I might be dreaming because there was no sense to what Mel was saying. "What things? What are you talking about?"

"I'm done playing nice," Mel whispered into the phone so it sounded like she was hissing. "And if you don't sign the bloody papers like you've been promising to do for a whole month now, I'm going to make your life very uncomfortable."

"Are you threatening me?"

An ominous silence followed, in which I imagined her dramatically putting her hand to her forehead or letting her eyes fill with tears, as she always did when she lost an argument. "It's Christmas Day," she said in the end. "I don't want to do this now."

"Mel, please," I said, even though I wasn't sure what I was pleading for.

"Look, I have to go." Her words sounded strangely desolate, and I felt a heavy clawing in my stomach, which might have been the processed food I'd eaten. Perversely, I wanted to ask her again to come and join me, to persuade her that we could have a good life together in the countryside, away from the foolishness and stress of London. But there was no point because I'd spent ages trying to persuade her of that before and she'd made it clear that she liked her life, which was another way of saying she didn't love me enough. "But I need the papers. Both sets."

"You know I'm never signing the other ones. Only the house ones."

She made a little noise that sounded like she was being strangled. "Cole, this is insane. You're making my life a misery."

"But what you're asking me to do would make me miserable."

She snorted. "You're not going to win, Cole, so I don't understand why you're persisting."

Sometimes arguing with Mel made me feel mad. She was capable of making me believe that my views were inconsequential and I was crazy to think they were worth considering. "You can't ask me to just give away my life."

"It's not your life," she shouted. "It's mine." Which of course was the root of the problem: I didn't actually matter to Mel.

She sighed as if everything hurt. And then the line went dead. I replayed the conversation as I finished my glass of prosecco, the sweet acid nestling behind my breastbone. It sounded as if Mel was now making up lies about me to her family, but I couldn't work out why, or what she might be saying. It wasn't like I'd done anything to hurt her. In fact, she was the one who'd done something incredibly hurtful to me.

But, if I'm honest, all throughout our relationship I've felt a little like I was failing a test. Mel has a photographic memory, not just for facts but also for emotions, and she expected me to be the same way. She was always hurt if I couldn't remember every single tiny detail— her likes and dislikes, her views, her feelings—and would get especially cross if I forgot that we'd gone somewhere together or misremembered a present she'd given me. Sometimes she was even annoyed when I thought differently from her. And it was exhausting because sometimes I did forget things, or disagree, and I don't know anymore if that's okay, or if I was a total prick who let her down.

I forced myself to be more proactive after that call, but still felt like I'd taken quite a few steps back from the equilibrium I'd begun to feel. I started every morning with a swim, I got enough sleep, and I ate good food. But still, one day I had to shout at a family standing right on the edge of the cliff for a photograph, their two young children literally inches away from the fifty-foot drop. And on another, I turned on the radio and was met with the end of a discussion about female safety. They were talking about the Walk for Women girls and the abuse they were getting online. I looked them up again and, sure enough, a couple of comments on their posts were sexual and revolting, which made me feel pretty ashamed to be a man. Then Mel texted a few days after Christmas, reminding me to at least sign the house papers. When I admitted that I'd forgotten again, she got quite abusive, saying she knew I wasn't good on details, but could I please just get the fuck on with it.

So, all in all, it was very nice when Lennie texted two days before New Year's Eve, and we agreed to go for a drink. When I got to the pub, she was sitting at a table by the fire with two pints in front of her, scrolling through her phone, which reminded me uncomfortably of Mel, who is obsessed with social media and always had an email to answer. It became impossible to have a proper conversation with her because she was always tapping away. She'd often shove her phone under my nose to show me a plate of food or an animal or a sofa or a view I couldn't place. At first, I'd make the appropriate noises but eventually I couldn't bear it and told her she was frying her brain, which produced a huge sulk, and every time I caught her looking at her screen after that she'd pull a face and tell me not to speak to her because I'd be appalled by her intellectual inferiority.

Lennie put her phone away as soon as she saw me, and we spent the first few minutes on a polite "how was your Christmas"–type conversation. She spoke in a very loud voice, her accent scratching the air, which made me feel embarrassed as I hate taking up too much space. But she also asked lots of questions about my job, like she was interested, which was a nice change.

"But what is it you do?" I asked after a bit, worried that she might think I was one of those self-involved men only interested in the sound of his own voice. "You said you don't have to be back at work till June. What sort of job lets you not go in for a year?"

She waved a hand in front of her face in a dismissive way that made me feel sad because women are so conditioned to make what they do seem unimportant. "I'm an artist, and I have a show in June."

I smiled because I'd been right. "Oh, right. What sort of art?"

"This and that." She took a sip of her pint, and I could tell there was something else she wanted to say. "So, how long ago was your breakup then?"

It was a fair question and of course she was going to ask, but still I felt sunk by the thought. "Six months."

Her eyebrows knitted together. "And how long were you together?"

"About seven years. We were married, actually."

She gulped at her pint again. "Okay. Right. What happened? If you don't mind me asking."

My mouth felt lined in sand, but I made myself speak. "No, it's fine. Mel, that's my wife, and I wanted kids, but we couldn't get pregnant.

"It must have been hard, having a baby on your own so young, with your mum dead," I said.

"It wasn't the best. But, you know, I'm glad I had Jasmine when I did. My life felt totally chaotic at the time so I didn't think it had anything to do with having a baby and just got on with it. But actually, I think it would have felt just the same if I'd had her ten years later and that would have freaked me out, because you're not meant to feel like that when you're grown up."

I laughed. "I'm not so sure about that. I moved to get away from the chaos and I'm well into adulthood."

"Ha, I like you, Cole. Come on, it's bloody freezing," she said, taking my arm and steering me toward the cottage. "I don't want you to think that I don't adore Jasmine. She's amazing, totally different from me, really studious and bright and all that. It's, well, it takes a lot out of a woman, having a child."

"Society doesn't appreciate the physical and mental toll of motherhood," I replied as we turned into the little gate. Lennie's life seemed so full and different to what I'd imagined, almost like it was bursting at the seams, when I'd imagined it calmly contained within the walls in front of us. She opened the front door and stepped up into the bright hallway and all I could do was follow.

"Could you stoke up the fire while I get the champagne?" she said, depositing all her outdoor gear on the end of the banister. Some of it fell on the floor, but she didn't bother to pick it up.

It was strange to be inside the cottage when I'd looked at it from the outside so many times, a bit like stepping into a painting you know really well. I was glad that it felt as cozy as I'd imagined, that the paint was flaking, the floorboards creaked, and, from what I could see, nobody had ripped out any original features and replaced them with some terrible modern shit. It had a wonderful authenticity about it that gave me the soothing feeling of being stroked.

I went into the sitting room, where the deep mustard yellow walls were even cozier than they looked through the windows. There were some embers still glowing in the bottom of the grate—which I'm pretty sure was the original—so it hardly took any effort to get it going again. By the time Lennie came in carrying the champagne and two glasses, a flame was already licking around a log. I took the glass she handed me, even though I'd had enough. Not being a heavy drinker makes me a bit of a lightweight, but it felt rude to refuse, so I took a sip.

"Is this what you're working on, then?" I asked, indicating the shrouded canvas on the other side of the room.

"Well, technically." Lennie sat down heavily on a chair by the fire. There was another opposite it, but I wasn't ready to sit.

"Can I see it?"

"Absolutely not." The words were so forceful I walked over to the mantelpiece to hide my discomfort.

"Sorry," she said, more calmly. "I don't mean to sound rude. I just never let anyone look at my work until it's finished."

"No, it's fine."

"It's silly, but it embarrasses me. I still feel like, well, like a fraud, calling myself an artist. I'm never sure if I'm doing it right."

"Is there a right way?" I was looking at a photograph on the mantelpiece of a young Lennie holding a disgruntled baby on her hip.

"Well, I wouldn't know," she said. "I never went to art school or anything like that, you see. In fact, after Mum died, I pretty much stopped going to school, not that I'd gone too much when she was alive. Everything looked pretty grim for a while because people aren't exactly clamoring to foster a moody, gobshite fifteen-year-old. And then I had Jazz two years later and I couldn't really see a way out. The only subject I was ever any good at was art and I found that drawing calmed me, after I'd gotten the baby to sleep. Then one night I was watching this late-night documentary about outsider art. This incredibly posh woman was being interviewed about the gallery she'd recently opened dedicated to underprivileged artists. Bring me your work, she said. So I did. I put my drawings in a plastic bag and went to the gallery the next day with Jazz screaming all the way. But, you know, Bea, the posh woman, took me on and I've been with her ever since. Although, it hasn't stopped me feeling like a fraud."

Life had undeniably dealt Lennie some hard blows, which reminded me of myself. She was clearly a person who had built a bit of a wall around herself to protect against life's knocks. Bad things had happened to her, and I could tell fear lurked just beneath her skin. Certain scratches would bring it rushing to the surface, which gave her a wariness. It made me think about her name and how she'd shortened it to an ugly boy's name, almost in an act of self-protection. And that made me feel sad for her.

"You're not a fraud," I said. "I mean, your story, that's so impressive."

She gulped and then I saw that she was crying, swiping at her eyes to stop the tears. "God, sorry. I'm not normally this pathetic."

I went over and sat next to her so I could put my arm around her. Lennie tilted her head up toward mine and, with the firelight dancing across her face, she looked so sweet and vulnerable that before I knew it, we were kissing. I regretted it almost immediately, even as our lips were still locked, because only an hour or so before I'd felt so full of Mel. Plus, I was worried that Lennie was a bit drunk, and I'd never take advantage of anyone who didn't completely know what they were doing. And also, it was way too soon for something like that to have happened between us.

Sex for me is very spiritual and also very specific. I've learned that I need to prepare myself mentally, otherwise it can make me nervous, which doesn't have a good effect on my body. I find it quite overpowering if it just happens, like there are no rules, and I lose all sense of myself. I need to be totally in tune with the women I sleep with, not only physically but also mentally. I know I'm different from most men in this respect. I'm an overthinker and an over-feeler and I don't like casual hookups or treating people badly. And, strange though it sounds, sometimes that makes things hard.

Mel was the only person that I'd been completely open with about all that stuff. And, at least for the first few years, we were totally in sync. We encouraged each other to talk about and explore our desires, and she was so open-minded and cool. But the busier she got at work, the more complicated sex became, so I was never entirely sure where I stood. There were weeks when she was so exhausted that she'd fall asleep as soon as she got home, and if I so much as brushed her arm, she'd get annoyed. But whenever she wanted to have sex and I didn't, she'd act like I found her repulsive, crying and shouting. Then by the end of our relationship, when we did sleep together, she was always distant and distracted, showering within minutes of finishing, and refusing to cuddle. Plus, IVF made her seem so delicate that I couldn't imagine us ever going back to those heady early days when we'd first met, which made me feel a little desperate, as I couldn't work out who we'd be if we couldn't connect with each other in that way.

Lennie drew away from me. "Look, to be clear, I'm not going to sleep with you." A surge of relief rushed through me. "But it's late and raining. You don't have to go home."

The rain had set up a steady patter against the window and it was warm and cozy in the cottage. Also, the thought of the walk home to my dark, empty cottage was a bit depressing. "Thanks, that'd be really nice, if you don't mind."

"Not at all," she said, standing up. "But I'm knackered, so I'm going to call it a night."

I followed her upstairs.

"You'll have to bunk up with me," she said, as we reached the landing. Her bedroom was straight ahead, with an inviting-looking black iron bed, covered by a quilted blanket and lots of fluffy pillows. Two wooden chairs were being used as bedside tables, small lights glowing calmly on each, making the room look peaceful and warm. She opened the only closed door to reveal a tiny room, which smelled a little damp, containing an unmade single bed. She shut it again. "I wouldn't inflict that on you."

"Your room looks lovely, Len . . ." But then I faltered. "Leonora. Sorry, do you mind if I call you that? I think it suits you so much better. It's a beautiful name."

"No one calls me that," she said, but then laughed. "But I guess I don't mind if you do."

A warmth expanded through my chest and I took a step toward her. "It's been hard to think of you as Lennie. I think you hide behind that name."

She frowned. "What do you mean?"

"Well, it's a hard, ugly name, and you're so soft and beautiful." She laughed, but I continued, "No, really. That's not some crappy, chat-up bullshit. I mean it. I know what it's like to be on your own; it makes you put up a hard front. But that can also obscure the real you."

She nodded slowly. "Maybe. I don't know. I've never thought about it like that before." She went to the bathroom to get changed, so I undressed quickly, except for my T-shirt and boxers, and slipped into the shockingly cold covers. She came back in a full tracksuit. "Sorry I should have warned you," she said as she got in beside me. "It's like an icebox in this room."

"It's nice," I said. And I meant it. If I could have imagined a perfect situation before I'd moved, this would have come very close. A beautiful cottage on the edge of a cliff, nature howling outside, and a warm, friendly woman next to me who wasn't trying to dissect my thoughts. I slipped my arm under Leonora's shoulders, and she sort of burrowed against me. I glanced down the covers and caught sight of all the lumps and folds her body made, which gave me an unexpected jolt. I don't mean that in a bad way, as she has a beautiful body and slimness is a problematic male contrivance of beauty, but it made me think about how if I lay on top of her, it would feel like I was sinking into her. She would be easy to get lost in.

The wind had picked up outside and the rain sounded like stones being thrown against the window. The bed had warmed, and a feeling of intense coziness enveloped me. Normally, when I'm safely tucked away from the weather, I think of all the homeless people who have to endure it and then feel horrible about myself. That night, though, it wasn't homeless people I thought of, but the Walk for Women girls. The photos accompanying their posts had revealed them to be very slight. They'd barely looked strong enough to carry their backpacks, and I couldn't imagine how they were faring in the storm.

"Have you heard about those girls walking along the South Coast?" I asked.

"Mmm," Leonora said.

"If I had a daughter, I'd hate to think of her doing that. I mean, doesn't it seem dangerous to you?"

"I guess." She shifted against me. "But, you know, most things are dangerous when you're a woman. I really admire what they're doing."

"You know they're going to be passing right by here soon. Apparently people come out to watch them walk. I've been checking the barriers all week."

"That's nice," she said, but her words were slurring slightly.

Leonora fell asleep almost immediately, her breathing settling into a slight snore. I watched the silver light of the moon on the ceiling for a while but knew that sleep was a long way off. I considered going downstairs and making a cup of tea but was worried about disturbing her. So instead I inched my arm out from underneath her and reached for my phone, flicking through a few news sites. But it was all pretty depressing, lots of catastrophe that I had no interest in being a part of.

After a few minutes I googled the Walk for Women girls and was immediately directed to their latest post, written only the day before. Thank you for all the concern, I read, which set my heart beating a little faster. We just wanted to let everyone know that we're fine and won't be put off continuing our walk. Neither of us were harmed, just shaken and saddened. To set the record straight: last night we were woken up by a man outside our tent, which we'd pitched at the edge of a forest. He was shouting and hollering and pressing himself against the fabric, which made it clear that he'd taken off his trousers. We called the police and shouted at him to go away, which resulted in verbal abuse. Unfortunately, he ran away before help arrived, but the matter is now being dealt with by the police. Far from putting us off, this incident has highlighted even more how much we need this conversation. Because the sad truth is what happened to us was very minor compared to the violence and degradation suffered by less fortunate women every day.

The rest of the post detailed services that help women experiencing violence, asked for donations, and talked about their route, which was nearing our stretch of coast. It was horrible to think about how scared they must have been, and I felt a surge of anger toward the man who'd done that. Leonora's daughter was the same age as Molly and Phoebe, and I couldn't imagine what it would feel like to have something like that happen to your own child.

Most of the comments under the post were supportive, although one man had written that they should consider their own safety more and were wasting police time that could be spent helping the women they claimed to be walking for. Another had pointed out that lots more men than women were murdered each year, but no one walked for them. And then I came across someone called ManintheWild, who'd written you'd be lucky to be raped. next time might be your lucky day bitches. I went back through their previous posts and saw he'd commented on every single one, each one vile and sexual. I let my phone fall against my chest and noticed that my heart felt tight and my mind sloshy, like my thoughts couldn't take root properly.

I had a nightmare about drowning, which bolted me awake early the next morning, earlier even than I usually woke for swimming. Leonora was still snoring, lying on her back, with her arms thrown out, so I had been pushed right to the edge of the bed and the cold metal was digging into my leg. I slipped out of the covers into the freezing air and dressed quickly.

But halfway down the stairs I thought that if I left before she woke, she might think I was one of those shitty men who disappear when denied sex, so went into the sitting room to find something I could write on. There was a pad and pencil on the sideboard, and I scribbled a few words saying that I liked to get up early to swim before work, but I'd call later, before propping the note in front of the shrouded canvas.

I knew it was wrong, but I moved the sheet covering the canvas. I was met with a beautiful, instantly recognizable scene, a stunning painting of the view from the cliff top, of the dirty white cliffs plunging into the sea churning below in a multitude of colors. The winter sun was nothing more than a feeling of light, and an impression of birds moved across the sky. It was exactly the sort of painting I would have imagined her creating, but still it made me feel slightly dizzy, because Leonora was clearly very talented, which made me feel a bit embarrassed about myself as I don't have an obvious gift like that.

My phone vibrated on the walk home with a text from Mel asking if I'd mailed the documents. Her tone was very businesslike, and I was depressed at the thought of her awake at 5:30 a.m. because it reminded me of every morning of our shared life, when I would wake to the sound of her tapping away on her phone or laptop. I could imagine her so clearly, lying in our bed, the room dark around her, her face lit by the screen, and it made me want to run all the way to London to tell her that there is no shame in admitting when you've gotten something wrong.

Not that Mel would ever admit to getting anything wrong. Over the course of our marriage nothing had ever been her fault, not even little things, like when she filled the sugar bowl with salt. And especially not the big things, like when she turned up late to our second implantation, or when she consistently refused to rest, never listening to the doctor's advice, which really is not a hard thing to do. The world will not fall apart if she's away from her desk for forty-eight hours. After our second implanting, we argued outside the doctor's expensive Harley Street office. I was begging her to come home, and she was saying she had a meeting that was impossible to reschedule. I remember standing on that bustling, dirty pavement and wanting to cry, thinking of our little embryo trying desperately to implant itself as its mother rushed about in high heels, sucking down the coffee I knew she'd lied to me about giving up.

"What could be more important than the baby," I'd said as a last-ditch appeal to her sanity.

But she'd replied, "Well, unfortunately, we have to pay that expensive doctor to stick a needle up my cunt because we appear to be broken, so you know, there's that."

A man dressed in a smart suit was hurrying past as she spoke, and I actually felt him flinch at the coarseness of her words.

I shook myself away from that train of thought because it felt grubby and disloyal. I didn't want whatever had happened between us to make me bitter or to remember her unfairly. Mel's commitment to her work was incredible and she must have felt so shitty at that time. But it was still okay for me to wish that she had listened to me and our doctor and slowed down to reduce her stress levels. Adrenaline is actually proven to poison an embryo. But however much I begged her to leave work on time, or work a day from home, or not go to every evening event, she always ignored me.

I deleted her message and put the phone back in my pocket.

My morning swim made me feel a bit better, and I still had time to check the trap before work. It's odd but even before I lifted the lid, I knew it looked different, as if vibrating with the life it contained. And, sure enough, when I peeked inside, there was a rabbit, quivering in the cold. I'd read all about the process and everything was well prepared, so I continued on autopilot. I lifted it out by the scruff of its neck and took it straight to the flat stone I'd found weeks before on the beach, with a mallet waiting patiently beside it. I brought the mallet down swiftly on the rabbit's head as the dispatch has to be done quickly to avoid any unnecessary distress. I also made sure I was feeling every moment, aware of the fact that I could have stopped but chose not to. It's part of the country code, that you be aware of your actions, so you can weigh if they're valid or gratuitous.

There was significantly more blood than I'd expected, and pieces of brains and fragments of bone splattered on my fingers. Without warning, my stomach turned and my bowels contracted, but I took a deep breath and focused because there was no way I could expect to become a self-sufficient man of the land if the sight of blood made me sick. I took the corpse to the outhouse at the bottom of the garden, which centered me. It was one of the things I liked most about my new country setup. In fact, I had been irrepressibly drawn to it when Holly had shown me where I'd be living after my interview. She'd even joked that

I was more interested in it than the house, which wasn't far from the truth. But it's so unusual, a proper brick structure tucked in the hedges, its solid door locking tight. And when you go inside, it's dark and musty, like an animal's burrow, so you feel completely cocooned from the world. A man cave, as the media would call it, although I don't think needing a space of your own is gender specific.

The butcher block was scrubbed, and the knives made a metallic ringing sound when I pulled them off their magnetic strip. I kept them well sharpened, so it was easy to cut off the rabbit's head, then slice through the belly. I was feeling totally fine by then and was able to pull out all the slithering, slimy organs, and smell their fusty, grassy scent without even the smallest flinch. I scraped the entrails into a bag, as leaving them lying around would attract foxes, then hung the body upside down on a hook I'd banged into the wall when I first moved in. I'd read up on how to use a smaller knife to create a slit in the skin, and it was then surprisingly easy to pull the fur down and off in one quick, skillful movement. It reminded me briefly of how I'd sometimes undressed Mel, in the beginning.

I felt so pleased with myself when I'd finished that I wanted to tell someone about my achievement. But there wasn't anyone, which made me feel panicked. To calm myself I pulled up the email I'd saved from Mel that she sent to me in the weeks after we first got together. At first, I kept it because it made me so happy, but after things turned sour and we split up, I found I couldn't delete it. Sometimes I panic at the thought that years will go by without us speaking and, if that happens, I know I'll need something to hang on to, something to prove that she did really love me once. I know the letter so well that I barely have to read it anymore, the words like pathways in my brain. But still, my heart jolted as it loaded onto my screen and I allowed myself to remember how it felt when I received it.

Dearest Cole.

I just wanted to officially say how much I love you. I've never gone out with anyone before who listens and thinks before they speak and is interested in ideas and wants to make things better. You make me feel special and valued and like you're not going to laugh at me or make me feel stupid, which, believe me, is something I've been made to feel plenty of times by plenty of men. It's so crazy—we've only known each other a few weeks—but you make me feel safe, which isn't even something I knew I needed to feel.

Thank you so much for opening up to me so fully last night. Your vulnerability will never be unattractive to me. In fact, it's one of the many things that makes you so different from every man I've ever dated before. Please, never be scared to show me all those sides of yourself and know I love you all the more for them.

I've been thinking about what you said all day and it makes sense. You're right, life is too full of stupid conventions and who's to say what's right or wrong, as long as everyone's happy. I want to try it.

Love you forever, Mel.

Holly sent me to check the barriers again when I got into work because the Walk for Women girls were due to pass in the next twenty-four hours. As I trudged across the freezing landscape, I checked to see if there had been any updates on the man outside their tent. They'd posted an hour before, but there wasn't any news, just a long post about male violence and female headspace. ManintheWild had been the first to comment, barely a minute after they'd posted, restricting himself this time to the very unerudite watch your backs slags.

The coast-guard cottage loomed into view as I climbed up the path from the beach and Leonora suddenly seemed like such an antidote to all the lunacy. The next day was New Year's Eve and I couldn't work out the point of both of us starting the year on our own. But when she answered the door, she was pale and red-eyed, which dried my mouth— perhaps it had been bad of me to simply leave a note earlier. It wasn't that I thought we were dating, but in the time since I'd last dated, the rules had changed so profoundly that I think it's fair to say it's hard to know where you stand anymore, as a man. For example, I would like to hold open doors and compliment my partner, treat them to meals, and carry their heavy bags, but things like that used to irritate Mel. Although she'd also get annoyed if she felt like I was taking her for granted, or not listening properly, or not making her feel special. Often, I feel very confused.

"Are you okay?" I asked quickly.

Leonora tried to smile. "I've been having a stupid row with Jasmine."

"What about?"

She half-laughed. "It's so silly. It's just Nina, that's her dad's wife, thinks she'd look good with short hair and now she's thinking of cutting it off." I couldn't work out how I was meant to answer. "I probably overreacted," she said, which made me realize it was probably better if I said nothing, a tactic I'd learned with Mel. "But she has exactly the same hair as I do, and it felt a bit wounding, to hear that this other woman, who must be acting as a sort of mother figure to her, suggested cutting it off. Like, she wants to eradicate me or something."

It seemed like an unlikely series of suppositions, but I could see how she'd arrived at them. "I'm sure it's not like that."

Leonora rubbed a hand across her face. "I really can't bear it if she does cut it. It'll feel so symbolic, somehow. Maybe I'm not as ready for her to fly the nest as I thought I was. You know, the other night I was lying awake, imagining someone breaking in, and I actually calmed myself down by remembering how I used to feel when Jazz was little. I barely slept for years then because it felt too dangerous. Like, if I let go for one second, everything would unravel." I felt lost in the conversation, and it was also freezing, which made me shiver. She put a hand to her forehead. "Sorry, I'm being rude. Jabbering on while you stand there in the cold. Come in."

I shook my head. "I can't stop. I was just wondering if you fancied doing something tomorrow night, for the New Year. If you still don't have any plans, obviously."

She smiled then. "No, I don't. And yes, I'd love to. If I'm honest I was sort of dreading spending it alone. Even though I've given it the big 'I don't care' to anyone who's asked. Why don't you come here? I'll cook."

I got caught up with the barriers, so it wasn't until after two that I made it home for lunch. I just had time to put the rabbit in to the slow cooker, tucking it up with onions and celery, which would make the meat so tender. And I swear it tasted better because I knew its origin. I couldn't resist checking the trap again, but of course it was empty, devoid even of a rat. Not that I was worried as when something has happened once, it's bound to happen again.

After lunch I went upstairs to sign the conveyancing papers. Intellectually I knew that we had to sell the flat because it was the scene of too much misery for either of us to want to live there. But the thought still made my heart ache. My best-case scenario had always been that Mel would realize her terrible mistake and want to come back to me. Although I'd promised myself that if it did happen, this time my needs would also have to be met. Ideally, we'd stay living in the country, and, of course, we'd have to start IVF again. None of this had felt like a pipe dream because, truthfully, I couldn't imagine Mel coping without me. She is a very erratic person who needs a lot of love and reassurance, and I knew my absence would have left a big hole.

Mel's solicitor had marked where I had to sign and date. But I caught sight of our address and it was like our flat flooded over me. I could see the honey wooden floors and the sunlight streaming through the kitchen window, the little table on the balcony, all Mel's lotions lined up in the bathroom and her grandmother's lacey quilt on the bed. God, I loved that flat. I spent hours, weeks, months making it perfect for us. I presumed Mel would buy a new place, but I couldn't bear it if it was a house with a garden, like we'd discussed when we'd been trying for a baby. I know I was the one who'd wanted a new life, but it seemed suddenly unfair that she was still in the space I'd created, and I was the one having to start again. But it's always that way, isn't it? Men are expected to be the ones to leave. As if men don't have an inner life or as much of an emotional connection to spaces and things as women do. Which means, when it comes down to the messy process of splitting up, it's the women who get to be coddled and cared for, even if they're the one who's fucked it up. Mel's salary was the reason we had been able to afford that flat, but the work I'd put into it made it as much mine as hers. And it wasn't only that—one of the big reasons Mel was so successful and earned so much was because I'd picked up so many of the pieces at home, something she never acknowledged.

Underneath the flat papers I saw the other ones, the ones that would turn off the power to our embryos until they'd melted into nothing more than effluence ready to be flushed down the drain. She was asking me to be part of such a brutal act I sometimes wondered if she'd had a breakdown or something. Because the Mel I fell in love with would never have wanted to do something so barbaric.

As I stood with the pen in my hand in my damp bedroom it felt like I'd been written out of my own life. I'd created a life for Mel that allowed her to be her perfect self but in the process forgotten about myself. My breath caught in my throat and my vision jagged, so I had to lean over the chest and the pen dropped out of my hand and rolled onto the floor. It seemed like too much effort to bend down and pick it up; it was much easier to fold the papers back into their box.

The next day I woke determined to be positive. The truth was Mel couldn't get rid of the embryos without my consent, and I simply wasn't going to sign. More than that, I had to stop pining after some-one capable of such a disgusting act. It was time to start focusing on the future. It was going to be a brand-new year at midnight, and it was time to move on.

I had a productive morning on the cliff, then went home for lunch. Holly called just as I was getting ready to go back out, saying that she'd received a notification from the coast guard about people sitting on the edge, just up from the coast-guard cottage. Halfway there my phone buzzed in my pocket and when I pulled it out, I saw that it was a text from Mel.

I'm going to have to get tough if I don't at least get those house papers soon, she'd written, also FYI I've asked my solicitor to start the divorce pro-ceedings asap.

My breath was tight in my throat as I imagined yet another stack of papers landing in my cottage. Her tone was so hard. She was starting to make me feel unsafe, like she wanted to get rid of me.

Two girls were sitting right on the edge, their legs dangling over the drop of the cliff, their shrill laughter piercing the air. Their phones flashed against the gray of the sky as they pouted and posed, and I marveled at their ability to be so casually unafraid.

"Hey," I shouted as I approached the demarcation line. They both turned to me, their foreheads creased in consternation. "You can't sit there. Seriously, it's not safe. You need to get back behind this string."

They stood very slowly, brushing the chalk off their jeans.

"Please, be quick," I said. "The cliffs here are very unstable."

The blond one reminded me of Mel, from the photos I'd seen of her as a young woman.

"Okay, okay, keep your hair on, mate," she said as they walked languidly toward me and stepped over the string. As soon as they were close enough, I recognized them: the Walk for Women girls.

"Didn't you see the notices?" I pointed at the bright signs I'd hung only hours before, determined not to let them intimidate me.

"Yeah, but, like, we thought it was an exaggeration."

"It's really not."

The blond girl rolled her eyes. "Right, okay."

"I'm not making it up. Erosion's really bad here and if you're standing on the cliff when it goes down, you don't stand a chance." They both screwed up their faces as if they didn't believe me. I waved at Leonora's. "See that cottage down there. It used to have a long garden and it's gone now. One day soon it will all disappear."

The blond girl held up her hand. "Could you watch your tone, please?" The conversation was starting to remind me of the millions I'd had with Mel in which she seemed to enjoy misunderstanding me.

I felt myself flush. "I'm sorry. But it's just that it's really stupid to get so close to the edge like that."

The blond girl snorted in such a rude way that I threw my hands in the air. They made quite a loud sound as they hit my legs, which made us all flinch. The other girl held her phone up to my face and we all heard the click as it started recording. It was an escalation I was totally unprepared for.

"I'd seriously advise you not to judge our intellectual capacity," she said, which was so far from what I'd been thinking that I felt completely lost.

"I think you've got this wrong," I said, keeping my voice steady, although I'd started to sweat under my clothes. "I'm not that type of man. I was just giving you a bit of advice that might save your life."

They both pulled themselves up a bit straighter, the way Mel would do when she was really digging into an argument.

"Don't talk to us like that," the blond girl said.

I motioned to the phone. "Can you put that down? You don't need to do that."

But the phone stayed in my face. "Don't come any closer."

"Oh, for god's sake," I said. "You're being ridiculous."

"No, you are," the other one said.

I felt a seam of anger bubble up. "Excuse me?"

"Don't raise your voice."

"I'm not." Although I realized I had, even though I didn't mean it in the way she was implying.

"You look fucking angry."

I felt tension in all my muscles. "I'm angry because I only came here to give you a perfectly reasonable piece of advice, for your own safety. And you've completely blown things out of proportion."

"Oh, I'm so sorry. Of course, it's our fault. You're not responsible for your actions at all, are you?" Her voice was dripping in sarcasm. I made a stupid grab for the phone, but they were quicker than me, leaping back, so I tripped.

"I'm not joking," the other one said. "Take one step closer and I'm calling the police."

I looked up into the gray sky and suddenly everything felt pointless.

"You know what?" I said, looking back at them. "Sit on the edge. Fall into the sea. I really don't care what happens to you."

I walked away from them down the hill, but my whole body felt lined in lead. Gender relations are so fucked. Sometimes I don't know how we're going to come back from it.

Leonora looked very nice when she opened the door that evening, dressed in a flowing black dress and lots of silver jewelry. Her hair was loose, with a red scarf keeping it off her face, and her skin was clean and fresh looking, like she'd just gotten out of a hot bath. And she was so pleased to see me, the tightness that had been threatening my head since my encounter with the Walk for Women girls loosened.

We went into the delicious-smelling kitchen and she poured some wine. Honestly, I reckon Mel cooked for me less than fifty times in our whole relationship. Not that I think the woman should cook for the man or anything remotely like that, obviously. But cooking for someone is undeniably an act of love, which I did for her often, and a nice restaurant or great takeaway is not the same. It doesn't fill the soul in the same way it fills the belly. We ate prawns smothered in garlicky butter, then pasta with eggplant and tomatoes, a fresh green salad, and, to finish off, a rich chocolate mousse. I liked how much Leonora ate, mopping up the sauce with thick slices of bread.

Mel doesn't have a huge appreciation of food, unless she's eating in a fancy restaurant, and then it's much more about the surroundings than the content. I think she sees it more as fuel. She's always been happy to start her days with nutritional drinks, to keep herself awake with huge coffees, and to buy ready-made meals on the way home from the office or order in. I tried to help her change her eating habits, especially when we got into IVF because all my reading pointed to the fact that chemicals and stimulants have a detrimental effect on fertility. But it was always an emotional topic, which I understood because she probably carried a fair amount of guilt about the whole thing.

After dinner, we moved to the sitting room, lit by fairy lights and candles, and opened a bottle of champagne. I stoked the fire while Leonora plugged her iPhone into a speaker and started playing a soothing playlist that made me think of the sea.

"Thanks so much for that supper, Leonora," I said. "I so appreciate the effort you went to."

She dipped her head like I'd embarrassed her. "It's a pleasure." But then she smiled. "I like you calling me Leonora, by the way. It makes me feel, I don't know, a bit special."

My blood felt warm. "I'm so glad. I really do think it suits you so much better."

She drew up her legs and tucked them under herself. "Anyway, tell me a bit more about your life before you moved down here."

Mel immediately ambushed my brain. I tried to think of something I could say that wasn't about her, but my mind felt blank.

"I used to work in PR," I tried.

"PR?" Leonora's eyebrows raised. "I wouldn't have put you down as doing something like that."

It was a nice thing to say, which made me smile. "Well, you're right, it didn't suit me. When I met Mel, I was sort of between things and she was already working in PR, so she helped me get a job. And, well, our life was pretty expensive, especially after we started IVF. So, before I knew it, I'd done more time at the agency than I would have for some pretty serious crimes."

Leonora laughed. "Does Mel still work in PR then?"

"God, yes. She'll be carried out of the office in a box. Which, you know, I'm not criticizing her for. But it's not my dream."

"It sounds like your ambitions weren't very compatible."

I nodded, even though it felt a sad thing to admit. "You could say that. Mel is totally committed to her career, which is super impressive in so many ways, but for me success is more defined by experiences and relationships. Before I met her, I was much more creative. Freer. I didn't feel the need to always be consuming."

Leonora screwed up her face as though she felt sorry for me, which made me feel better. It was so nice to talk to someone who got it. It had been uncomfortable being married to someone so driven because extreme ambition can eclipse so-called smaller desires. I felt a shot of respect for Leonora as well, as she'd clearly followed a passion rather than a career, happy to live more modestly as a result. Maybe without the relentless consumer grind I would be able to find my passion as well.

"Mel sounds very different to you. And like, maybe, she didn't appreciate that difference. It sounds as if you've been through a really rough time."

"You don't know the half of it."

Leonora screwed up her face. "What do you mean?"

"You know how I told you we were doing IVF before we split?"

She nodded, and momentarily I wondered how much of a betrayal it would be to talk about what Mel had done. But it was my story as well. "The thing is, we actually started on a third round. In fact, we got really far. We had three viable embryos and were all set to have them implanted. But then, the night before it was due to happen, Mel had a complete freak-out. Like, worse than I'd ever seen her. I tried everything to calm her down. And it seemed to work. She asked me to go and get her this special pasta from a nearby deli." I'd been speaking to my lap, but made myself look up and Leonora's eyes were fixed on me. "Anyway, I went, of course. And on the walk there I convinced myself that it was all going to be fine. What she was going through was so horrific, it was no wonder she was freaking out. There were some tulips in a bucket outside the deli and I picked up a couple of bunches because they're Mel's favorite. But when I got home, she was gone. She'd even taken some clothes. I tried ringing and texting, but nothing. She didn't get in touch with me till ten that night, only to say that she wouldn't be coming to the implantation and needed time alone."

The air felt alive when I'd finished speaking and neither of us spoke for a bit.

"But you've spoken properly about it since?"

"Not really." The extent of Mel's betrayal felt heavy on my shoulders. "She moved in with her best friend, Siobhan, and never came home. And she wants to have the embryos destroyed. She wants me to sign these papers agreeing to that, as obviously the clinic needs both of our permission to do it."

Leonora's eyebrows raised up her forehead. "But you don't want to?"

"I can't. We invested so much in them. It would almost feel like murder."

Leonora's cell phone rang, which made us both jump. "Oh, shit, that'll be Jasmine. She said she'd call. Sorry, you don't mind if I take it, do you?"

"Of course not." I had another sip of champagne, but I felt it in my head, which is never a good sign.

"Jazzy," she trilled as she picked up the phone. "How are you, love?"

Leonora left the room and I heard her climb the stairs. I thought I should get my phone, too, in case anyone wanted to get in touch with me, so I went into the hall to retrieve it from my jacket pocket.

"Stop fretting, Jazzy," Leonora was saying from upstairs. A little shiver ran down the back of my neck, my muscles fluttering in an invitation to pain. I told myself to move on, but of course, I didn't, and stayed listening at the bottom of the stairs. "I'm fine. I can handle it."

I made myself go back into the sitting room, but it felt a bit darker, and the muscles across my shoulders and up my neck were tensing in a sickeningly familiar way. I sat back down and leaned my head against the soft chair with my eyes shut, but my heart had joined in, thumping out at me through my ribs. People talking in another room reminded me too much of all those furtive business calls Mel would take all weekend, shutting herself away, apparently so as not to disturb me. Once I even found her typing away on her phone behind the marquee at a wedding, and, when I asked her if she couldn't stop for just one day, she'd cried and asked me when the fuck I wanted her to work, which was so weird because I'd never stopped her doing that in the first place. I wondered where Mel was then. It was nearly midnight on New Year's Eve, and it seemed almost disgusting that I couldn't place her. I suspected she'd be at one of our friends' houses, Kate and Siobhan's probably, maybe Jake and Joy's. Probably they were all together. Maybe there was even a single man there, a friend of Jake's, as he'd never really liked me, who was into sport and laughed loudly and earned heaps of money.

I opened my eyes and sat forward, which released the pain so it shot across my chest and up into my head, reminding me of a few easily googleable fatal illnesses. And, despite all she'd done to me and the fact that I was sitting in Leonora's house, all I wanted in that moment was to lay my head in Mel's lap. Except it was possible that I would never again do that, a thought that opened a chasm in me, as if I were spinning, unconnected to anything. What was the point of me without her, walking over hills and breathing fresh air while she was laughing at another man's jokes in the center of one of the biggest cities in the world, all those bodies and houses and appliances between us?

Leonora shrieked with laughter upstairs and the pain took dominance in my head, little flickers in my peripheral vision that I knew would grow and grow. This headache felt mean, I could tell it was going to throw its full force at me. In an attempt to calm myself, I focused on my phone, but it was as blank as ever. It was ten to midnight and not one person had wished me a happy new year. I pulled up Mel's number without any real consideration, jabbing out a text and pressing Send before I'd stopped to consider if it was a good idea. But then I could almost see her reaching across Kate and Siobhan's kitchen table for her phone, her face dropping when she saw the text was from me, saying something like, "Oh god, Cole's just wished me happy new year, what should I do?" The conversation would falter, and Jake's friend would say his ex-wife couldn't move on as well. They'd talk about me for a while, and Siobhan would say it was the right thing to do, not answering, it would only give me false hope.

I heard Leonora counting down upstairs as the numbers ticked over on my blank screen, my worried face reflected in its cracked glass. Eventually the call finished, and she burst back into the room.

"I'm so sorry about that. Jazz wanted to see the new year in with me in my time zone."

Even in those few seconds her phone was constantly pinging, so I knew hundreds of people were thinking about her.

For the first time since the split, I thought that I'd been stupid not to keep up with any of our old friends. But then it struck me that it was unlikely anyone would choose me over Mel anyway, as she'd always controlled our social life, never inviting my old friends to anything, meaning everyone we knew together really belonged to her. I couldn't work out if it had been deliberate or just something that happened but, whatever the reason, it had very effectively marooned me.

I stood and made my way over to Leonora, accepting her kiss, but only really able to concentrate on Mel kissing Jake's friend, swigging from a bottle of champagne, and linking arms with Siobhan. I imagined her saying something along the lines of, "This is going to be a better year." And everyone around her understanding that it was because I wasn't going to be part of it. Leonora's phone bleeped even louder.

"Shit, sorry. Let me mute it." But when she looked at the screen, she smiled. "Oh, look, the Walk for Women women are live streaming."

I looked at the dark image on her phone, which took a few minutes to work out because the lights in my vision were expanding, distorting my sight. But inevitably, Molly and Phoebe came into focus, waving a bottle of champagne at the camera, their faces large and bright.

"So we just wanted to say Happy New Year to you all," they said. "Apart from all the men who are sending us vile comments online, all the men who've hurt us and our friends over the years, the man who came to our tent last week, and the prick of a man who attacked us here earlier."

The vice around my head squeezed tight enough to make me worry that the blood vessels were going to pop. I had an image of Leonora splattered in my gore.

"We made a mistake, that's all. You didn't have to react that way. In fact, your anger is dangerous and a form of violence. I looked in your eyes and saw how much you hated me. How much you no doubt hate all women. If you haven't already hurt a woman, I expect one day you will."

There was a strange slithering in my guts, as if a snake were crawling through them. They surely couldn't be talking about me, but also I remembered their phone in my face. What they were saying was insanity because the anger had come from them, not me.

"Some men get off on intimidating women," the blond girl went on. "Some men use their physicality to try to frighten us into submission. Some use their fists; some use their words. But it's all the same. It's all unacceptable and it all contributes to a culture in which violence against women is seen as normal, almost natural."

I glanced at Leonora but she was absorbed by the screen, her brow furrowed and her teeth worrying her lip. I wanted to tell her that everything they were saying was bullshit, but then I'd have to explain how I knew that.

"Things are going to change," the other girl said. "We recorded our encounter today and we'll release it tomorrow, because, you know, we don't want to ruin the vibe tonight. But make no mistake, we've had enough of the angry men."

It was as if we'd slipped into an alternate reality in which everything was back to front. Except that's the way things are now. My wife runs a PR company and I know how it all works.

They turned the camera away from themselves and panned outward. At first I thought they were in a dark cave, but then I realized I could see the white tips of waves and hear the sea crashing against the cliffs.

"Oh my god, they're sitting on the edge," I said, moving toward the door.

"Are you going to try to find them?" Leonora called after me. "I know where they're camping 'cos they posted a picture earlier, by the Long Barn. I'll come with you."

But that made me stop. If we found the girls together, they'd recognize me, and then Leonora would know that I was the so-called angry man. It would make her hate me, which would be completely unfair. I knew I'd never be allowed to tell the proper version of the story. And it was all so fucking confusing because I want nothing more than to support and empower women, but surely that doesn't mean I should lie on the floor and let them walk all over me.

"I guess there's not much point," I said. "I mean, they could be anywhere."

"They've stopped now anyway," Leonora said, putting her phone down on a table. "But, man, that sounds savage. I hope he didn't hurt them."

"I'm sure he didn't. Most men don't want to hurt women, you know." I felt exhausted. My headache was beyond redemption and I knew it wouldn't release me until it had done its worst. "I'm sorry. I'm going to have to make a move. I've got a terrible headache."

She looked immediately crestfallen. "Seriously. Oh god, I'm sorry to have been so insensitive, leaving you alone at midnight, especially after what you told me."

"Oh, no, really it's not that," I said. "I get migraines and I can feel one coming on."

She screwed up her face. "Poor you. They're the worst."

Mel was never that understanding. In fact, I think my headaches used to irritate her, but still it wasn't enough to make me stay.

"I'm really sorry," I repeated, as I went into the hall. The jags in my vision were becoming wild, and I wanted to make it home before it closed completely. "I hope I haven't ruined your night. Everything was so nice. The food was so good."

"Don't be a plum," she said, with a wide, genuine smile. I smiled weakly as I stepped down into the night. The fresh air did make me feel a little better, the cold like a medicine, but it was nowhere near enough. She was still in her doorway waving at me when I reached the gate. "Sleep well!"

All I could do was weakly raise my hand. I wanted to sit down and cry, but it was too cold, which made me think about the girls all alone in their tent at the top of the hill and how ridiculous everything was. I couldn't work anything out; why Mel hadn't answered my text or why the Walk for Women girls were lying about me. My heart was pounding in my ears and my head was so woozy I was worried I might actually pass out. Which seemed like a stupid thing to do right next to a river, dangerous even. I turned away from the beach, deciding that all in all it would be safer to take the slightly longer walk home, up the hill toward the Long Barn.

I woke on New Year's Day lying on top of my bed, but fully dressed. There was mud on the knees of my jeans, a cut across the back of my hand, and all my muscles screamed with an overexertion I couldn't place. My vision was back to normal and the pain in my head was dull, but my heart was still beating too fast. I tried reaching for memories from the night before but the more I fought for them the more distant they became. There was a terrifying blank between leaving Leonora's and dragging myself up the stairs, pulling my body upward by the handrail.

I pulled off my jeans and maneuvered myself under the covers because I was also freezing. I rolled onto my side and saw my phone on the table next to the bed, which was something, because I must at least have had the sense to take it out of my pocket before I lay down. I pressed the home button, but the notification center was blank, which reminded me of the text I'd sent Mel the night before. Pinpricks of embarrassment flared along my skin.

I considered sending her another to apologize—I could say I'd felt nostalgic in the moment or something. But I doubted she'd buy that. Mel not only knew me well, she also would demand an explanation and always wanted a little more than I felt able to give. She enjoyed interrogating me down to the bones of myself, constantly asking how I was feeling or what I was thinking and dissecting arguments we'd had years before. And I wanted to give her everything, I really did. But often, even when I really thought about whatever it was she was asking and replied appropriately, it wouldn't be enough, which freaked me out because the truth was there wasn't anything more.

We were told that our infertility was "nonspecific," which is obviously the worst kind, as it means they don't know why it's happened or how to treat it. I'm not sure how any couple survives IVF. Watching Mel go through it was a bit like watching a horror film. The drugs affected everything about her—her skin became red and sensitive, her hair fell out, her fingers swelled, her back ached, her head split, and her mind ran away into a dark corner. One minute she'd been screaming and yelling, the next under the covers weeping. She'd accuse me of terrible things and then cling to me, begging me to forgive her. And the white sticks with their fucking blue lines that never materialized, the blood on the sheets, the howling behind locked doors. But no one ever acknowledged that it was hard for me as well. Not as hard as it was on Mel, obviously, but still hard. We would sit in the plush waiting room surrounded by posters advertising counseling, all with pictures of weeping women on them. And when the nurses asked how we were coping, they always looked at Mel and directed their questions toward her. Sometimes I wanted to scream at them to look at me and give me just one second of compassion.

Because, the thing is, I desperately, completely, horridly want a baby. I yearn for one. I dream of strapping him or her to my chest, and long for the sleepless nights and the dirty nappies and the food smeared across the walls. I want little arms to reach out for me. I want to know that I'm the only one who can quiet tears or rock a tiny body back to sleep. I want to look into a perfect face and see myself reflected back. I want to know that parts of me will remain after I'm gone.

I stayed in bed much later than usual on New Year's Day. My ghost baby hovered in the corner of the room, just out of sight, so in the end I gave up trying to see it and let myself cry. I wondered how Leonora would react if she could see me. It would be nice to think that she'd bring me tea and stroke my head, but chances were it was more likely she'd be a little disgusted. It's strange how men are asked to be sensitive and understanding now, but when we really are, when we say how we're truly feeling, women don't actually like it. I think, subconsciously, they want us to hold their hands and understand their emotional contradictions, but they also still want us to be strong, to bang our chests with our fists and protect them from shit. That's what I think Mel wanted from me and, let me tell you, it's a hard ask, expecting someone to be all things at all times.

I knew I should get up and do something constructive to start the new year. A year that I'd tried so hard to make bright in my mind, but which was beginning to look like the same pile of shit as the last. I pulled my knees up into my chest. My life seemed like nothing more than a series of mistakes, when I'd only ever tried my best to be kind and do the right thing.

I probably would have stayed in bed all day if my phone hadn't started ringing around lunchtime. I leaped for it as if it could save me. At first I couldn't make out what Leonora was saying. The wind from the previous night still hadn't died down, so it sounded like a steam train on the other end.

"Cup your hand around the phone, Leonora," I had to shout several times. "I can't hear you."

Eventually she must have taken my advice because suddenly her voice became clear.

"Cole," she shouted, "I need your help."

"Has something happened?"

"I don't know. Where are you?"

"At home."

All the hairs on my body were standing at attention, and I felt hot despite the cold air all around me. I heard her pull in a breath, as if attempting composure.

"I'm by the Long Barn. Can you come?"

"Are you okay? What's happened?"

Her voice broke slightly. "Please, Cole. I'll explain when you get here."

I pulled my jeans back on and found my coat and boots discarded by the front door. The air was gray and freezing and, along with the exertion of running, my lungs felt like they were on fire. My head

wasn't recovered enough for the exercise and my brain jangled disconcertingly against my skull. But I felt a strange urgency, little flickers of
something that could be a memory firing through me.

When I reached the barn, Leonora was bending over an orange tent,
the flaps at the front gaping open. She straightened as I approached and
put a hand to her head, which was covered by a blue wool hat.

"Thanks for coming. I was just out for a walk and found this. It's
Molly and Phoebe's tent. You know, the Walk for Women women?"

The tent was instantly recognizable from all their posts, but I
couldn't immediately work out what Leonora was saying.

"I won't report them for camping here. I won't even say anything
about that stupid video they did last night. As long as they move on."

"No, that's not what I mean." She shook her head and gestured at
the scene. "Doesn't it look, well, abandoned? Even like there could have
been a struggle?"

I stepped past her and looked inside the tent, where everything was
in disarray. "What are you thinking?"

"I don't know. But this is weird, right? I mean, why would they leave
all their stuff like this? And the tent open?"

"Maybe they've gone to get something?"

She looked at me like I was stupid. "Where from? There aren't
exactly any shops nearby. And anyway, it's New Year's Day, most places
will be shut." My body flushed with heat and my head felt too delicate
for whatever was going on. It had a sense of fullness, which it sometimes does after a bad attack, so everything is almost blotted out. But
she carried on, "I know they've been getting abuse online. Some man
came to their tent in the middle of the night a few days ago. And then
that idiot shouted at them on the cliff top just yesterday. I think we
should call the police. I really don't like the look of this."

It was true that the scene had a bad feel to it, but I couldn't tell if
that was real or perception. "Right, I mean, you're probably right."

She walked over to the side of the barn and turned away to make the call. I used the time to dip back into the tent and have a quick look for their phones. Because I wasn't discombobulated enough not to realize that I was in a dangerous position. They had lied about me in their stupid midnight vlog and there is no benefit of the doubt offered to men anymore. But, of course, their phones weren't there.

"Hey, they said not to touch anything," Leonora said from behind me.

I darted back out. "Sorry, sorry. I was only looking to see if they'd left anything that might tell us where they've gone."

"Did you find anything?"

"No, but one of them left their wallet."

"Shit. Shit, I hope nothing bad's happened."

The police arrived disconcertingly quickly, their blue lights flashing into the murk of the day. There was a thick moisture in the air that threatened rain, and standing still had let the cold seep into my bones. The policeman who reached us first was young but had a serious air about him. A policewoman stood a bit behind him, a notebook open in her hands.

"DS Croxley," he said, holding out his hand to Leonora. "Ms. Baxter?"

Leonora shook his hand. "That's right."

"So, talk me through what's going on here."

She pulled in a deep breath. "Well, I was out for a walk and came across this tent which looks, well, you know, abandoned. I know it belongs to the Walk for Women women because I've been following them online."

The policeman screwed up his face, but I saw the policewoman behind him nod. They both moved over to the tent.

"Have either of you touched anything?" The policeman asked over his shoulder.

"I have," I said. "I'm sorry, I didn't think. But one of them left their wallet."

"Hey, Stu," the policewoman said. "Look at this."

He went over to her, bending over a pile of rocks next to the tent. He straightened back up quickly. "Okay, we should secure the scene."

His colleague walked away to speak into her radio, but we all heard the word *blood*.

He turned to me. "Sorry, and you are?"

"Cole Simmonds." My voice sounded weak.

"Were you with Ms. Baxter when she found the tent?"

"No, she called me and asked me to come. I just live at the bottom of the river."

"And this was at what time?"

"About two thirty?"

He turned back to Leonora. "What time did you find the tent?"

"About ten or fifteen minutes before that." She took a step toward him. "Molly and Phoebe, the women doing this walk, they've been getting quite a bit of abuse online. Last week a man, well, rubbed himself against their tent in the middle of the night. And just yesterday a man shouted at them right here. They've posted about it all online."

DS Croxley turned back to the policewoman. "Can you fill Adam in on all of this so we can have a look when we get back to the station?"

"Has something happened to them?" Leonora asked. "Did you find something bad?"

"I'm really sorry, but I can't go into any details right now," Croxley said. "We need to get forensics up here. In fact, I'm going to have to ask you both to leave. I take it you live nearby?"

"Yes, we both do," Leonora said. "I'm in the coast-guard cottage and Cole is by The Wildlife Hut."

He nodded. "Good. If you could give your details to DC Williams, then we'll arrange a time to take your statements, if things progress."

We did as he asked and then walked down the hill toward the cliff edge. The light was gray but bright, an eerie shimmer distorting everything ever so slightly.

"What the fuck is going on?" Leonora said as we reached the string demarcation line. We were standing in almost the exact same spot I'd been with the girls twenty-four hours earlier.

"I have no idea."

She looked across at me. "They sounded worried."

"I know."

"Do you think someone might have hurt them?"

"I don't know."

Leonora sort of swayed into me, holding on to my arm. "I feel a bit dizzy," she said.

I put an arm round her shoulder. "Come on, let's get you home."

The light was starting to fade as we made our way down toward her cottage, the brightness that had been there earlier totally vanished, the clouds low and dark. The temperature had also dropped dramatically so a mist was starting to work its way up from the ground. You could feel the impending frost in the air.

"I'm so sorry," Leonora said as we made it through her front door. "I'm being totally pathetic."

"It's fine," I said. "You've had a shock. Let's get you warm."

I took her into the sitting room, where I sat her on the sofa with a blanket over her knees, then got the fire going. "Why don't I make us both a cup of tea."

"Thanks so much, Cole." She turned her face up to me and I was taken aback by how young she looked, as if she'd been washed clean. I don't think Mel ever thanked me in all the time we were going through IVF for the way I'd cosseted and coddled her and made her feel warm and secure. Sometimes she'd even shout at me to go away and say she felt suffocated. She made me feel as if I got everything wrong, so I basically spent the last two years of our relationship constantly feeling like I was failing her. "Actually," Leonora said, "I could do with something stronger than tea. There's some gin in the cupboard above the sink, and tonic in the fridge."

I poured us both quite a strong drink as I looked out over the sea. It was that time of year when night almost obliterates day, and I could feel the darkness drawing down. I sent a quick text to Holly and she replied that she was aware of the situation, but there was nothing to be done until we heard more from the police. The air in the sitting room had warmed nicely by the time I got back, but Leonora looked worried.

I sat next to her. "Are you okay?"

She held her phone up. "The police just called, asking if I saw or spoke to the women at all."

Something hard dropped through my stomach. "Did you?"

"No." She rubbed her forehead. "But it definitely sounds like they're taking it seriously."

"It might all be a misunderstanding," I said. "The girls could right now be sitting warm and comfy in a pub somewhere."

"Yeah, maybe." She tapped a nail against the side of her glass. "But how often do missing women just turn up, unharmed?"

I looked out of the window at the blackness. I'd read that the coast guards believed one room in their homes had to face away from the sea or else they'd go mad. The metallic tones of the news theme made me turn back to the room. The missing girls were the third story, after the ongoing war in a faraway land and the financial crisis. But it was the story the newscasters appeared to enjoy covering the most, almost salivating over the details in a way that made me feel sick. Molly and Phoebe's eager faces stared out from various photographs, many taken from their walk, but some from parties and their graduations. In each one, they looked impossibly vulnerable. I thought about the rabbits in my trap and how easy it is to break small limbs, how quickly sharp knives cut through flesh.

"I never saw my mum's body," Leonora said after the report had finished. The words circled through the room, and I stayed quiet because sometimes speech needs time to settle. "The police advised against it, which I obviously knew meant he'd beaten her too badly.

Although now I sort of wish I had because everything I've imagined since is probably worse than the reality."

"I'm sorry."

The muscles on her face were working hard, her jaw clenched tight. Eventually the tears won so I pulled her into me and rubbed my hand down her back.

"Oh god," she said into my chest. "This has made me feel really scared." I could feel her actually shaking against me, so I held her a bit tighter, and she burrowed into me. She felt so small and weak, which made something contract at the base of my stomach. She pulled back. "Would you stay the night, Cole? I'm really sorry to ask. I just don't think I can bear to be alone."

Her lip was quivering and her eyes were huge as she waited for my answer. It made me feel like maybe there were other possibilities out there, that I didn't have to spend my whole life fighting and apologizing and being wrong. I leaned across and kissed her before I'd really considered if it was the right thing to do, but she responded, though it was tentative. The feeling was electric. I was taking control of a situation and being strong and making things better. I didn't need permission. No one was telling me what to do or denying me something or mocking me. I could just be this best version of myself.

But then Leonora pulled away. "I'm sorry. I'm not in the right headspace for this right now."

I reached for her hand. "It's fine."

"I do like you." She hesitated. "It's just today's been a headfuck."

I leaned forward and kissed her forehead. "It's okay, Leonora. I totally get it."

She stroked a finger across the back of my hand. "What happened? That's a nasty cut."

"I tripped on the walk home last night." As I said the words, I did have a vague sense of landing heavily, and it had to have been what happened.

I made us both sandwiches and we went to bed early. I could tell from the way she moved that she was exhausted, and I drew the curtains tight against the sea before she could look out. We lay in the creaky iron bed together and it felt much more comfortable than last time. Leonora lay on her back so I could see her eyes shining in the darkness. I felt for her hand under the covers.

"I don't have to swim in the morning, if you'd rather I was here."

"That's kind, but don't worry, I'll be fine." She squeezed my fingers. "Don't you get scared, being out in the sea in the dark, alone?"

"Sometimes," I admitted. "But that's part of it. Forcing myself to do something scary."

"What are you most scared of?"

"This is going to sound silly. But mermaids."

"Mermaids?"

"Have you ever seen photographs of the mermaids Barnum exhibited?"

"Yeah, I think so."

Horrific images swam into my mind, the distended human forms with rounded spines and bald heads, the scaly tails and sharp teeth, the infuriating opposite of what they were meant to be.

"My mum had a series of pictures of them hanging on her study wall. And now I can't go in the sea without thinking about them."

Leonora rolled onto her side, propping her head up on her elbow. Her face looked serious in the darkness, as if she was working something out. "Don't you think Barnum was very canny in showing those grotesque mermaids?"

"Why's that?"

She lay back down and spoke into the night. "Because people have always wanted horror stories. The power of fear is so potent."

I swam as usual in the morning, barely feeling the cold, as if the heat from the night before was still inside my body. Physically I felt back to normal as well, which always makes the memory loss seem more bearable. As I thrashed through the sea I even wondered if Mel had ever been as important as I'd made her out to be all this time. By the time I got to the Hut, Holly was bursting to talk about the missing girls. She told me that the search had resumed at first light, but nothing had been found yet. And she'd heard a rumor from her brother, who worked for the local police, that they'd found Molly's blood at the scene. Holly is one of those people who finds it hard to be quiet, so I knew we were in for a long day. Plus, our whole work schedule was disrupted. Head office wanted us on the cliffs and beach all day so we could help where needed.

I spent the morning on the cliff top fielding photographers and news crews who were getting in the way of the police operation. A large white tent had been put over the orange one and yellow police tape was sealing off a whole section of the field. As the morning progressed, I noticed a few women walking by. Someone had left a bunch of flowers wrapped in shiny plastic by the tape.

My plan was to drop in on Leonora at lunchtime to check she was okay, but when I arrived at her cottage, a police car was parked outside. Through her window I saw her sitting with the officers from the day before and thought I shouldn't disturb them. I felt very restless when I got home; I ate a quick sandwich and then checked the trap. I wasn't expecting anything, so it felt like a gift when I opened it and saw a plump rabbit sniffing the air, much better than the first one. The dispatch was also much cleaner and more efficient. I darted back inside to get the outhouse key, before taking the rabbit corpse over. But when I got there, something wasn't right. At first I couldn't put my finger on what it was, but then I saw that the chain I used to secure the door looked different. My heart set up a steady thump because it didn't make sense. I undid the lock and dangled the chain in front of me. I was sure that I'd bought enough length to double it through the handles, but what I held only allowed for a single loop.

I opened the door tentatively, but inside nothing was amiss. The outhouse has one main room and a small anteroom off to one side. The lock on that door was still secure and I couldn't face the idea of opening it, so I only looked around the main space. All my things were exactly as I'd left them. Although, there was a faint tang in the air of something I couldn't put my finger on. But it was so mild I wasn't sure if I was imagining it or not. I took a few deep breaths and made myself stand still. Surely I hadn't come out to the outhouse on New Year's Eve, and, even if I had, that wouldn't explain the chain being shorter. I reasoned that I must have misremembered the chain length, especially since the key had been on its hook in the cottage and everything else was as it should be.

As I was scraping the rabbit's guts into a plastic bag I heard my name being called. At first I thought it must be my mind playing tricks on me, but then I heard it again and knew Mel was really there. I could tell by the way she was shouting that she was annoyed. Marriage does that to a person. It gives you a superhuman ability to detect moods from the slightest movement or sound. I considered hiding but knew if Mel had driven all the way down here she wasn't going to be put off by me not being home and I had no desire to have her poking around.

I took a deep breath to steady my nerves, then locked up and rounded the side of my cottage. The first thing I saw was a large van with blacked out windows in my drive. Mel was looking up at the cottage, so she didn't notice me at first and I was able to take in the fact that she appeared to have gotten even thinner, which meant she probably wasn't eating properly without me. She was wearing tight jeans tucked into tall black boots, a yellow jumper, and a white fluffy coat, a strange choice for the countryside.

"New car?" I said, which made her turn around. I saw the surprise on her face as she took me in.

"Cole" she said, "goodness, I hardly recognized you."

I involuntarily put my hand to my face and stroked my beard, which probably had gotten a bit out of control. Also, my clothes hadn't been washed for a couple of days and definitely had mud on them and possibly blood, too, from the rabbit. That reminded me that I was carrying a bag of guts, so I dropped it quickly by my front step.

"Didn't have you down as the van type," I said. "What happened to the sports car?"

She glanced over at the vehicle. "It's in the garage. This is all they had."

I knew how long it took Mel to create her perfect face, but still, and despite myself, I was impressed by how polished she looked. "What are you doing here?"

"Could we go inside?"

Mel hadn't wanted to be near me for months, so this was a surprising development. But still I opened the door to my cottage and led her through to the kitchen. The debris from my sandwich was on the table, which embarrassed me, which in turn annoyed me. Mel took off her coat and draped it and her bag over the back of a chair as she looked around the room. I'd loved my cottage, but it sort of withered under Mel's gaze. I knew she'd be noticing the damp above the back door and the way not all the cupboard doors aligned, the steel sink, and the rickety fridge. I had a sudden urge to bundle her out of the door so she couldn't contaminate the space with her judgment because all the things she would hate about it were the things I loved, and I couldn't bear it if she ruined that for me as well.

"Would you like a cup of tea?" I asked.

She pulled out a chair and sat down. "Yes, please."

"Sorry, I only have normal milk." She was happy to eat processed, ready-made meals and drink liters of coffee, but god forbid a bit of dairy or gluten made its way inside her.

"Don't worry, I'll have it black." She fished her phone out of her bag and put it on the table next to her.

"You hate black tea."

"It's fine."

She winced when she took the first sip, which made me remember that she hates twice boiled water. She used to go crazy if I made her tea without filling the kettle with fresh water, even though I could never taste the hollowness she claimed was there when you boiled it twice. Like the ghost of tea, she used to say. Now that the rose-tinted glasses had started to slip, I wondered if emotional manipulation was her strong suit.

"It's nice, this place. Good find." She smiled at me over the mug.

"Yes, yes. I think I've thanked you enough times."

I wished that Mel hadn't found me the cottage and the job. It had felt as though she was trying to get rid of me when she'd emailed the listings about a month after she moved out. But it's true that I'd felt paralyzed by the task of finding a new place so I hadn't started looking. And, I had to hand it to her, as soon as I opened the link, I knew it was exactly what I wanted.

"I'm glad you're happy about where you're living, Cole." She paused and I braced myself. "It's just, I still haven't managed to settle into a new place of my own because I need to sell our flat first. And I can't sell the flat until you've signed the papers. And the people who're buying it have said that if they don't get the papers back by the end of the week, they're going to pull out."

I tried to remember if Mel had always sounded so patronizing when she spoke.

"I'm sorry. I've had quite a bit on." She raised an eyebrow. "Two girls went missing here yesterday, you know."

Her brow contracted. "Yes, I heard about that on the news. I thought it sounded near to here."

I pulled at the neck of my jumper, which felt suddenly tight. "It was. About a fifteen-minute walk." I sipped at my tea, but it was too hot and burnt my tongue. "In fact, a friend of mine found their tent and called me, so I was there when the police came."

She frowned. "Did they question you?"

"Of course they questioned me. But I couldn't tell them anything."

She hesitated for a moment. "Did you do anything fun on New Year's Eve?"

"I had supper with a friend. In fact, the one who rang me when she found the tent." It took a superhuman effort not to ask Mel what she'd done. "Anyway, have you really driven all the way down here to get the flat papers?"

It seemed so unlikely because she never took the day off work for anything, apart from holidays planned long in advance, and even then, she was always contactable "in an emergency," which basically meant anything and everything. She never took the day off for birthdays or illness, or even fucking IVF appointments.

A vein twitched at the side of her head. "Yes, Cole, I drove all the way here because I can't take it if the buyers pull out. I cannot go through the stress of putting it back on the market again. I'll have to take drastic action."

"Drastic action? Are you threatening me, Mel?" She rolled her eyes. "You never answered my text on New Year's Eve."

"Are you serious? What, you're not signing the papers to pay me back for that?"

"Don't be childish, Mel."

She ran a hand through her hair so I could see her dark roots. "Listen, I don't know what you think is going on between us. But we're not going to be friends after all this."

Her words felt like daggers, but I held firm. "Did Siobhan tell you to say that?"

Mel sat up straighter. "Actually, you know what, I do have my own fully functioning brain and can make up my mind about most things." I raised my hands in a symbol of supplication, feeling already exhausted by her ability to fight about anything. She stuck out her bottom lip. "Look, I just need those papers, all of them. And then we can stop having these conversations. Hell, we can stop having any conversations."

Her meanness made me act totally out of character.

"You're not going to believe this, but I posted the flat ones yesterday."

"What? You didn't think to let me know?"

"I'm sorry. I didn't realize it was all so urgent."

"It was there in all the emails." Her voice had risen in the way it does when she gets angry.

"Look, don't worry. You'll get them tomorrow at the latest."

"Fucking hell, Cole. It's the first day of work after the break and I had to cancel loads of meetings to come here." She rubbed at the top of her nose and looked so serious I nearly laughed. But instead, I apologized, although really I didn't even care if we lost the sale because all she'd have to do is ring the bloody estate agent. I'd spent so much time before I left fixing things and repainting and generally making it as easy as it could be for her. Her face was set hard. "I still need you to sign those other papers as well."

"I'm not going to sign them." I could feel a weight descending through me that I knew was going to be very hard to shift after she'd gone. Her eyes welled, but she bit on her bottom lip to stop herself from crying. "You'll thank me for this one day. I think you'd hate yourself if we destroyed them. It's a heat-of-the-moment reaction."

Her brow furrowed. "It's not. I've told you a hundred times I want to get rid of them. I'm not going to change my mind."

"I can't bear to do that to them."

She rubbed a hand across her face, which looked pale suddenly, so I could see the darkness around her eyes. "I can't do this again, Cole. They're a collection of cells. We're not doing anything to them because they're not sentient beings."

"They have the potential to be." I was quite close to tears myself and my voice had risen in pitch, not that it moved her.

"Every sperm you ejaculate has that potential. You know, saying that, you're not many steps away from being pro-life."

I snorted. "Don't be ridiculous. You always do that. You always exaggerate to the point where the argument is lost." She shook her head. And something about the casualness of the movement made all the old desperation flood back, extinguishing the anger, so I wanted to fall at her feet again. It was all so confusing I wanted to give up and cry. "Look, Mel. I'm not sure you've really thought this through. But I have, a lot, and there is a solution. You could still carry our baby without us getting back together. And I'd do everything when it's born. It could even live with me full-time, if that was better for you, although obviously you could see it whenever you wanted to, or we could arrange a custody agreement. I'd even move back to London if that's what it took."

She simply stared at me for a moment, but then the tears broke free. "What the fuck?" she hissed.

"Mel, please. Please, just consider it. I just want to discuss it."

"You can't put something into my body, Cole," she said. "And then make me carry it for nine months. Then give birth to it. I mean, do you know how insane that sounds?"

"It's not insane," I said. "It's less insane than killing three potential babies."

She made a sound that was almost a scream. "What do you think I am? Some sort of fucking vending machine?"

Her hands were shaking and her face had gone very pale, which is usually the sign that she is on the verge of a complete freak-out. And Mel's freak-outs are hard to navigate; they can even turn violent.

"Please," I said. "It's not such a mad solution when you think about it. I really, really don't want to lose my chance to be a father. This could be the last chance for both of us."

She shut her eyes for a second, but when she opened them she'd stopped crying. "You, Cole, are literally the last person I would want to be the father of my children. In fact, no woman in their right mind would want to have children with you. Having those embryos in that freezer is making me ill. I think about it all the time and it's totally fucking with my head."

"I'm begging you, Mel," I said, all my dignity departing.

"You need fucking help," she spat across the table.

I forced myself not to reply to her vileness. "Or, if you don't want to carry them, we could find a surrogate."

She almost snarled, her lips pulling away across her teeth. "Fuck you, Cole," she shouted as she stood up, grabbing her coat and bag. "I am so done with you. Honestly, it would be better if you weren't here anymore."

She ran to the door and, even though I followed her, she was in the van before I even got outside. She didn't look at me as she started the engine and revved away, her face set like stone. I felt incredibly strange and also freezing as I watched her screech away. I should have been back out on the cliffs helping with the search, but I was dazed. I went back inside, but the cold had penetrated the bones of the building, making my whole body shiver, my teeth actually chattering. I stumbled into the sitting room and lit the fire, wrapping a blanket round my shoulders as I waited for it to get going.

A wave of pure tiredness washed through me as I tried to make sense of what had just happened. It was almost unbelievable how quickly things could deteriorate with Mel, her rudeness an open wound that still had the ability to shock me. And her threats were starting to feel very real. I wondered even if she could be dangerous.

M el texted later that evening, when it had been dark for a long time. I still hadn't turned on any lights, although the fire had dyed the walls orange and heated the air nicely. An infinitesimal part of me let myself believe that she was texting to apologize, but the larger part knew that I'd been hiding from the truth for too long and my wife was not someone to be either trusted or appealed to. I opened the message with shaky fingers and was rewarded with the words:

I'm going to contact my lawyers in the morning to see if I there's any way of getting your name removed from the permission so I can have the embryos destroyed myself immediately.

The scales fell completely from my eyes then, and I finally saw Mel for who she was, for who she'd always been: a bully. The text was nothing more than the grown-up equivalent of a big kid lashing out at a smaller one on the playground. I fell forward over my legs, dropping my head between my knees to stop myself from passing out. But when I shut my sore eyes, the image that appeared behind them was of Leonora and it calmed me. I had made a pact with myself to move forward and yet here I was still repeating the same destructive patterns with Mel. Leonora and I had undeniably formed a connection the night before and it seemed suddenly so obvious what I should be doing.

I heard a fox screeching outside my front door, which reminded me that the rabbit guts were still in a bag on the doorstep. When I went to retrieve them, the light from the hallway lit up his dark eyes and pointed nose, which gave me a little fright.

It was about half past nine when I let myself out of my cottage, dressed for the freezing cold, with the plastic bag of guts in my hand. The moon was at the beginning of its cycle, a fingernail of light in the black sky, but the night was clear so its silvery sheen still melted into the air. The ground was hard already, and I could see the sparkling beginnings of a frost starting to form on the ridges of dried mud on the path. I walked up the hill toward the Long Barn, where I figured I could dispose of the guts in a field. But when I got to the top, it was all lit up by searchlights. The white tent was illuminated like a beacon, with two policemen standing by the tape surrounding it, laughing at something on their phones.

I cut down a side path toward the sea, but bizarrely came across a group of women sitting around a campfire. They'd pitched two tents and one of them was strumming on a guitar, the music floating upward. I stuck to the shadows as I passed because I couldn't face a conversation. I couldn't even work out what they were doing there.

Before I knew it, I was basically at Leonora's front door. The lights were on in the sitting room and Leonora was in the chair by the fire tapping away on her phone. She looked pretty shattered and, from the path, her eyes resembled two dark holes. My heart tipped at the thought of her scared and vulnerable on her own, and I hated myself for being so distracted by Mel that I hadn't contacted her. I pulled out my phone and tapped out a quick message:

Sorry, been a hectic day. Hope you're feeling okay. Can come round now if you want some company.

I saw her reading my message, her shoulders hunched over. But then, she let the phone drop into her lap, sighing as she leaned her head back against the chair, shutting her eyes and massaging her temple. I don't know what I'd expected her response to be, but it wasn't that. My breath hitched at the thought that she could be pissed off with me for not getting in touch all day. She didn't know that I'd come by at lunch-time or what had happened with Mel. As far as she was concerned, I'd known how upset she was about the girls and not made any contact.

She stood, tucking the phone into her back pocket, then went around the room turning out the lights. I moved up the path in time to see the light from the kitchen being extinguished, and I guessed she must be going to bed. I checked my phone, but she still hadn't replied, and I started to get that same creeping desperation that so many women have produced in me, Mel especially.

I slipped down the side passage, past the dark, empty kitchen, where the light from the moon revealed the remnants of Leonora's supper, some bread and cheese. There's something intensely personal about see-ing what a person puts into their body, almost more personal, I think, than seeing their naked form. It says so much, doesn't it, about how much we think we're worth. Leonora's supper spoke of a lack of care and that made me realize that I cared. I didn't want whatever it was that we'd started to end. I moved to the small back garden, where I could see the lights on upstairs, in the bathroom and the bedroom. Leonora appeared at the bedroom window and lingered at the view for a few minutes. She leaned right up close to the glass, her breath misting the pane.

I felt very sad then, because it had taken me too long to work out what was going on and what I needed. It was suddenly obvious that I'd gone for the wrong women all my life, starting with Laura, my first proper girlfriend, who literally never said what she meant and tied me in all sorts of knots. I met her during my first year of university and we went out for nearly a year. But she ruined that experience, manipulating every-thing I did, so I can't bear to even think about that time, which should have been some of the happiest years of my life. I think she got inside my head so much that it had set off a pattern in my relationships. I don't think I've ever felt entirely safe with a woman since, even though I kidded myself that I was with Mel. It was time to be honest with myself: I'm not an alpha male and I think these alpha female types shrink me somehow. Someone calmer and quieter like Leonora had always been what I'd needed. And then I felt angry because I should have been in her room, comforting her, rather than standing alone watching her from a freezing, dark garden.

History is littered with bad men doing bad things to women. And, the truth is, they've ruined it for the rest of us, who just want to love and nurture. They've created a world in which sometimes the only options left for us are the desperate ones. I walked over to the back doorstep and emptied the guts onto them. The rich scent of blood immediately flooded the air and I imagined foxes all around following their noses. They would fight and screech under Leonora's window and she would be reminded that it's nice to have a warm body next to you in a bed, and that being loved and cared for is what life is all about. I left the garden and hurried away from the cottage. As I took the path down to the beach, I resolved that I would start again the next day. I'd forget about Mel and show Leonora how much I liked her. I would concentrate on positives rather than negatives.

The sea looked amazing, the light of the moon picking up all its little undulations. I stopped for a moment to look at it but was overcome by tiredness and sat on a large rock. I pulled out my phone and saw a missed call and message from a number I didn't recognize.

"Mr. Simmonds, this is DS Croxley. We'd like a quick word with you about the disappearance of Molly Patterson and Phoebe Canton. Could you give me a call back at your earliest convenience? We can arrange a time for you to pop into the station, or we can come to you. Many thanks."

My heart clenched and the muscles along my shoulders twitched. Obviously they'd need to talk to me; it was normal procedure. I knew it was a bad idea, but I clicked on Mel's message again, which seemed even crueler on second viewing. It, in fact, seemed bizarre that what she wanted to do wasn't as severe a crime as whatever it was the police were investigating. But I was able to look at it all with calmer eyes now that I had my newfound understanding inside me. She wasn't what I needed, but whatever else happened, I couldn't let her just dispose of our babies.

It was obvious that I was going to have to be the grown-up, so I typed out a considered reply:

I'm sorry for springing that idea on you today. I can see how it might have come as a bit of a shock and I should have been more sensitive. But I do think it's worth considering. I don't want to get back together either, but this could be the last chance for both of us to have a baby. My offer will always stand to be the primary caregiver and I think we could work really well together and create a happy, if unconventional, little family. Please can we talk about this more? Any time that suits you.

Almost immediately she texted back:

There is nothing more to speak about and I will never change my mind. I'm going to do everything I can to get rid of those embryos, starting with stopping paying the clinic to keep them on ice.

I tried to google if it's possible to destroy embryos without the father's consent, but my reception wasn't good enough for any pages to load. My mind felt like it had come loose from my body, as if there was nothing keeping it steady and I could drift into the air at any moment. I stood because otherwise I would have passed out. I was hot and shaking and knew there was only one thing left that could calm me.

I put my phone on the rock and stripped off all my clothes, walking directly to the shore, where I confused the sound of breaking waves with mermaids calling to me. It was hard to tell how big they were in the dark, but they were obviously pretty large, and I absolutely knew I shouldn't go in. I ran at the sea because the worst danger occurs when the waves break. It was easier than I'd feared and the water held me up, which calmed me because it proved I was strong and capable and should trust myself more. I swam out a bit farther and for a few minutes I enjoyed feeling my body responding to the waves, letting myself be taken up and down.

But the cold also brought me to my senses. What I was doing was dangerous and I didn't want to hurt myself. Mel's threats weren't worth risking my life for, especially not when I had a good life almost within touching distance. I turned back toward shore and, out of habit, glanced up at the coast-guard cottage. But the view jolted me by how wrong it was. For a second, I thought the world had tipped upside down because the edge of the cliff was alive with little pinpricks of light, as if the stars had fallen to earth or a million fireflies were dancing in unison. It had to have something to do with the missing girls, but I couldn't work out what.

The sea roared in my ears, wrapping around my ankles with mean hands, and every swell looked like a body heading toward me. I started to make for the beach but had clearly swum farther than I'd realized. Every stroke felt closer to a hundred so I exhausted myself quickly, the water was finding its way inside me and clogging my senses, while my muscles screamed and begged for release. A wave crashed on top of me, pushing me under and turning me round. But I bobbed back up and pushed on.

I put my foot down and it mercifully connected with the stony bottom, but it was immediately tugged away and I was pulled inside another wave. My back smashed against the ground, and I was dragged across the sharp stones, my left leg twisting underneath me. This time when I emerged, I was farther in. There was a large rock in my path, which I wrapped my arms around as the next wave crashed down on my back. I gasped for air as it receded, my whole chest screaming for oxygen and an irony taste of blood in my mouth. I knew I had to move before the next break, or I would die.

My legs were shaking when I stood but the water only came to my groin. I could hear the next wave rushing behind me so I half ran, half swam into shallower water. The wave knocked me off my feet, but I was able to dig my fingers into the seabed and hold my ground. And then all I had to do was haul my tired, broken body a little farther until I was safe.

I lay on my back, gulping at the air, looking up into the night sky. I felt ridiculous, but also a little angry. I was being driven to behave in a stupid, reckless way because my wife had a vendetta against me. Or maybe against men in general. I didn't know anymore. Maybe all women hated all men? Maybe they even had good reason? At that moment nothing seemed clear.

And I know, historically, it's been hard to be a woman but, my god, it's hard to be a man right now.

Okay, let's make one thing clear. My name is Lennie, not fucking Leonora. Every time I heard him say that I wanted to smash his self-satisfied face in because it is no one's right to take away your name. Men have been doing that for too fucking long.

But there's a time and place for those thoughts. You don't live a life like mine without learning patience. Just like you don't live a life like mine without learning what people want from you. Then again, you don't live a life like mine without also learning what you want from people.

And I'm not afraid to take what I want. Because people like me know what we're owed by the Coles of this world. We know their time is up and they haven't worked that out yet, which gives us a major upper hand.

two

T he night is hot, which makes the open bathroom window a bit more plausible. Not that any woman sleeping alone in a basement flat in Lewisham, or anywhere for that matter, would ever casually leave a window open. I hope Cole realizes that and hasn't gone far, although I didn't actually spell it out for him, so he might be walking round the block or something. I turn over to stop my thoughts from racing, but that's worse because then I can feel my heart thumping against my ribs. I'm desperate to shut the window, but we've come this far, and I don't want to look like I'm backing out.

Cole is unlike any man I've met before and I'm so excited by where our relationship is going. The sex thing is the only cloud in an otherwise clear blue sky and I'm not too sure it counts as a cloud anyway. It certainly doesn't when you compare it to all the shit Luke put me through.

By the end of the year I spent with Luke, I felt a little mad. I sometimes still wonder if it was all a game to him because I don't know what else he could have gotten out of it. He lied even when telling the truth would have gotten him the same result. He was never where he said he was, never turned up on time, didn't contact me for days, and, if ever I complained, he told me I was overbearing and reading too much into things. After we split up, I genuinely thought I was done with men, but then I matched with Cole on TwoHearts and he looked so nice in his profile that, well, he restored my faith in the male species.

The first time we had sex, Cole went limp halfway through, something that had never happened to me before. It made me feel so embarrassed and ashamed, I wanted to grab my clothes and run. I'd been on top and all I could think of was how disgusting I must have looked, my fat sagging off me. But Cole cried before I could, which stopped me in my tracks. I don't think I'd ever seen a man cry before, not so openly and unabashedly. I mean, plenty of men have made me cry, but it has never been the other way around. Then he started incessantly apologizing, which made me nervous because when a man does that it usually means he's done something bad. But after hours of coaxing, what he admitted was shocking but also very sweet.

On our first date, he'd said that his parents were dead, but that night, he confessed that it wasn't true. He told me the saddest story about how he'd only said that because the truth was too embarrassing, that they'd never loved him. I held him tight as he recounted the loneliness of his childhood and his mother's inability to show him love or affection, and how it made him very scared of not being enough. He had experienced his share of bad relationships as well, with women who didn't understand him or take the time to dive deep. He went out with this girl, Laura, at university who really did a number on him. I mean, it was years ago obviously, but he still looked upset when he told me about her. She'd acted really into him at first, but then went all cold and asked for space. But she'd still flirt with him at parties, and on one drunken night they slept together. He thought they'd be getting back together, but then found out that she was spreading lies about him, saying he'd treated her badly, when it had actually been the other way around. I think it really confused Cole and made it hard for him to trust women. I've met that type of woman, and they give all of us a bad name.

But I am determined to be the person who helps Cole overcome all his trauma. To show him that there are good women out there who will love and nurture him like he deserves, because he really is a special person. Well, I mean, not good women, just one good woman: me!

I encouraged him to explore what it was about sex that scared him. To really think about what he wanted. I told him that we would create a safe space in which nothing was off-limits, and I'd take everything seriously. And I know doing what he wants is going to bring us so much closer. As Cole says, sex is a convention and anyone who doesn't understand that is closed-minded. Things are different when you agree to everything first and they're only done within the context of an exclusive, loving relationship. And, god, it's so cute, the way he has to feel a genuine connection in order to have sex. I mean, I'd literally never met a man who thinks that way. So, I want to make this right for him; it's important that I make this right for him. Also, I don't want to fuck this up because I can't start another relationship with a man who might not be arsehole Luke, but still thinks the size of his watch matters, or sends me soul-destroying late-night texts canceling our plans, or worse, asks if he can come round at midnight. It's probably a cliché, well it's definitely a cliché, but I'm about to be thirty-seven and I'm exhausted by dating.

I hear a thud in the bathroom, the sound of the shampoo bottle I keep on the windowsill falling into the bath. I knew Cole would knock it over when he climbed in and I wanted to have a small warning. My heart speeds up and a sickness nestles into my gut, but I force myself to breathe deeply and not to be stupid. *It's your boyfriend,* I repeat to myself, *your boyfriend who tells you every day how much he loves you and buys you the most thoughtful surprise gifts and is an excellent cook and doesn't mind sitting through house renovation shows.* This is the least I can do for him. And anyway, I'm being stupid. I've been round the block a few times—I'm no prude.

The door to my bedroom inches open and my heart leaps into my throat because what if it isn't Cole, I mean what the fuck would I do then? The figure who emerges is dressed all in black, hood up so his face is in shadow, but it's definitely Cole so I lie still. He walks over to the bed without speaking and I try to catch his eye, but he's looking at my body, his face set so hard my stomach clenches. He leans over and pins my arms by my side, my skin twisting slightly under the pressure. I don't dare move because it might spoil the moment. Sweat breaks out on my skin and my heart is thumping so hard. It feels like I'm scared but, as Cole said, I'm not actually; excitement and fear are very similar emotions.

He straddles me and I wish he'd take off his clothes, but he starts to undo his belt, which makes me think that this is going to be it. I'm not sure I'm ready. I don't even know if we're going to kiss and that makes me feel funny, although surely that's part of it? He pushes a knee between my legs to part them and I can hear his excitement in the pitch of his breath. My arms are hurting and his hood is dusty because it's the middle of summer and he hasn't worn it for so long. My nose is already tickling, which happens sometimes when I'm trying not to cry. And then, I sneeze. It's such a loud sound that he pulls back. I laugh and immediately see him deflate. He's told me about women laughing at him before, so I want to actually kick myself. He rolls off me, pushing his hood off his head and I can see the exasperation on his face.

"Shit, I'm sorry," I say, sitting up in the bed.

He smiles. "It's okay. Just killed the mood a bit."

"No, I know. It must have been the dust."

"We don't have to do this, Mel. I don't want you to do anything you're uncomfortable with."

"But I'm not." I can feel myself heating up at the thought that I'm letting him down.

"I mean, maybe you need more time, which is totally understandable. But, honestly, it's nothing to be scared of. Sex is such a convention, when you think about it, and there's a real freedom in not letting yourself be dictated to by all the things you've been told are right or wrong."

"Absolutely," I say, irritated that Cole now thinks I'm uncool and uptight, when we've already had this conversation so many times. I've never had a man check in with me before. Not that anyone has done anything wrong, but still, it's nice to be checked up on. And now I've ruined the moment. "It's nothing to do with that. I promise."

My phone bleeps and I involuntarily reach for it. I'm in the process of setting up a new business and I've recently approached all the clients I work with to ask if they want to come over with me. It's not from any of them, but the estate agent, apologizing for the late email and saying that my offer on the flat has been accepted. I give a little squeal of delight and look up at Cole. He's smiling sardonically, leaning up on an elbow, looking very handsome.

"They've accepted the offer," I say.

"Great," he says, although his smile looks tight. "Guess it's good you left your phone right by the bed, or we'd never have known that."

"Oh god, I'm sorry." I put it back on the table, although I'm itching to answer. "I'm sorry it's been so manic lately, but you know, once my business is up and running and we're moved into the flat, it's going to be amazing."

I hold out my arms, so he leans over and wraps me in a hug, kissing the side of my neck. "Don't apologize. I admire your work ethic."

"We should have a big party when we get the flat," I say. "Before it's all done up, I mean. I'd love to meet your friends."

He laughs. "You wouldn't really. They're a bunch of losers."

I have, of course, met his two flatmates, who do fall on the loser scale, but there must be others. "How about your university friends?"

"We sort of drifted," he says. "You know how it goes."

And I do because that happens to all of us, although I met my best friend, Siobhan, at university and can't imagine ever losing touch with her. But men are different. I've noticed they often don't form emotional connections in the same way. "Oh, by the way, I spoke to Paul about the job and he's up for meeting you next week."

"That's great." But I see I've sunk him again and I hate myself.

"You don't have to go. I don't mind either way. I mean, your photography's so beautiful, maybe you should just keep going with that. And the flat's going to need loads of work and you're so good at all that stuff. You've got a much better eye than I have."

We've only been together a few months, but he's going to move in because, as Cole says, when you know, you know. He shakes his head and the movement travels down his body.

"Come on, Mel, I'm not going to let you keep me. I don't think I'd be able to look your parents in the eye if I did that."

"Oh, fuck that." I feel a sharp desire for him in that moment because he's so sweet and vulnerable and not at all frightened of showing that side of himself, which makes him such a rare bird. I straddle his lap, letting my hair fall onto his face as I kiss him. But I can feel that his body isn't responding. After a minute, I pull away.

"Sorry," he says. He's gone red. "It's just, you know..."

I'm ashamed that I've disregarded all the things he's told me, all the nights we've spent talking about this, all the planning that's gone into this moment. I even emailed him a bloody love letter, which I haven't done since I was about fourteen. This is all a big deal for him and I'm acting like some over-sexed, over-hyped woman, not thinking about what he needs at all.

"Shit, Cole, I'm sorry. I got carried away."

He bites his bottom lip. "Would you... I mean, is there any way we could try again? Totally fine if you don't want to, of course." He looks so adorable in the moonlight. I'd do anything for him.

"I want to." I lie back down and wave him away with my hand.

He stands and pulls the hood back over his head, obscuring his face. I'm not sure if he smiles at me before he leaves. I hear the front door shut and I'm alone in the flat again, with the open bathroom window. I know he'll be back in a minute, and this could be fun, sexy even, but I can't stop my heart from firing and the sickness from returning to my belly. Like an idiot, I get this mad urge to burst into tears.

My wedding day is the best day of my life, everything exactly as I always imagined it would be. The sun shines, my diet has worked so I look amazing in my dress, everyone has fun, the band is brilliant. And Cole's speech is so heartfelt that nearly every woman in the room cries. I feel luckier than the luckiest person alive.

As we take to the floor for our first dance, he pulls me into him, melding our bodies together as he says, "You're the love of my life, Mel."

"And you're mine," I say back.

He leans into my ear. "I can't wait to have a baby with you."

When I get home the lights are low, the table is set, and Cole is standing over the stove.

"Wow, smells delicious," I say as I hang up my coat. I was much messier before I met Cole, but he's right, there is something great about an ordered life.

He doesn't turn. "It's only risotto."

"I'll be two secs," I say, heading for our bedroom.

"I didn't realize you'd be this late."

"Sorry," I shout as I swap my suit for jeans and a shirt. "But it's so manic at the moment." Truthfully, I could have stayed at work all night and still not finished everything, but all work and no play makes Jack a dull boy, as Cole likes to say.

He hands me a glass of wine as I go back into the main room, a large open space with our kitchen running along the back wall, a table in the middle, and our sofas at the end. Cole was adamant that we knock the two rooms together and every time I walk in, I'm so glad we did.

The doorbell rings before we have a chance to say anything else. I ignore Cole's slight sigh as I buzz Joy and Jake up. I get why he finds them a bit much, but also I've known Joy since we were teenagers and she's been there for me through lots of shit. They come into the flat full of their usual bluster, apologizing for being late and brandishing bottles of wine, which I suspect Jake will drink the majority of, another thing

Cole dislikes about them. I hang up their coats while Cole asks them what they want to drink, large red for Jake, as usual, and curiously, fizzy water for Joy.

"Shit," Joy says as we sit down, scratching at a white mark on the shoulder of her black shirt. "Milly was losing it when we left. The babysitter could barely pry her off me."

Jake raises his eyes. "You need to leave her with other people more. It's not surprising she has attachment issues." He's already halfway finished with his first glass of wine.

"Well, I don't know many people I could leave her with," Joy says, her voice strained.

"Oh, come on," Jake says. "I'm sure your mother would jump at the chance."

"No, she wouldn't. She lives two hours away and has a life." I can hear the tension in Joy's voice, but no one else seems to have noticed.

I should probably offer to watch their daughter, but sip at my wine instead. The truth is Milly terrifies me, with her loud, irrational presence that takes up all the space in any room. Of course, I can see she's adorable, but she's also a bit of a terrorist in my friend's life. Joy is always exhausted, always worried, never fully present.

Cole sets the risotto on the table, along with a bowl of green salad, and starts to dole it out. Jake pours himself another glass, tipping the bottle in the direction of Cole, who shakes his head with a tight smile.

"God, I need this," Jake says. "Work's hell at the moment."

"Yeah, I know the feeling," I say.

"How's your new job, Cole?" Jake asks as he accepts his plate.

Cole shrugs. "Oh, you know, it's a job."

I notice Joy shift in her seat. "Have you thought any more about going back?" I ask.

When she looks at me, I can see that her nose has gone red. "Actually, there's no point now." She smiles over at Jake and pats her stomach. "We've just found out we're having another."

I don't look at Cole, but I feel him flinch across the table. He's been wanting to start trying since we got married last year, but I haven't felt ready. I've blamed it on my business, which is true in lots of ways, but also I'm not sure I'm personally ready either. I jump up and rush round the table to embrace Joy. "Oh my goodness, that's the best news, congratulations."

"In for a penny, in for a pound," Jake says. His face is already flushed.

"Not that it affects you that much," Joy says as she sits down.

"Well, someone has to keep a roof over our heads," he says.

I do glance at Cole then, but he's staring at his plate, jaw clenched. I feel a rush of love for him because he'd never say anything like that to me.

"This risotto's amazing," Joy says. "What did you do to the onions, Mel?"

"Oh no," I say. "Cole made it."

Joy actually puts down her fork and stares over at Cole. "You made this?"

He nods. "I fried them with cumin."

"Bloody hell," Joy says. "Hang on to that one, Mel."

The evening passes as it usually does. Jake drinking more than he should, getting louder with each glass and regaling us all with his opinions, while Cole gets quieter. At some point, Jake starts talking to him about football, which makes me cringe because Cole knows literally nothing about sports. Joy chats about things that sound so boring I don't know how she doesn't jump out of the window most days. And by ten she's so pale I worry she's going to pass out at the table. She manages to get Jake to put down his glass and stand up around eleven, by which time he's not entirely steady on his feet. But finally, they leave, with lots of thank-yous and you-must-come-to-ours-soons.

"Fuck," I say, as I shut the door. "Sorry, they were both on fire tonight."

"It's fine," Cole says as he starts to clear up. "Joy's sweet."

I go to him and put a hand on his back. "Thanks for doing that." He turns to me, but there are tears in his eyes. "Shit, what's wrong?"

"It's . . ." He goes and sits back at the table, so I follow him. "I mean, I wish it was us who were pregnant."

My heart stretches across my chest. "Oh, Cole, I know. Only you know how it's been with my business and everything."

"Yes, but we're thirty-eight, Mel. We need to get on with it. Especially if we want more than one." He takes my hand. "I mean, you do still want kids, don't you?"

I take a breath. "Of course. Just, doesn't it seem like such hard work to you? I mean, sometimes I hardly recognize Joy. In fact, I hardly recognize any of my friends who've had babies."

"I get that it's scary," Cole says. "But it's so important to me and you always said you wanted them. If you've changed your mind, then I think you should tell me. It would be better to make a clean break of it."

My head does a little spin and I reach for my wine glass, which is still half-full. "What are you saying? That if we don't have kids we can't stay together?"

He looks directly at me. "Mel, you know how much I love you. But I've never lied about how much I want kids. You know what it means to me." And he's right, he's always made his position completely clear. It's me who hasn't been entirely honest. I've never told him that I find the whole concept scary, that I'm not sure I'd be a good mum, that I really love my job and can't imagine anything else making me feel so fulfilled. "I know you're worried about giving up work," he says, as if he can read my mind. "But I'd never expect you to do that. I think what you've achieved with your business is amazing and I can see how fulfilled it makes you. I'd never take any of that away from you. I'd be completely happy as the primary caregiver and going part-time. Whatever is necessary. If I could be the one to get pregnant, I'd do that as well."

"Oh, Cole," I say, leaning over and kissing the side of his face. He really is one in a million and I'd be a total bitch if I denied him something he wants this much for my own selfish reasons. "I'm sorry I haven't considered you in all of this."

He gives me a tight smile. "It's okay, you're very busy."

"Look, let's go for it," I say, in a rush of emotion. "You're right, we're not getting any younger and there's never going to be the perfect time as far as my business is concerned. But it's in a good place and I could step back for a few months to have the baby."

His whole face changes like a light's been switched on inside him, which makes me feel even worse. "Do you mean that?"

"Yes." I laugh.

He stands and takes my hand, pulling me up. I think he's leading me toward our bedroom, and I get a rush that maybe we're going to simply have sex. Maybe this is all it would take? But we go to the bathroom, where he opens the cupboard above the sink and takes out my pack of birth control pills.

"Come on, then," he says excitedly. "Let's get rid of them."

I laugh. "Well, okay, I guess. Chuck them in the bin."

But he's taking the strips out of the packet. "No, let's do this properly."

"How?"

He holds them out to me. "Flush them down the toilet."

I laugh. "Seriously?"

"Yeah, go on. It'd be . . ." He looks round the room. "Symbolic."

The air feels thin as I take them from him and stand over the toilet. I press against the back of the strip and the first pill falls into the water. I keep thinking he's going to tell me to stop, but all I can hear is his excited breathing as he watches over my shoulder.

I drank a little more than I intended to, a combination of overexcitement and nerves after I saw which table I was sat at. The names on the place cards belonged to men I've admired for years, each running such successful and lucrative businesses, and I couldn't believe the organizers had seen me in their same league. On my left is Robert Stevens, CEO of one of the biggest marketing companies in Europe, and on my right, Albie Schneider, head of strategy at one of the largest advertisers in the world.

"All she fucking does is complain," Albie is saying. We've been sitting here for a couple of hours now, so I asked about their wives, producing laughter from both of them.

"I mean, you'd think she was going down a fucking mine," he says. "I say to her sometimes, 'honey, if the facials and lunches and shopping are so hard and make you so miserable, then just stop. It's not like any of us need you to do it.' She threw a glass of very expensive wine at me last time we had that argument."

I do briefly think about mentioning the four children he told us about earlier, one of whom has special needs that require a lot of attention. Robert laughs and leans across me, so I shrink back a bit in my chair. "My wife has this little lifestyle blog."

"Oh, what's it called?" I ask, as I follow quite a few of them, often salivating over perfect cups of coffee positioned on sheepskin rugs, artfully arranged photographs, statement flowers, and tables set for the Gods.

"Shit," he rubs a hand across his mouth, "hang on, I always forget." He gets out his phone and scrolls down. "Yes, here it is. @LoveinLife."

"Oh, I follow her," I say. "She's great. She's got loads of followers and her posts are beautiful."

Robert frowns. "Well, if you follow her, perhaps then you can explain what the fuck it is?" Both he and Albie laugh again.

I worry this is a trick question because he must know what his wife does. But he's looking at me expectantly. "Well, like you said, it's a lifestyle blog. She takes really stunning photos and shows her followers how she lives." It does sound a little lame when I say it out loud so I laugh as well.

"But what's the point of it?" He pours us all another glass of champagne. "I mean, I've asked her directly and she can't really give me an answer, beyond, I kid you not, 'spreading positivity.' And, of course, getting free shit, which she could just buy anyway."

"I guess she's building a brand," I say. "I mean, these things take time."

"Oh, come on." Robert leans back in his chair. "You're a smart cookie. You know that it's all a waste of time. She's never going to become a powerful brand or make any real money. Proper influencers are professionals."

I disagree with him, but it's easier to stay quiet and hear myself being described as a smart cookie by one of the top people in my industry. I get a warm rush of pleasure knowing that I'm not like their wives, that I don't have to find things to occupy my time, that they find me interesting and appealing and the work I do meaningful.

I'm still buzzing when I get home. Cole is up, watching something on the TV. I go to him and fall onto the sofa, kicking my shoes across the room.

"Someone's in a good mood," he says as he mutes the TV.

I kiss him deeply on the lips. "It was great. I was seated next to some really big hitters. And look." I pull out my phone. "Albie Schneider, you know the head of KPG, he's just followed me on Twitter."

He wipes his mouth. "Congratulations. What a fantastic achievement."

I put my phone down, feeling a little pathetic because Cole hates social media and his reactions always make it seem puerile. Which, of course, it is, but it's necessary for my work and, if I'm totally honest, I also really enjoy it. In the same way that I like reality dating shows and fashion magazines and cat memes, all of which I know Cole is probably right to hate. I smooth his hair off his forehead and feel that he's clammy.

"Are you okay, sweetheart?"

"My head's not great, actually."

"Oh no, one of the bad ones?" The ferocity of Cole's headaches scares me. I want him to go to the doctor, but he says he's always had them and if there was anything seriously wrong with him, he would have known by now. But I'm not sure I've ever seen anyone in so much pain and sometimes he even forgets little things he's said or done during an episode. I pull at his hands to make him look at me. "What's brought it on? Please talk to me."

When he returns my gaze, his eyes are sad. "I guess, well, it's not that much fun sitting here alone waiting for my beautiful, clever, amazing wife to come home from a fancy dinner with successful men."

At first I think he's joking but then see that he looks properly hurt. "Oh my god, you can't be serious." I turn to face him, pulling my legs up under me so I'm kneeling on the sofa. His mouth has turned down at the corners, which tugs at my heart. "Cole, sweetheart, you can't think that. You know I adore you. In fact, when I'm at these dinners, I always can't wait to get back home to you."

He rubs his hands across his face and lets out a deep sigh. "It all feels a bit meaningless at the moment."

It feels the opposite to me. My business is doing really well, we can afford nice things, we're going on holiday to the Maldives later this year, and our marriage is good. I lean in close to his ear. "Do you want to slip out and I'll get into bed and accidentally forget to lock the door?"

He doesn't even look at me when he shakes his head, which is good because he doesn't see the relief on my face. "Not tonight." He stands and takes his mug to the kitchen.

I follow. "Cole, seriously, I'm sorry if I've upset you."

He straightens after turning on the dishwasher. "Have you given any more thought to IVF?"

The clock above his head tells me it's gone midnight and I'm a little too drunk to have this conversation. "I mean, yes and no."

He half smiles. "We've been trying for over a year now and we're not getting any younger. We'll both be forty soon."

I press my body against his, forgetting momentarily that he doesn't respond well to that sort of thing. I quickly pretend all I wanted was a cuddle and rest my head on his shoulder. "If it means that much to you, then let's give it a go."

"I don't want to force you into it. I mean, I want you to want it as well. But if you don't want kids, then you should be honest."

I pull away from him and see the pain in his eyes and hate myself for not saying anything sooner because I know how important it is to him. "Of course I want them."

He rubs his temples. "I'm not sure our lifestyle is that compatible with getting pregnant."

His words make me feel dirty in my smart dress, reeking of alcohol and the sneaky fag I had while I waited for my cab. But also, there's something I've been wanting to talk to him about for a while now. "I'm not sure it's our lifestyle. I think, I mean, maybe, the way we have sex isn't helping me get pregnant."

His eyebrows knit together. "Pregnancy doesn't work like that. And I thought you enjoyed it? I mean, you just suggested it yourself."

"I do enjoy it," I say quickly, because I can't think about it too much and I do want to make Cole happy. It's not as if he ever does anything I don't agree to. But also, I get this creeping sensation on my flesh when I think about it the next day. And sometimes when I watch the news or listen to other women talking, I feel disgusted with myself. "I just, I don't know, I'd like to do other things as well."

His eyes well with tears. "I'm sorry I'm a failure in that department."

"That's not what I said . . ."

"But you know how it is for me. I need it to be that way. I thought you understood."

"I do. Of course, I do." I force myself not to cry, because Cole hates seeing me upset.

He takes my hands. "I really don't want to make you do anything you don't want to, Mel. You know I couldn't be prouder of how hard you work and everything you've achieved. But having a family is the most important thing to me, and I think you should be honest if it's not the most important thing for you."

I feel a little dizzy with the way the conversation has switched. "Don't say that. I've never imagined my life without kids." Which isn't exactly true, but close enough, and anyway, it's what all our friends are doing, and Cole would be the best dad.

He runs a finger down my cheek. "And we've discussed it so many times. It's not as though your life would have to change that much. I'm going to do the lion's share of the caring duties."

"I know, I know." My heart swells at the thought of Cole with a tiny baby, like the poster I had on my bedroom wall as a teenager of a ripped man holding an infant. And, really, he's so much more evolved than any other man I could have ended up with. I should stop being so closed-minded.

"Maybe that's the problem," he says, dropping my hands. "Maybe it's a bit of turn-off thinking of me changing nappies while you're having dinner with men who run global businesses?"

That makes me feel hot, because the thought of being married to someone like Robert or Albie is horrific. "Don't be insane, it's a turn-on if anything."

"I can't help feeling I'm a bit of a disappointment sometimes." He swallows hard, which makes me think he's trying not to cry. "I mean, you mix with all these super high achievers who could give you everything you ever wanted. I'd almost understand if you'd rather be with one of them."

I take his hands. "Honestly, that is so far from the case. I'm with you because of how principled and different you are. Because you don't do all that traditional male crap. Honestly, forget what I said."

He smiles weakly. "If I'm honest, I'm worried." There's a horrid catch in his voice. "I lie awake at night scared that we'll never get pregnant."

That makes me feel terrible because I'm the one delaying it. He first mentioned IVF a few months ago and I haven't done anything about it.

"Let's look into it tomorrow," I say.

He lifts my hand to his lips and kisses it very lightly. "I love you, Mel."

My heart flutters. He does so much for me and he's so wonderful and supportive. I shouldn't have said anything about the way we have sex, which is fine. A tiny part of me wonders how I will ever fit a pregnancy, let alone a baby, into my life, but I'm being selfish. Cole's right, nothing is more important than family. I am determined to give this wonderful man the happy family his own cow of a mother so cruelly denied him.

"I love you too," I say.

When I leave the office, it's been dark for a few hours already, even though it's not yet nine. I text Cole to say I'm on my way home and he asks me to get an Uber, but I tell him it's fine, there's still lots of people about. Of course, this isn't so true when I get out at our station and experience that little frisson of fear that every badly lit, windblown street gives to any woman walking home alone. But I cross my bag over my body and put my head down. I try not to hear the ringing my shoes make against the pavement, like an alarm call into the night. I also try not to think about the young woman who disappeared a few weeks ago on her walk home not far from here. Although, I tell myself, as I turn onto a totally empty street, that had happened later, closer to midnight.

At the end of the street, I pause by the green. It shaves a good fifteen minutes off my walk if I cut across it, and the path is lit by streetlamps, but it also clearly breaks all the walking-home-alone safety rules. I go for it, but when I'm halfway across, I notice that the streetlamps are positioned too far apart and, in fact, when you walk under one anyone who's around can see you immediately.

Moments later, I become aware of a presence. It's not that I can hear footsteps or anything like that, it's more an instinct that I'm not alone. I glance over my shoulder but can't see anyone. I hate myself for taking this route and try to speed up, but my heels are not conducive to walking quickly.

My heart tightens and my breath isn't filling my body with enough oxygen, so I start to feel light-headed.

It happens so quickly that I know there's nothing I could have done. As soon as I'm in shadow, an arm wraps around me from behind. It covers my mouth and pulls me into a strong body. In those few seconds I know with total clarity that I'm going to die. And if I don't, it might be worse to remain alive after this man is finished with me. I regret every stupid decision I've ever made, every time I've failed to tell people that I love them, every lost moment, every wasted dream.

But then the man lets go of my mouth and spins me round. It's Cole. I feel such intense relief that my legs give way, and he has to catch me. He leads me over to a bench, where I let my head drop between my legs, gasping at the cold night air.

"Mel," he's saying. "Shit, Mel, are you okay?"

I look up at him. "What the fuck were you thinking?"

"I'm so sorry." He looks totally crestfallen. "I knew you'd walk across the green, even though I've told you not to a thousand times. I wanted to prove to you how stupid it is."

I sit up but my heart doesn't return to normal. "But that's . . . I mean that's sadistic, what you just did."

"Oh, come on." He reaches for my hand, but I don't let him take it. "I'm sorry."

"Did it?" I can barely bring myself to finish the sentence. "Did it turn you on or something?"

He looks shocked. "No, don't be ridiculous. I wanted to prove to you how much danger you put yourself in walking across the green in the dark."

I'm not sure I believe him, but if he's lying, then surely I'd have to stand up and not just walk home alone, but also out of our flat forever.

"The only danger I'm in is of having a heart attack, thanks to you," I say.

He laughs and puts his arm around my shoulder. "Come on, Mel Bell. I'm sorry, I didn't think it through. And anyway, it was probably an especially stupid thing to do right now. Dr. Leggart did warn us that the hormones might make you feel anxious."

I stand and start to walk, and he follows me. It's true that I have felt like shit since I started the injections for IVF. Maybe I did overreact. And I mean, he's right. It is stupid of me to walk across the green alone in the dark. I certainly won't be doing it again, which is probably a good thing. All I want to do now is get home and have a hot bath.

"It's fine," I say, as we reach our street. "Forget it."

I am late and I can't be late. Acid refluxes up my throat as I shove my phone deep into my bag, so I can pretend that I'm not needed anywhere else. I can't imagine how disappointed Cole will be as I race up the ornate wooden stairs. I try to formulate my excuse, but the only thing I can come up with is the truth, which I know is unacceptable. Cole was right, I shouldn't have gone into the office this morning. But also, if I hadn't, Gemma would have sacked me and she's one of my best-paying clients, and, if nothing else, this IVF is ruinously expensive because I felt too guilty making Cole wait longer for the NHS after I dragged my heels about starting.

I race past the couples in the waiting room, their expressions gaunt, their earliness entirely appropriate, and I want to apologize to everyone. The stupidly expensive New Year's holiday we went on might as well not have happened for all the tension I'm feeling. In fact, it might as well not have happened anyway because Cole sulked his way through it, tutting at what he called the artificial atmosphere of the resort. I thought it was beautiful.

He's standing in the inner waiting room, and I can see by the set of his shoulders how worried he is, and it makes me want to cry. Although that could be the bloody hormones, which have really kicked in this past week. I'm at the stage where I feel close to hysteria most of the time, only slightly better than the murderous rage I feel at the beginning of the cycle. I can't really decide.

He spins round and I clock the clench in his jaw, which usually means he's trying to stave off a headache.

"I'm so sorry," I say too shrilly. As the woman looks up from the discreet reception desk, I swear she raises her eyebrows slightly.

"I've been trying to call you," he says. "I was so worried."

"I know, I'm sorry." I am so hot I think I might faint. "All that stuff with Gemma was insane. It's been a total nightmare. I'm not sure that the press won't run with the story anyway."

He presses down the air in front of him with his hands. "It doesn't matter. You're here now. Do you want a glass of water or something before we go in?"

I do but I shake my head. "No, no. Let's not keep him waiting any longer."

"Your phone *is* off, right?"

"Shit, hang on." I plunge my hand into my bag and fish it out. There's two missed calls from Gemma, one from my assistant, Maya, and a text from her that reads: Sorry, I know you're at the hospital, but call when you can. I glance up at Cole because I really should make the call before we go in, but his eyebrows are knitted tight together, so I mute the phone and drop it back into my bag.

"Right," he says, looking at the receptionist.

She picks up the phone and tells the doctor I've arrived. I try not to think about what might have happened with Gemma this time, filing it all away in my mental to-do list that grows longer and more complicated every day. Because Cole is right, I do work too hard and it's not fair to him. When we're together now, I have to think about the best way to get things ticked off the list without it seeming as if I'm working and, more importantly, without him noticing.

We had a horrendous argument at a wedding a few months ago after he found me answering emails behind the marquee. He was so angry I thought he was going to completely lose it, so I screamed at him to leave me alone before he could. But also, I felt angry myself, because every time I'd tried to answer emails on the train down, he'd sighed like I was killing a kitten. It all made me feel a little desperate, trapped in something I didn't understand and unable to work out what I was doing wrong.

"You can go in now," the receptionist says to us.

As Cole and I sit down, I realize that I'm not fond of Dr. Leggart. He doesn't even look up from whatever it is he's writing. Be a bit more fucking polite, I want to shout. I'm paying you enough bloody money. But then I feel embarrassed at my thoughts. These hormones really are on fire today.

"Nice of you to join us, Mrs. Simmonds," he says finally, looking at me over his glasses.

"Ms. Connelly, but call me Mel," I force myself to say, a dance we've already repeated quite a few times. Cole takes my hand and squeezes it gently. It reminds me of the hours we've spent laughing at how old-school Dr. Leggart is, which makes me feel better, so I squeeze back. Dr. Leggart raises his fluffy eyebrows, so then I feel bad. "I'm sorry. I had a nightmare at work. I got here as quickly as I could."

"Implantation is a delicate process," he says, steepling his hands together in front of him. "Far be it from me to be dictatorial, but it's not ideal to rush in here and then expect it to work."

"No, I know. I'm so sorry."

"You're very lucky to have an appointment so soon after the last round. It would be a shame to waste it."

"We know and we're very sorry," Cole says, his hand now tense in mine. "As I think you know, Mel runs her own business and is often pulled in lots of different directions."

"Yes," I repeat. "I'm so sorry." My eyes go to the photograph on his desk of his wife and two daughters in a snowy scene, skis propped up by their sides, their bodies indistinguishable in huge suits. I surprise myself by thinking about how I could do with a wife.

"So, your last round was in October of last year?" Dr. Leggart says, looking at something on his computer.

"Yes," Cole answers.

"As I said, you're lucky to have gotten in this early."

I look at my husband and the doctor and wonder if anyone is going to acknowledge that this has nothing to do with luck, but that I paid more. But then I wonder about something else, because I do feel significantly worse this time round. Sometimes it feels like my skin's on fire and my blood runs with anxiety.

"Is it safe to do them this close together?"

"Perfectly." Dr. Leggart stands in a way that makes me worried he hasn't even heard my question. "Anyway, shall we get started?"

As I'm changing behind the curtain, I hear Dr. Leggart tell Cole how brave he is to stay and watch. I try to smile at the nurse who comes in, but I can't be too present during the process because if I am I get these weird thoughts about being part of an experiment. I've googled it and Dr. Leggart definitely isn't doing anything dodgy to me as I lie on his table, but I'm not sure that makes it any better. The humiliations my body endures would be a prosecutable violation in any other scenario. Except in this one, I am expected to be polite and say thank you and pay for it.

"There," Dr. Leggart says when he's finished. "Let's keep everything crossed."

I want to ask if he's joking, but I'm wearing a paper gown and lying with my legs spread open, so it doesn't feel appropriate. I look at Cole and he smiles so deeply at me that I can see the love in his eyes. But still I get this strange sensation that I'm not real, that I'm nothing more than a bag with a hole in it, or a machine that needs to be made to work properly.

"If you can spend the next forty-eight hours in bed that would be optimum," Dr. Leggart is saying, which is completely and utterly laughable. If I lose Gemma as a client, there is no way I can pay the exorbitant fees he demands. I get a sudden urge to shout into his fat face. Stop it, I reprimand myself, pull yourself together. He's probably a perfectly nice man and you're being a hormonal bitch.

I check my phone when I'm behind the curtain getting changed and there are two more missed calls from Gemma and Maya and one from Zoe, which makes me really worried because she never gets flustered. I don't listen much as Cole and Dr. Leggart say their goodbyes, as I'm going through all the different things that could have happened in the hour or so I've been unavailable. But I do manage to say thank you and to promise to take it easy. Cole takes my elbow as we emerge onto the street, and I scan the traffic for a taxi.

"I think that went well," he says, which makes me want to hit something because my insides are raw and tender. "Anyway, let's get you home. I went to D'Angelo's this morning and got your favorite organic squash pasta. I thought I'd do a tomato sauce."

My limbs feel stringy, and I hate myself as I say, "Oh god, Cole, I'm so sorry, but it's all kicked off at work. I'm going to have to go back in for a couple of hours. But I'll sit still, I promise, and I'll come straight home as soon as I can."

He couldn't have looked more shocked if I'd hit him. I hate disappointing him this way. Women have been such a disappointment to Cole all his life, starting with his mother, and I so wanted to be different.

He rakes a hand through his hair. "I understand that your work is really important, but I don't think that's very fair, Mel. Dr. Leggart specifically said you need to rest."

"Yes, but I can't." A fizzing desperation is building inside me. "If I lose Gemma as a client then we're a bit screwed."

He snorts. "If you lose Gemma as a client over this then she's not worth having."

"Cole, please," I say. "Don't make me feel bad about this."

"I'm not making you feel bad. I just don't know what's more important than our baby."

A bolt of anger rushes through me so, before I know it, I shout, "Well, there's the fact that we have to pay that expensive doctor to stick a needle up my cunt because we appear to be broken, so there's that."

His face falls so spectacularly that I regret what I've said immediately and start crying. Big, heaving sobs that wrack through my body so violently I'm not entirely sure why I'm this upset.

Cole puts his arm around me. "Come on, sweetheart, this isn't like you. It's just the hormones talking. You know how you get."

I let him pull me into him and he's right, this anger isn't like me, and can only be because of the hormones. As I lean my head against his chest, I realize how tired I am and how much I probably do need to rest. And, of course, Cole is right: nothing is more important than the baby. He raises his hand, and a taxi pulls up. As we drive away, he puts his arm back around me and kisses the top of my head, laying his other hand gently on my belly.

When we get home, Cole says he's going to put lunch on, so I should get changed into something more comfortable. I say I'm going to have a quick shower, not because I want one, but because the water will mask the phone call I need to make. It's not that Cole minds in principle, I tell myself as I turn on the taps, but in this specific context he's right to mind. Maya passes me on to Zoe, who is as calm as usual. She's diffused the situation the way I should have thought to do this morning, which makes me feel a bit panicked because I've never not done the right thing before. She tells me not to worry and to rest up. Then I call Gemma, who gushes about Zoe and tells me she's going for a celebratory lunch with her boyfriend, who was the cause of the fucking problem in the first place.

There's a knock on the door and Cole shouts through, "Just checking you haven't drowned in there. Lunch is almost ready."

"Yes, sorry," I shout back.

I have to stand under the shower for a minute, otherwise it would look odd. I smile at Cole as I make my way to our bedroom, where I pull on a tracksuit and some thick socks and towel-dry my hair. I glance in the mirror and see that I look like death, but I just rub some cream on my face. Cole claims I look better without makeup, which can only be a lie and pisses me off. I enjoy looking good and I'm not sure why that's a bad thing. I used to argue with him about it but, quite frankly, I'm too tired to think about it now. I make myself turn my phone facedown as I sit at our kitchen island, even though I can't quite believe the crisis has really been averted. Cole puts a steaming bowl of pasta in front of me and then sits down with his own.

"Thank you," I say, looking at him so he knows I mean it, which makes him smile.

He's getting little lines around his eyes and his hair is graying at the temples, but I think it makes him look more handsome. So many of my friends are married to such awful men who can't work the dishwasher or keep their dicks in their pants or drink responsibly or wake up for their children during the night or even be regularly at home. I'm flooded by how lucky I am to have this sensitive, serious, charming husband who properly cares about and looks after me. I feel bad about being dismissive or thinking bad things about him. We eat in silence for a while. The sauce he's made is silky and delicious, even though I've never really liked the squash pasta. I much prefer the mushroom.

"I'm sure it'll work this time," I say with a surge of optimism. Because I desperately want to give Cole the happy family he was denied as a child.

"I hope so. We have to make sure we give it the best chance."

We've talked a lot about what will happen when the baby's born and we've agreed that Cole will go part-time, as obviously it wouldn't make any financial sense for me to step away from my business. Sitting opposite him, though, I realize that I wouldn't mind if he gave up work altogether. I think it would make him happiest. And I want him to be the happiest he can be because he deserves it. My heart swells with the thought of how modern and content we'll be.

"You know," I say, as I spear another juicy piece of ravioli. "I've been thinking. I know you don't enjoy your job. Why don't you just give it up when we have the baby. Or maybe I could help you set up something new. You were such a good photographer when we met, perhaps you can go back to that? But, I mean, only if you wanted to. It would be fine if you just wanted to look after the baby."

A muscle twitches under his left eye. "I don't think there's any 'just' about looking after a baby, Mel. In fact, I think quite a bit of feminist thinking would shoot you down for that."

I try to laugh. "Sorry. Stupid choice of words. You know what I mean."

He looks at his bowl and sets down his fork, although he hasn't finished. When he looks up at me his eyes are glistening. "Is there no part of you that wants to be a full-time mum?"

The question lands against my solar plexus. "What do you mean?"

He smiles. "Nothing. I only wondered if you've ever thought about it."

"Not really." I try to keep my voice light, but the question is absurd. We both know that if I stopped working, we'd have to completely change our lifestyle. Surely neither of us wants that. Also, I love my business. "I thought you wanted to be the main caregiver?"

"Oh, I do." His tone is breezy, as he takes our plates to the sink. "But I wondered if it'd ever crossed your mind."

I take a sip of the water he's put in front of me and see that my hand is shaking slightly. "No," I say, as forcefully as I can manage.

"Yup, that's what I thought."

His back is turned to me as he rinses the dishes, so I can't tell if he's joking. For the first time I worry that not wanting to be a full-time mother is a failing on my part, something fundamentally unnatural and weird about me. But also, even if I did want that, Cole couldn't support us. It feels as though I'm losing either way. When he turns back, Cole's all smiles. He leans against the kitchen counter as he dries his hands.

"There is another option, you know."

"What's that?"

"Well, we could both look after the baby."

"Of course, we'll both look after the baby." I laugh, although the sound isn't jolly.

"No, I mean, properly. Not one of us being absent for seventy percent of its life."

"It's hardly seventy percent," I say as I try to do a few mental calculations.

Cole raises an eyebrow. "I've been doing a lot of reading up on the IVF process and it's actually quite similar in theory to the stuff I've read about bringing up a child."

I can feel a headache building across my shoulders and up my neck. "Right?"

"Stress is such a fucked-up thing. All that cortisol and adrenaline is poison to the body, especially to an embryo." My hand instinctively goes to my stomach as if to protect the would-be baby from myself. "And it got me thinking. This flat is worth quite a bit now, what with everything we've done to it. We could sell it and live almost mortgage-free in some parts of the country."

I look down at my hands resting on the wooden countertop Cole spent about three weeks polishing and waxing. "Where?"

"Oh, I don't know. Cumbria for one."

"Cumbria? That's miles away."

"Well, I don't know. There are a few places." I know they'll all be miles away, but I don't say anything because he's gone a bit red, and I don't want to make him feel stupid. "We could end up near your parents."

I love my parents, but I couldn't live near them. I think of the hours of study it took to get away from the small town I was born in and the years of hard work that went into building my new life.

"What would we even do in Cumbria, or wherever, anyway?"

Cole shrugs like he hasn't thought about it, though he obviously has. "I don't know. Take on a small holding, maybe try our hand at farming. If we had enough land, we could open fields for camping in the summer. That's really lucrative. It would be so good for you and our children. Imagine not having all the stress of public transportation and business meetings and client calls and budgets or any of that shit ever again." I can't think of anything to say because I cannot for one second imagine myself wearing wellies in the middle of a muddy field with animals and children and a bloody campsite. I'd laugh if I weren't trying so hard not to cry. I can see the excitement in Cole's eyes, though, and I don't want to piss on his bonfire. And maybe he's right, maybe I do need a change of pace. What if I only think I love my work? What if, really, I'd love a life in the country more? It certainly sounds more wholesome and would probably be best for the kids. I'd have to be a monster not to want the best for them. "Anyway, you look exhausted. We can talk about this another time," he says. "Why don't you go and lie down, and I'll bring you a cup of herbal tea."

I'm relieved at the let off. "Oh, that would be lovely." I stand and pick up my phone, but Cole steps forward and holds out his hand.

"What?" I laugh.

He stretches his hand forward. "Not the phone."

"Oh, come on. I'm going to check a few emails and then I'm going to sleep. I promise."

His eyes well, and when he speaks his voice is shaky. "Please, Mel. I don't know how much longer I can go on monitoring you like this. I just don't understand why you ignore all the advice and still put yourself in the way of stress when you find it so hard to deal with."

I'm surprised to hear him describe me as someone who finds stress hard to deal with, when I run an entire business by myself, but maybe he's right? "Come on, Cole. Today's been a nightmare. I need to answer some emails."

He lunges across the island, and I don't work out what he's doing until he's grabbed the phone out of my hand.

"What the fuck are you doing?" I shout.

"I just can't cope with this." He starts to cry. "I try and try to make everything as easy as possible for you. All I'm asking is that you play your part and make an effort not to get stressed, especially straight after an implantation."

I feel confused. He does do a lot and maybe I do let the stress get to me. But if something else has happened with Gemma, I've got to know about it. "Look, I know you're amazing and I know I could relax more. But I can't pretend my business doesn't exist," I say, as calmly as I can.

He snorts. "As if we could ever forget that."

"Yes, because there's a lot to pay for."

"Oh, here we go." His tears are dripping off his chin, making me feel like a complete bitch. "I'm sorry I'm not as successful as you, Mel. I'm sorry I'm such a terrible disappointment."

My internal organs are stretching uncomfortably. "You know that's not what I mean."

He throws my phone onto the island and turns away. "You know what, I give up. Knock yourself out."

"I don't even like the squash pasta!" I shout pathetically at his back, hating myself more as I speak. "If you remembered anything about me at all, you'd know that the mushroom is actually my favorite."

I grab my phone and go to our room. But as soon as I shut the door, I feel disgusted with myself because it seems crazy to be arguing when we've just had a potential baby put into my stomach. And Cole's right, I always insist on pushing myself to a breaking point, ignoring all the effort he puts into making things easy for me. The floor feels spongy and my vision blurs around the edges as I lie on our bed, letting my phone drop to the floor as I curl onto my side.

The restaurant was a bad idea. Neither of us wants to be here and Cole physically cringes as we step into the opulent reception. But I can't bear the idea of spending another evening in our flat with blood dripping out of me and so I let the fawning waiter show us to our table.

"I wonder where they're flying in the mangoes from at this time of year," Cole says as he scans the menu. "Bloody hell, you could feed a family of four for a week on one bottle of wine."

I shut my menu. "We can go. It's posher than I realized."

But he shakes his head. "No, no. Let's get some food in you at least."

I don't put up a fight because the bleeding and the guilt are exhausting. Dr. Leggart said it's just one of those things, but I think we all know it's my fault. We order, and Cole sighs at the glass of wine I ask for, sticking pointedly to mineral water.

"Why don't you have one? It would do you good to relax," I say.

"I don't need wine to relax," he says. "It doesn't help anything, you know. Anyway, I think I've got a headache coming."

"Well, I'm going to have one. It's been a terrible week."

"Of course it has."

"I didn't mean only for me."

"I know you didn't."

We stop speaking, one of those awful silent married couples you sometimes see in restaurants. I'd always thought they had nothing to say to each other, but now I wonder if they're quiet because the only things they have left to say are too painful. The waiter puts our food in front of us. We've both gone straight to mains, and I doubt either of us will have dessert. My wine glass is empty, but I refuse another, despite longing for one because the alcohol hasn't yet touched the edges of my anxiety. My chicken is coated in a creamy sauce that makes me feel sick.

"Did you speak to Dr. Leggart about when we can start the next round?" Cole asks.

"No." I don't tell him that I couldn't face making the call.

"It's fine. I'll give him a call tomorrow."

The chicken defeats me and I put down my cutlery. "Perhaps we could give it a bit of time." I'm worried about what might happen if we start another round too soon, not just to my body, but also to my mind. I've started getting these weird compulsions to dig into my skin and see what lies beneath. Not that I've done anything and not that I would, but I feel unsafe.

The skin around Cole's eyes looks tight and dark. "Do you think that's wise?"

I scratch along the inside of my arm, leaving a red welt on the skin that we both notice. "I wouldn't mind a bit of a break."

He raises his eyebrows slightly. "What, as in time off work?"

"I mean a break from the IVF."

His shoulders slump. "Oh, right. Silly of me to think . . ."

"I can't, Cole. We lost the Beaumont account today." He shifts in his seat but doesn't say anything, so I give him another chance. "If I'm going to go on paying for the IVF, I can't take my eye off the ball."

"God, Mel," he huffs. "Not everything is about money."

The muscles across my back are stiff and tight. "Cole, Felix rang me. I know what you did."

He flinches. "I'm not going to apologize for that, Mel. I was protecting you."

"By sending him loads of abusive messages? And then going to his house and shouting at him? With his wife and kids there?"

"Perhaps if he'd answered me, I wouldn't have had to do that."

"He didn't answer because he didn't want to engage in something so absurd."

Cole's eyes narrow. "Mel, you're being naïve. I've seen you two together and he's completely inappropriate. You're too sweet to do anything about it."

Even breathing feels hard. "He's a nice, friendly man."

Cole snorts. "Honestly, Mel. He's not being nice or friendly."

"He loves his wife."

"That doesn't stop most men."

The muscles in my neck are now clenching in sympathy with my back. "He's not like that. He said his wife wants him to go to the police."

"Except he hasn't, which should tell you all you need to know."

I rub at my neck to try to stop the pain. "It was so embarrassing. I liked him. But also, he was a good client who paid well."

Cole lays his hands flat on the table. "I'm sorry I can't help more with that."

His tone is accusatory, not that I meant it like that. Maybe he was protecting me in some way, which might be sweet. I can't work out that sort of thing anymore.

"Look, we've had this conversation so many times. There's no point in you getting a better job and then giving it up in a year or whatever when the baby's born."

"It would be different if we moved," he says. "I mean, if we were in the country, not only would it be healthier, but it would also be cheaper."

I sometimes wonder if he really is serious about moving. It's such an insane idea. "I'm not moving on a whim," I say, allowing the irritation I feel about Felix to creep into my voice.

"A whim?" He looks genuinely hurt.

"I don't know where this idea came from. Our whole life is here in London. All our friends, my business. It's our home. I don't think it's very fair of you to expect me to walk away from all that."

"Fair?" His face is creased. "I don't know what you're talking about, Mel. I'm trying to make things better and you're making out I'm forcing you to do something terrible."

Moving to the country would be terrible for me. But he's right. He's only suggesting it for the best reasons. "Sorry, I know. I'm just tired."

Cole indicates my plate. "You've hardly touched your food." I try again but the cream sticks to the inside of my mouth. "Anyway," Cole says. "The baby comes before the move. We need to get back in front of Dr. Leggart as soon as possible."

My insides burn at the thought. "It's a lot, physically, I mean."

"Yes, but we're forty-one. Time isn't on our side."

My food looks far away and I'm not sure my hand is going to reach. "No, you're right."

He reaches across the table and puts a hand over mine. "I do love you, Mel. I hope you know that everything I do is for you. What you're doing is incredible. You're my superwoman."

And, somehow, it's been agreed that it's all going to happen again, which makes me want to upend the table and scream at all the people in this elegant room.

"Do you think maybe we should speak to someone?" I say tentatively. My friend Siobhan thinks I should speak to a therapist about what I'm going through.

Cole frowns. "Who?"

"A therapist, I guess?"

"A therapist?" The word sounds hot in his mouth. "Why on earth would we do that?"

I feel very weak and hold on to the edge of the table. "It might be good to speak to someone neutral about all of this, to sort of get a handle on where we are, what we both want."

"So we don't want the same thing now?"

"No, of course we do. But maybe a professional could help us make sense of the best way to get there."

He runs a hand through his hair and his eyes look a little wild. "To be honest, I'm quite shocked you'd suggest that. I mean, with everything you know about my mother."

My heart speeds because I know I have to tread carefully. "I'm sure there are lots of different types of therapists. Not all of them will be the same as your mother."

But he shakes his head and now there are tears in his eyes. "I thought you understood, Mel. There's no way I could trust a therapist after growing up with that woman."

I feel desperate so I ask the question I've thought about many times over the years. "All the things you've told me about your childhood sound horrible, but why do you hate her *so* much?"

He pulls a breath in so sharply I think it must hurt. "I guess the best thing I can say is that she wasn't exactly what you'd call a natural mother." He barks a sound that I think is meant to be a laugh. "You know, for most mothers nothing is more important than their children. But she was always helping other people, listening to their problems, writing her bloody reports. She never put me first. And then, when I got older, she never stood up for me. She twisted everything I said. Always made me feel inadequate and wrong. I couldn't possibly go through that again."

I feel a little stunned by his words and not for the reasons he might think I am, but more because his description of being a "natural" mother sounds terrifying. It sounds like falling down a dark hole with nothing to grab on to. But if he's right and that is how "natural" mothers feel, then what if I'm not a natural? What am I even doing?

"I'm sorry," I say, quietly. "No, of course you couldn't."

A spiraling panic begins in my stomach because I think I must be wrong about so much and that makes me feel very lonely. I try to regulate my breathing with internal counting, but my head feels full, and my palms are sweaty. There is a truth nestled deep inside me that keeps rearing its ugly head. I'm not sure I want to be a mother. But saying that is surely admitting to something sordid and disgraceful. And it would also mean losing Cole and I'm not sure I'm ever going to meet another man like him again. I don't want to be alone, but I also don't want to share myself. Because that's what a baby is: a part of me, emerging from me, feeding from me, needing me every day forever and ever.

A woman at the next table stands to go to the toilet and I follow her progress through the restaurant so intently I can't be sure it's not me making the journey. When she disappears from sight, I think it's me that's gone and am overwhelmed by the sense that the real me is lost within the bowels of this awful restaurant. I look back at Cole, but he's eating, his eyes trained on his own plate. I am so, so frightened. Frightened of letting everyone down, frightened of who I might be, frightened of what might happen to me. Fear stalks my every waking moment. Sometimes I remember those seconds on the green when Cole came up behind me and it feels like a release. It might have been easier if a bad man had gotten me that night, because at least that type of fear is tangible and easy to process. Sometimes it feels like a better option than the constant terror of my current situation.

C ole is tentative when he pokes his head around the door. "What are you doing in here, Mel?"

I sit up and pull the covers with me so they come under my chin. My body is shredded with exhaustion from not sleeping the night before and crying too much.

He comes over and sits on the bed. "Are you ill? You look shattered."

"You don't remember why I came in here last night?" My voice sounds hoarse.

He looks around the room as if there might be a clue. "I remember I got one of my bad heads and went to bed."

My eyes feel lined in sand. "You don't remember waking up in the middle of the night?"

His eyes widen. "No. What happened?"

I can't tell if he's telling the truth because I don't see how he could have forgotten. His bad heads have given him memory lapses a few times before, but they've been little things like how we got home or what we ate. He's never forgotten a whole conversation. Then again, we've never had a conversation close to the one we had last night.

"Cole," I say slowly. "You frightened me last night."

His face creases in genuine concern. "Oh my god, did I hurt you?"

"No, nothing like that."

"What happened then?"

"Can you really not remember?" I stare hard into his eyes and he doesn't look away, which makes me feel a bit better because he seems genuine.

"Mel, please, you're scaring me. What happened?"

"You woke me up in the middle of the night. You were moaning so loudly, and when I asked you what was wrong, you completely turned on me. Started screaming and shouting about how I never listen to you and that you're done trying to help me. You called me some awful names."

Cole drops his head into his hands and I see a tear leak out from underneath them. "Shit. I can't believe that."

"It was really scary." As I speak, I can feel myself in our dark bedroom, Cole's eyes wide, saying things I never would have imagined him thinking. He could have been possessed. "Seriously, do you not remember anything?"

"No. The last thing I remember is getting into bed and you giving me two Tylenol."

I shiver because my memories of the night are way too sharp, like a knife against my skin. It feels horribly lonely to think that we could have experienced such different versions of the same moment. An image flashes into my mind of Cole waking next to my bloodied corpse.

"But I definitely didn't touch you?" he asks again, as if he can read my mind.

I shake my head. He didn't touch me, but that doesn't mean I didn't think he was going to. When I got out of the bed, he lunged toward the space I'd left, although I can't be sure that he was trying to get me. That was when I went to the spare room and he didn't follow, although I heard him muttering on the other side of the wall for a while. I thought about wedging a chair under the door handle, but it seemed too dramatic, something that would be impossible to get over.

He grabs on to my foot through the covers. "Mel, I am so sorry. I don't know what to say. I love you. I don't think anything bad about you."

"You said I was a selfish bitch." I watch the words land on him like arrows.

"You know I don't think that."

"But why would you say it?"

"It wasn't me."

"You were so angry." We sit quietly for a while and I look at the sunlight trying desperately to find its way past the blinds. "You didn't seem like you," I say finally. "It felt as if you were capable of anything."

Cole drops his head again, his shoulders rounding, and I feel a stab of pity for him. I've lived with him for nearly six years now and he's never shown a trace of the person I saw last night, which means it has to have been an aberration. I rub a hand down his back and he pulls me into him, wrapping me tightly against his chest so I can feel how fast his heart is beating.

"What can I do to make this better?" he says into my neck, his breath hot against my skin.

"You need to go to the doctor," I say. "These headaches aren't normal."

He pulls back from me and looks me straight in the eyes. "Of course. And I'll do whatever they say."

"Mrs. Simmonds," the nurse says, and I stand because I've given up that fight.

Cole stands as well, but I wave him down. "Please, Cole, it's too suffocating having you in there as well. Stay here."

I ignore the hurt expression on his face because the last round was hell, with Cole hovering over me, asking if my breasts were hurting or if there was any dragging in my pelvis for days before my period came. And this time he's frantic, tripping over himself to make sure I don't have to do anything, which I know is sweet and lovely, but he's watching me like a hawk. I feel guilty if I have a cup of coffee or stay an hour late at the office or basically do anything that he wouldn't. He even bought a bloody blood-pressure monitor. Every night, almost immediately after I walk in the door, he makes me use it, writing down the results in a little book and sighing at the reading.

The nurse tells me to lie down on the bed as I shut the door behind me. "It's only one injection today." The needle glints on the other side of the room, looking larger than usual. "And then tomorrow the implantation. How exciting." Her chins wobble as she talks, and I unfairly hate her.

I lean my head back and shut my eyes, but that makes the spinning sensation worse, and I don't want to risk falling asleep. When I do, all I dream about is blood and needles. Sometimes that's all that fills my mind during the day as well. Sometimes I look at my arm and imagine all the skin peeled away from it, so I'm just a mass of bones and flesh and nerves. When I try to talk to Cole about it, he says I need to rest more and that I should take a couple of weeks off work, but I worry that if I don't stay busy, I might actually lose my mind. And anyway, if I do get pregnant, I'll have to take months off, so I have to keep everything going while I can because what Cole doesn't seem to appreciate is that I am my business. It's only so successful because of me.

The nurse comes toward me with the needle. "Isn't he lovely," she says.

I have no idea what she's talking about, which is happening to me more and more lately. I get lost in conversations even though that's not something I can really afford to do. "Who?"

"Your husband." She rubs at my exposed arm with a cotton pad soaked in disinfectant, which stings my eyes. "I've watched him since you've been coming in and he's so attentive. So thoughtful. Honestly, he puts lots of the other husbands to shame." She sticks the needle into my arm and plunges the handle so hormones flood into me. I can almost feel their progress, all their strange synthetic weirdness rushing through my blood, changing and altering me in the hope of making me work. "Well, you're a very lucky girl." She withdraws the needle and puts a bit of cotton wool over the spot. "Just give yourself a moment."

I feel incredibly cold, and I worry that she's mistakenly injected me with liquid nitrogen or something. I get this moment of clarity, like emerging from a thick fog, and I can see exactly how my life is going to play out if we have this baby. Cole will be at the school gates and the doctors' appointments, pushing the swings in the playground. And forever more people are going to tell me how lucky I am, in the same way they do when they realize that Cole does most of the cooking and cleaning at home. I suddenly see how unfair these compliments are because it'd be ridiculous if he didn't, considering I work much longer hours than he does. And yet our friends fawn over him, as if he's solving world hunger. I look around the expensive office that I'm paying for and realize that no one is ever going to tell me that I'm doing well. In fact, they'll all judge me for not being around more and for putting my work first. One day my own child might think the same thing about me. It is, I realize with a sickening jolt, never going to be all right.

Cole leaps up as soon as I get back to the waiting room. "Are you okay? You're really pale."

"I don't feel great, actually," I say, wondering if I'm going to make it out of the building.

"Oh god, I hope you're not coming down with anything," he says as we step out to the street, and I try not to hear the irritation in his voice.

We hail a taxi and I lean into him as we inch our way through the London traffic, the numbers on the meter soon becoming farcical. I'm actually shivering when we walk through our front door, my teeth chattering in my head with the sense that I will never be warm again.

Cole puts his hand on my forehead. "We need to get you into bed."

But I am stuck, unable to move forward. "I'm scared," I manage to say.

"It's going to be okay, sweetheart," he says very gently. "You've just got too much going on. Anyone would find it stressful." I start crying then, the sort of thick tears that clog your head. "Oh, Mel, please. You know I hate it when you cry. What's wrong?"

The question floods me with relief. I think if I can tell Cole what's really wrong, he can help me to make it go away.

"I just don't think it's ever going to be fair," I say and am surprised by how raggedy my voice sounds.

"Fair?" Cole screws up his face.

"I mean, everyone's always going to think you're so great, aren't they? Our child is going to love you more than me."

"What are you talking about?"

I try to order my thoughts. "I feel like a slab of meat, Cole. And I don't think I can stand another needle or tube or finger invading my body. It's a form of torture, and if I have to do it again, I'm worried I'll lose my mind. When I sleep, if I sleep, I dream about sharp needles and oceans of blood and broken bones and torn ligaments."

"Mel, stop." He puts his hands on my arms, but that only makes me cry harder. "You have to calm down. This isn't good for the implantation tomorrow."

I shake him off me. "No, you don't understand. You have to listen to me. Everyone's going to judge me. If I don't manage to get pregnant, then I'm going to be seen as a lesser woman. But if I do and I go back to work, which I have to, which I want to, then everyone will judge me for being a crap mother. But you'll always be a hero, just for doing what a million women do everywhere every day."

"Mel, you have to get a grip. This is the hormones talking."

"It's not the fucking hormones," I scream. "It's what I think."

He turns away for a moment, but then turns back. "You know this isn't exactly a walk in the park for me, either. It's not fun being on the end of your frankly psychotic moods. I never know where I stand. And it's a total nightmare watching you make everything ten times harder for yourself and absolutely refuse to accept any advice."

The tears are beating down my cheeks, like I'm in the middle of a storm. "I can't believe you said that."

He throws his hands into the air and they slap against his legs. "I look after you so well, Mel. I try to be as kind and good as I can be, not because I think I should, but because I actually want to be that man. But it's never enough. You always need more. Yet you throw it all back in my face by filling your life with unnecessary stress. And then you break down because of course you're exhausted, but it's not the fault of the IVF."

I try to think of a way to get him to understand what I'm saying. It is vitally important that he understands me.

"I don't know what you're talking about. I have to work hard to pay for the bloody IVF."

"Oh, here we go!" he shouts. "That's the real nub of it isn't it? I know you hate me for not being able to provide for you financially. God, sometimes I hate myself."

It is so far from what I mean that I don't have the words to continue. "This isn't going to work. I can't do it anymore."

"You can't do what?" We have barely made it beyond our front door.

"This." I run my hand up and down my body. "IVF."

He looks like I've hit him. "You want to stop the IVF? The day before our third implantation? When we have three viable embryos waiting?"

For a moment I think he's got it and I want to fall at his feet in gratitude. "Yes. It's going to kill me. Or if it doesn't, it's going to erode my fucking soul. Cole, this is a horror story. Please, please help me."

I can see the effort it's taking for him to calm himself. "Mel, sweetheart. I know it's the most disgusting, invasive treatment and I love you so much for doing it. If I could go through it instead of you, I would in a heartbeat. But think about the bigger picture. Remember why we're doing this. We're going to have a baby and nothing is more wonderful than that."

I look into the corners of the room, expecting to see snarling monsters lying in wait, but it's just our clean Farrow & Balled walls. "What if having the baby kills me?"

He pulls me into him and wraps his arms around me. "Oh, sweetheart, that's not going to happen. Lots of women feel that way. It's totally natural to feel scared."

My heart thumps from the pressure of his hug. "I really think we need to see someone. Before we go on with this."

He loosens his grip and takes a step back. "Are you suggesting a therapist again?"

"Yes. We need someone who can help us sort this out. I don't think we understand what the other one is saying."

Cole snorts. "I can't have this conversation again, Mel. It's really triggering for me."

My eyes feel huge and swollen. "Come on, we could find a good one. It's really important to me."

But he shakes his head. "There's no way. No way I'm letting some do-gooder poke around inside my brain in order to tell me everything's all my fault. That was the story of my whole childhood and I can't go through that again." I can't think of a way to answer him, but he steps forward and rubs my arms. "I think you need a good rest."

"I've had enough rest."

"Well then, some food. What can I make you?"

I realize then that he is never, ever going to understand. That, in fact, he doesn't want to understand because it will mean giving up what he wants. And if I don't get away, I will become irretrievable. I have been slowly losing myself since we started this journey and soon there will be nothing left. And then it hits me. Cole has never forced me to do anything, but he must know that I haven't enjoyed it. I think back on the dark nights and the open windows and the footsteps down corridors and the fear in my throat and it feels the same as when I was lying on that bed earlier as the nurse stuck a needle in my arm. I'm not sure if I ever wanted any of it and I can't work out how he's made me do it all.

"You know what I really fancy?" I say as calmly as possible.

"Anything you want."

"Some of that squash pasta from D'Angelo's." I wait to see if he'll remind me that it's the mushroom one I like. I think I might even give him another chance if he does. But he smiles.

"Of course. It'll only take me fifteen minutes. Why don't you have a shower while I go and get it."

"God, would you? That's so sweet of you."

He kisses my forehead. "I'm sure you'll feel better after that and a sleep." He picks up his keys and turns to smile at me as he leaves. "You know, you don't have to go through this alone, Mel. You can always talk to me. We can devise a plan together so you're less stressed. I'm sure Zoe could take on more responsibility at work. It's all a question of putting the right systems in place."

I nod. "I know. Thank you."

As soon as I hear the front door shut, I go to order an Uber to Siobhan and Kate's house, but then I remember that Cole is able to track it when I do that and switch to a local cab company. I rush into the bedroom and shove a few essentials into a bag. I text Siobhan as I stand by the window waiting for my car and all she texts back is Finally, which makes my stomach turn.

The car arrives before Cole gets back and I cry all the way to Siobhan's.

oday I need to get up because I've spent a week crying in bed and it's not getting me anywhere. Siobhan and Kate couldn't have been nicer, and Zoe and Maya are running the office, but I need to get my life back. Cole's rung incessantly and turned up on the doorstep once, but I can't face speaking to him because I don't know what to say yet. It's clear that Siobhan and Kate are not his biggest fans and when I told them about the way we have sex, the shock was obvious in their expressions. They use words like *controlling* and *gaslighting* to describe him, which are so opposite to all the things I've ever thought about him. But also, this week is perhaps the longest time I've spent apart from him since we met, and the distance is helping things to come into focus.

The air is still heavy with the coffee and toast Siobhan and Kate must have had before they left for work, so I go into the kitchen and make myself some. Their back garden is bursting into a riot of color, and I watch a bird hopping about on their little patch of grass as I try to eat. But everything still tastes metallic and there's a blockage in my throat so I can't swallow properly.

I start to cry, again, which is all I seem able to do at the moment. But I am overwhelmed by the loss and I'm not even sure how much was mine to lose in the first place. The Cole I thought I married might not exist, which is a confusing thought, because I don't think he's been lying to me or doing anything terrible. Although, when I said that to Siobhan last night, she told me that it is terrible for anyone to think they're always right. And I know Cole isn't the same as those sweaty men in Hollywood or scheming politicians or predatory bosses, but, as Siobhan reminded me, he is a privileged straight white man, which means the world was designed in his image.

This week I've also found myself thinking a lot about Cole's mother and it's ignited a hot anger. Because surely she's the person who set him up for failure by making him feel so insecure and never teaching him how to love. Siobhan put me in touch with her therapist a few days ago and I went to see her yesterday. She was so lovely, but I couldn't stop thinking about how this is what Cole's mother does for a living, too. That lots of people must trust her with their minds.

In the early years of our relationship, I tried to build a friendship with Cole's parents, but they never reciprocated. They always made sure they were away for birthdays and Christmases, and invitations to visit were few and far between. Things were perfectly pleasant when we were with them, but I always got the feeling they were longing for us to leave. Cole said it had always been that way and they'd never shown him any real love or affection. He said he presumed he'd been a mistake and that the predominant feeling he had during his childhood was that he was getting in the way of his mother's work. Over time it became easier not to bother and it wasn't like I needed another family, as my own are warm and open. But now I wonder if that was stupid of me, and I should have pushed Cole harder to resolve things with his parents because it's clear our relationship would have benefited.

I have a shower to try to calm the rising anger that has become so much a part of me, but it doesn't work, and, in my head, I scream at Cole's mum as the water pounds on my back. The internal argument continues as I get dressed, so by the time I'm back downstairs I'm a mass of agitation. Ordinarily I'd run those feelings away, but the past couple of years have eroded me to such an extent that I don't trust my ability to make it around the park. My phone glints where I'd left it on the kitchen table. I decide that not contacting Cole's mother is letting her off the hook. When

I call her, she doesn't know that we've split up but agrees to see me that day, at lunchtime.

Clara's office is as groomed as she is and, as I sit in the plush waiting room, which reminds me of Dr. Leggart's, I think about the fact that the rich don't have to be ill or upset in the same way as everyone else. I feel extremely nervous when the receptionist tells me to go in, but it's obvious that Clara is feeling the same way. She's as gracious as ever, coming out from behind her desk to kiss me as she tells me I look well, which we both know is a lie. But her hand hovers around the neck of her pristine silk shirt and her mouth is a tight line.

"I'm so sorry that you and Cole have been having a hard time," she says as we both sit.

"Are you?" I made the decision on the way over that if I was going to do this it had to be done properly. I wasn't going to spare her feelings.

She clasps her hands on the desk in front of her. "Of course I am."

"I'm surprised. You haven't shown much interest in our relationship up till now."

"Ah," she says, her eyes narrowing slightly. "I see."

"I'm very angry with you." My heart is fast against my ribs, and I can feel sweat breaking out under my T-shirt, but Clara nods, which makes me continue. "I think things would have been very different with Cole and me if you hadn't been such a bitch." The word rings around the smart office.

"Go on," Clara says.

"Well, I mean, what sort of mother abandons their son the way you have? He's so hurt, and it's me who's been dealing with the fallout."

Her eyes widen. "I'd hardly call Cole abandoned."

I do wonder momentarily if sitting here is wise, but also someone has to answer for what's happened to me over the past few years. "Emotionally, I mean. You didn't even know we'd split up. And Cole says you were always unavailable to him during his childhood, which I don't see any reason to doubt, considering we've been married for five years and, honestly, I think I've been to your house, what, maybe eight times."

Clara smooths her beautifully dyed hair off her forehead. "Cole said that I was unavailable during his childhood?"

I worry that I'm going to cry. "Do you deny that?"

"Well, not entirely. I worked hard, if that's what you mean. But surely you must understand that? And his father's job was much more manageable, so he was able to stay home most of the time."

"Of course, I'm not questioning you working." I'm starting to feel hot.

"Well, I would also contest the idea that either of us were emotionally unavailable when Cole was younger. I'm sure we didn't get things a hundred percent right and maybe sending him to boarding school was a mistake, but we thought it was for the best at the time."

"But . . ." I think of all the stories Cole told me. "What about when you left him at school for the holidays? Or how you ignored him whenever you had clients? Or how you refused to touch him? What about the lock on your bedroom door?"

Clara's face twitches. "Oh dear," she says. "Mel, I'm not sure how accurate Cole has been in the telling of his childhood. We thought he'd stopped doing this."

The worst part is that I don't immediately doubt what she's saying. "Are you telling me that those things never happened?"

She takes a sip of water from a tall glass on her desk. "Not in the way Cole told you and, yes, sometimes not at all. For example, we never left him at school for any holiday. And I certainly hugged him a lot as a child. It's true that he was very difficult about my work and sometimes I did have to shut the door on him. But he wasn't left alone and, also, I'll never believe that I should have given up my whole life to spend every second with him. And, as for the lock on my bedroom door. That came later, when he was a teenager." Her lip wobbles and she touches her forehead. "He used to get bad headaches that caused him to sleepwalk. Or, at least, that's what he said. And whenever Geoffrey was away, I'd wake up to find him standing over me. In the end I put a lock on the door." I make an involuntary sound that pulls Clara forward, as if she'd leap across the desk if she could.

"Geoffrey and I did think about talking to you, in the beginning. But you and Cole seemed so happy, and we'd never seen him like that before. We thought maybe things had changed and he had just needed to grow up. We let ourselves believe that you could have a good life together. You know, you're so strong and independent, we thought that was probably what he'd always needed."

The world doesn't feel entirely real, as if there's a film between me and the room. "What do you mean?"

Her eyes dart behind me but then she forces herself to look me in the eye. "We loved Cole very much when he was young. We still do, of course, but it's . . . well . . . complicated."

"Why?" I ask, keeping my voice steady.

"Do you really want to know?" I imagine her telling her clients there are some things that are better not to know.

"Yes."

Her hands clasp together again, the force turning her knuckles white. "Cole was a very difficult child. Incredibly needy and demanding. He didn't sleep through the night until he was nine. It's why I stopped at one, in fact. But we loved him, and our parenting might not have been perfect, but it was fine. We sent him to boarding school for secondary because he was always a loner and we thought it would do him good, but he never seemed to make any proper friends." She sighs. "His school was all boys, but they began admitting girls in the sixth form. We got the first complaint in the first term of lower sixth."

"Complaint?" The sickness that had started in my stomach rises up my throat.

Clara's eyes are glistening, and I can tell she wants me to leave more than anything. But she nods. "Over the two years of sixth form, five different girls accused him of inappropriate behavior. It was never anything terrible, more pestering, being overly attentive, staring, that sort of thing. The last one claimed he put his hand up her skirt. His possessions were searched, and they found a notebook listing everything about the girls, in detail. The school didn't take it as seriously as they would have done now, and, to my particular shame, Geoffrey and I encouraged them to make it go away. Of course, we had to meet with the girls' parents, and Cole was basically never allowed to be alone with them again, but, looking back, he should have been expelled. It would have been much better for all concerned if he had been." The room has started to rotate, so I hold on to the arms of my chair. Clara pours me a glass of water and hands it over, but I'm shaking so much it spills down my chin. "I'm sorry," she says, her voice thick with her own unshed tears.

"Go on. Tell me everything."

She pulls in a breath. "Before he went to university, we talked endlessly about respect and consent and responsibility. But I think I knew that he didn't fully understand."

"And yet you didn't try to help him in some way?" My vision is starting to dim, and her voice sounds far away.

"I have made lots of mistakes," she says, and I can see the time she's spent thinking about this in her eyes. "I did try. But not enough. He was my son and I loved him, despite what he's told you. I kept telling myself that he was a teenage boy who was finding his way. And Cole is very charming, which can be confusing. I would be shocked if you told me he's ever done anything to physically hurt you."

I think of all the nights he's crawled through windows and around closed doors, how he's tied my hands above my head. But she's right, I agreed to all those things. *I don't want you to do anything you're not a hundred percent comfortable with.*

"I take it something happened at university?"

Her hand goes back to her neck as if she wants to push the words back inside. "You know he never graduated? That he was asked to leave in his second year?"

"No."

She shakes her head and one tear escapes, which she hurriedly swipes away. "To put it bluntly, although Cole would disagree with my terminology, he stalked a girl while there. On and off for about six months. They dated for a few months, but she ended it because she found him too intense. But after that he'd turn up at her room, write her letters, send her flowers, beg other students to speak to her on his behalf. Her friends told her to tell someone, but she said she felt sorry for him and didn't think he was dangerous. She only reported him when she woke up one night to find him standing over her bed. He ran away as soon as she screamed, but she was obviously terrified."

"Oh god," I say and then I have to lean forward because I think I'm going to faint. Clara stands and comes over to me, running her hand down my back and helping me sit up. I see the effect of these memories all over her taut face. "Who was the girl?"

"She was called Laura."

"Laura?" I repeat. I think of all the stories Cole told me about Laura, all the ways she made him feel small, all the lies she told, all the manipulations. "Are you sure? I thought they went out for nearly a year."

Clara shakes her head. "I'm not surprised Cole's told you about her. He feels a great sense of injustice about that time. I expect he's told you that she was manipulative as well? That she gave off mixed signals and lied about what she wanted?" I nod. "I went to visit Laura after everything came out and, well, all I can say is that she didn't fit Cole's description at all."

"But she never pressed charges?"

"No, she was adamant that she didn't want to. She said nothing had actually happened and she wanted to forget about it."

"And was she, like, okay?"

"As far as I know. I found out that she graduated, but I don't know what happened to her afterward." Clara leans against her desk. "He came back home after that. But, like I said, he was adamant that he hadn't done anything wrong. He kept dwelling on how unfair it all was. He maintained that he had been nice to her, a good boyfriend, that she wanted to be with him. He wouldn't even admit that it was wrong to break into her room. He kept on saying he never would have hurt her, that it was a game that I was obviously too conventional to understand. And the fact that she never went to the police seemed to reinforce Cole's belief that he hadn't done anything wrong. It was all we ever talked about and there were times when I thought I was losing my mind."

I stand quickly and Clara does the same, reaching out as I recoil from her. I should feel sorry for her, but all I can feel is Cole standing over my bed, lying on top of me, being inside me. *Sexuality is just a convention,* he repeats in my head, *people who think otherwise are so boring.*

I take a deep breath because I need to see this through now. "Go on."

"After a year or so we encouraged him to leave home. We thought it would do him good," she says, her voice croaky. "But we didn't abandon him, we helped him find a flat and gave him money. I offered him all types of therapy, but he always refused."

"But didn't you worry about what he might have been doing?"

"Yes, of course. But then he met you and we thought . . . I mean, we hoped . . ." I know she wants me to tell her that was the right thing to do, but I stay silent. "Oh god, I've thought about this so much, Mel," she says, and her voice is so strained it sounds hoarse. "I'm sure I don't need to tell you that Cole sees himself as this kind and caring person. And he's not pretending. In so many ways he is. His kindness is genuine. But, also, he finds it very hard to accept when things are denied him. He doesn't take responsibility for anything. Everything is always someone else's fault." She rubs at her forehead, and her eyes are red. "Over the years I've wondered if he has a personality disorder, maybe narcissistic or anti-social. Neither definition quite fits, but you learn with psychology that humans rarely fit neatly into categories. But, truthfully, sometimes I think that giving him a diagnosis could be a let off. Because he's the same as so many of the men I meet every day, and all the ones who govern us."

I remember something my therapist said, an echo of what Siobhan had also told me, when I'd wailed about how weak I'd been. Men like Cole believe they're right because society has told them that they are their whole lives. And, as a result, they find it difficult to be told "no." I look at Clara, shaking with fear at what she created and know how easy it would be to blame her for Cole. We always look to the mother when they must have enough of their own shit to deal with, and I can't understand how we go on expecting individual women to erode thousands of years of bullshit. The only saving grace in this horrid mess is that I didn't get pregnant. I'm still not sure I understand what happened to me. But I do know that it was wrong, and I've been complicit in it. My stomach rolls. I make for the door, but Clara calls after me.

"Please, Mel, I'm so sorry. If there's anything I can do, please—"

I stop, with my hand on the door handle, because I realize there is one thing I need from her. "What's Laura's surname?"

Clara looks down. "Oh, I can't, I mean, I'm not sure I remember."

But I hold my ground. "Cole has this thing," I say, my voice shaking. "He can't have sex unless we play this very particular game."

"Please," she says, her hand held up in front of her.

"Well, at least I thought it was a game," I say. "I'm not so sure I'd call it that anymore. He likes to pretend we're strangers and breaks into our flat. Sometimes he ties me up. He likes it best if I act scared, which, if I'm honest, hasn't ever been an act."

Clara sinks into her chair and a sob echoes out of her. Her head falls into her hands, but I can still hear it when she whispers into her desk, "Laura Perkins. She lives in Bristol."

I make it back to Siobhan's and climb straight into bed, not bothering to remove my clothes. My mind feels like it's being blended, everything from the past six or so years since I met Cole whizzing together so quickly I can't quite catch hold of any of the strands. I shut my eyes against the images playing on a loop, but they won't go away. I'm worried that I will forever feel hot breath on my neck and fear in my heart, that love will never be easy for me again.

Laura is wearing her bank uniform when we meet at a coffee shop in Bristol, and she's careful to tell me that she only has an hour. She looks older than she is, her hair a little straggly and the skin around her mouth tight. But she smiles when she sees me and I catch a streak of pity in her eyes, which is fair enough, because I married him. I've already explained why I want to speak to her in the messages we've exchanged over the past couple of weeks, so it feels a little like I know her already when I sit down.

"I think I've sort of been waiting for this moment for years," she says, after we've exchanged a few pleasantries and received our coffees. "The older I've gotten, the angrier I've felt with myself for never going to the authorities about him. But I've never known what to do about it. It always seemed too late."

"But you spoke to the university, didn't you?" I say. "I mean, he had to leave, right?"

She nods, but her face contracts. "It's just, it wasn't enough. The fear he left behind in that room has followed me everywhere. I don't think I've slept through the night since it happened. And after I had my kids, it got really bad. I'd be up a hundred times a night checking no one was in their rooms."

"I'm so sorry," I say.

"I second-guess myself a lot," she says. "Sometimes I think Cole pulled the rug out from under me and made me realize that life is unsafe. Wherever I am, on motorways or in the quiet woods or even behind locked doors at home, I don't ever really feel safe." I recognize myself in Laura and it's uncomfortable. She looks over my shoulder and squints against the low sun. "Fear is a disease. It gets inside you and attacks you. I truly believe it can get into your blood and infect every part of you. On my worst days I can't get out of bed. The fear makes me so weak, it takes away my power to think straight or hold up my own body. And I hate myself so much for that. That I let what he did to me continue to affect me and my family."

"Oh, Laura, I'm so sorry," I say. "You know none of this is your fault, don't you?" This is something Siobhan says to me a lot and I've yet to work out if I believe it.

She half laughs. "It's definitely my fault that I felt too embarrassed to do anything about it."

"You did all you could."

Laura tears open a packet of sugar, letting the little white crystals fall onto the table. "No, that's not true. I should have gone to the police."

"There's no guarantee anything more would have happened to him."

She looks me straight in the eye and my skin runs cold. "He didn't leave after I screamed."

My hand goes to my throat. "What do you mean?"

She presses her lips together so forcefully, I can see the bones of her skull. "I mean, I didn't say no. But I didn't say yes either." A single tear drips down her face. "I think I was so shocked and scared that I sort of let it happen. And afterward, he acted as if it was something we'd both agreed to. That's why I went to the welfare office in the morning. I knew I'd go mad if he stayed on campus."

I look down at the trail of sugar and try to process what she's saying, but my mind is refusing to make the connection.

"Apart from my husband, you're the only person I've ever told," she says.

"I'm sorry," I say, pathetically.

"He's wanted me to go to the police for years. You know, before I spoke to him about it, I didn't even think of it as rape." My stomach hollows. Because, of course, it's rape, but something about that word being spoken out loud makes me feel like I'm going to die. "I'm sorry, Mel. If I'd gone to the police he'd have been charged and you'd never have gone through everything you did."

I start to cry, so she moves her chair round the table to put her arm around me. I lean into her, and for a moment, it feels okay. But I can feel a bigger part of me withering. A black cloud is building in my stomach, which I worry is going to keep expanding until it fills me all the way up. If I find a way to carry on, I worry it'll be with this darkness forever inside me. I worry it's going to change me and define me, that I will always be alone, always be scared.

There are few places I would want to be at less than Alexandra Palace surrounded by hundreds of people, watching awards being given out to artists I know nothing about. But Paulo Rossi are sponsoring the event, and Paulo himself has flown over to present the big prize, and since his is the biggest makeup brand we represent, I have to be here.

I don't think Paulo has asked me one question all night, which actually I'm grateful for as there's no way I'd be able to tell him anything that's been going on in my life. But now I know all about his wife, his son, his daughter, the exact shades of lipstick they're putting out next year, and his dog's favorite food. I pour myself another glass of wine as he makes his way to the stage, even though I should probably stop. My therapist told me it was a good idea to come tonight, as did Siobhan, Kate, my mother, and my sister, but I'm not sure they were right because I'm an alien in an environment that used to feel like home. My dress hangs off my too-thin frame and the layers of makeup haven't done anything to hide my dark eye bags and newly acquired lines. But I'm here and that will have to do for now.

As Paulo makes his speech, my mind wanders to the frozen embryos, which the clinic have said they legally have to keep on ice for a year while Cole and I come to an agreement. This thought sends me back under the covers at least once a day because, the truth is, you never know how the law is going to change and I won't feel safe or free until they're gone.

"Lennie B," Paulo shouts from the stage, which makes me look up because I've heard of her. Well, anyone who knows anything about popular culture has heard of her. Every time she has a new exhibition, those massive shapes end up all over the media, with people debating if they're any good. Siobhan and Kate even have one of her prints in their kitchen.

She ambles onto the stage dressed in a long flowing sort of caftan with DM boots sticking out from the bottom. Her hair is thick and wild and lots of gold jewelry shines across her face and body. She looks every inch the bohemian artist. Her speech is short and sharp, which gives the impression that she's not that bothered by the prize, but then again, I expect she's won plenty of them over the years. Commercial bollocks, Cole says in my mind, and I want to bang my head on the table.

I sigh as Paulo maneuvers her over to our table when they come off stage, the expression on her face an indication that she feels the same way as I do about the thought of more polite conversation. But Paulo is not a man who is easy to say no to. When they arrive, he introduces her to the table, and we all congratulate her while she sticks out her bottom lip. I force myself to stand because I'm good at my job and go over to her after the conversation has fragmented and Paulo is pulled in another direction.

"Congratulations," I say when I reach her side. She bobs her head and sets her mouth. I hold out my hand, which she barely shakes. "Can I get you a drink?"

"Nah, I'm good." She's looking over my shoulder for a way out.

"I'm Melanie Connelly, Paulo's PR." I catch her grimace, but I plow on. "It would be amazing if I could talk to you, or whoever represents you, about some joint publicity to do with this prize."

She snorts. "I don't do press."

I think of the acres of column inches I've read about her. "Oh, sorry, I thought I'd read quite a few of your interviews."

She reaches for one of the chocolates on our table. "Not for years. Anything you've read lately is regurgitated bollocks dreamed up by some lazy PR or journalist to shift a few more copies of their sad magazine."

I try to smile, but my mouth feels stuck. Cole is heavy inside my head again, all the things he's ever said about my job ringing in my ears. I'm not saying it's wrong, I hear Cole say, but have you considered the implications of what you're selling? Or, what happens if we have a daughter and all she's interested in is what Gemma fucking Pritchard has for breakfast? My therapist says I have to stop judging myself by Cole's standards, but what if he's right? My throat tightens and I realize I am going to cry. I quickly turn away, but not before the first tears spill.

Lennie puts a hand on my arm. "Oh, shit, mate, I'm sorry. I'm having a crap time at the moment, which turns me into a proper bitch. That was really rude."

I swipe at my eyes, but they won't stop leaking. "It's fine. I'm having a crap time as well. It's not you."

She clunks her award onto the table and pulls me by the arm. "Come on, we could both do with a drink. There must be a bar in this place."

We find one tucked away in a little room and Lennie persuades a nervous-looking young man to pour us both a large whiskey while we sit on stools not designed for female heights.

"Thank you," I say as I sip at the warm liquid. It goes almost straight to my head. "I'm sorry you're having a crap time. What's happened?"

She wraps her hair into a bun and fixes it with a band from her wrist. "Oh, well my daughter's moved to Paris to be with her dad for a bit. It's not a big deal, really. I mean, her dad and I were never together so she needs to get to know him, and she's studying out there. I know it's good for her and everything, but it's still hard."

"How old's your daughter?"

"Twenty-two."

"Wow, you don't look old enough."

She shrugs. "I'm not really. I was seventeen when I had her."

"Oh, right." I try to imagine what it must feel like to give birth to someone who eventually leaves and realize I've never properly considered anything about motherhood. "Was it everything you expected?"

Lennie squints over her glass. "Was what?"

"Having a child?"

"Oh, right. I've only got ambiguous, annoying answers to that I'm afraid."

"Is there any other type?"

Lennie laughs deeply, actually tipping her head back. "Okay, so, she's absolutely the love of my life and I would die for her and I wouldn't change having her for anything. All those clichés are a hundred percent true. But also, it's the hardest thing I've ever done. I mean, relentlessly hard, both physically and emotionally, and sometimes, often, in fact, I'm sure I've fucked it all up and that she'll hate me one day, if she doesn't already. And, when she was little, there were times I couldn't believe I'd done this to myself, nights I spent crying with exhaustion. I'd have given my right arm for a few hours off. All those clichés are also a hundred percent true." I look down at my drink, vibrating in the low light and find myself crying again. There are never any easy answers when you're a woman. "Shit, I'm sorry," Lennie says. "Have I put my foot in it again?"

"No." I look back up at her dark eyes, which seem kind. "No, no. It's just that my crap time is that I've been unsuccessfully doing IVF for the past two years and I've recently left my husband."

She sits back a bit. "Oh god, I'm sorry."

"Actually, that's not even why I'm crying," I say. "I'm crying because it took me so long to leave the bastard."

She leans back into me then and draws her lips into a smile. "Now that sounds interesting." She motions to the young man for more whiskey. "I want to hear all about it."

Lennie is very easy to talk to and the bar is a quiet escape from the noise of the party echoing comfortably around us. And the whiskey is smooth and warm, slipping through my chest in an expansive way that opens me up, so I find the words fall out. I tell Lennie things I haven't been able to articulate fully to anyone else yet. I tell her about the way Cole likes to have sex, the unlocked windows, the dark hood, the rope he'd started to carry, the way he'd put his hand over my mouth when he came. I tell her about the IVF, the needles, the blood, constantly feeling that I'm broken. I tell her about the words that have been used about me, the conversations that have happened behind my back. I tell her that the only emotion I feel regularly these days is guilt, about how I've let everybody down, about staying in London instead of moving to the country, about maybe not wanting to be a mother. I tell her about Laura. And finally, I tell her that I am terrified, all the time, of everything, from the smallest moments to the largest problems.

It's late when we finish speaking. The noises of the party have subsided, so I suspect most people have gone home. The young man at the bar certainly looks tired. I am drunk, but in that clearheaded way, where you might not be able to walk in a straight line, but your thoughts are perfectly ordered.

"Do you know how powerful what you've told me is?" Lennie asks.

I smile because I feel anything but powerful. "I just feel exhausted."

She pats my hand. "I'm not surprised."

"You know what the worst part is?" I say. "Most people who look at my life would think Cole is one of the good guys."

Lennie's eyes are sparkling. "Of course. The bar is so low for men. All they have to do is a bit of bloody washing up, or ask how you're feeling, and everyone thinks they're the second fucking coming." I laugh. "Listen, I have an idea I'd love to run past you when we're both a bit more sober." She reaches for a napkin and fishes a pen out of her bag, passing it over to me. I write my name and number in big blue strokes.

"What's the idea?" I ask.

She shakes her head. "It's too complicated to go into now. And we're too drunk. It's to do with my new show."

"Aren't you going to do more shapes?"

She shakes her head empathically. "No, I'm done with them. Which could be a really bad decision. My gallerist certainly thinks so. But I've been doing them for so long and I think they've served their purpose."

"How so?"

"Okay, this is going to sound super pretentious, but when I was younger, I didn't know you could have dreams or principles or desires or any of those things. Even after my work started selling, it took me years to realize that I could take up space in the world. You know, that it was as valid for me to be here as all these pricks." She throws her arm back at the rarefied space we're in. "And I think that's why I ended up creating those fuck-off mammoth shapes. They took up space."

"I've never thought of your work that way," I say.

"Well, nor did I, for years. It only struck me recently. And then I thought, you know what, I've created the space I need to be heard. Now I have to say something I want people to hear."

"And what is it that you want people to hear?"

She tilts her head. "Well, it's complicated. It has to do with violence. And fear."

I laugh. "I'm certainly an authority on that."

She nods. "I've been avoiding my own fear for a long time, well pretty much all my life, really. I guess you've heard about my mum?"

"I think so. She was murdered?"

"Yeah, by my stepdad. And I've spent most of my life running from fear as a result. But I don't know, I feel now might be the time to let it catch up with me, to see the worst it can do. Or, rather, the worst I can do to it."

I can't work out what she's saying. "I don't understand how I can help. Do you need help promoting the show or something?"

She laughs. "Nah, nothing close. Look, let me formulate the idea properly before I say any more."

And for the first time in a long time a spark of hope shoots through me, like a tiny electrical current. I want to hear more.

I knew Cole was the one from the first moment I heard about him. As I sat opposite Mel telling me all about him at that stupid awards ceremony, a sense of destiny (if that doesn't sound too bollocks) started to creep over me. The creation of art is so often lots of small stops and starts—three steps forward, five back. An idea that feels like it has potential dissolving into smoke. Loose threads that refuse to bind together however hard you try. But there are also those rare but glorious moments when everything falls into place and you know you were right to hang on. Those heart-stopping flashes when you think you might be on the verge of creating something good. That's what Mel's story made me feel. And I knew immediately that only Cole could give me the ending I'd been chasing for so long.

APPLE BREAKING NEWS

Internationally acclaimed artist, Lennie B, forty, has been identified as one of the people who found the abandoned tent of missing women, Molly Patterson and Phoebe Canton, on New Year's Day, along with local man, Cole Simmonds, forty-three. Both live very close to where Molly and Phoebe went missing in East Sussex. Police have yet to comment.

From: Beatrice Westerfield <Beatrice.Westerfield@thewestgallery.com>
To: Lennie Baxter <Lennie@LennieBart.com>
Date: 3 January, 12:35
Subject: WTF & Observer

Lennie!

Just seen the news—was it really you who found the tent?? Shit, tell me all.

Also, I've had a call from Nate at the Observer and they want to do a piece on you. Great timing, as I'm about to start whipping up interest. I told Nate all about your self-imposed isolation and where you're living, and he went mad for it. He googled your cottage and is salivating (his word) at the thought of the shots they could get of you there. And of course that was before all of this broke—maybe they could shoot where you found the tent? But tastefully obviously!! They'd love to get this done in the next week or so but are happy to fit it around your schedule. Let me know!

xxB

And of course HNY. Hope it was fun??

From: Lennie Baxter <Lennie@LennieBart.com>
To: Beatrice Westerfield <Beatrice.Westerfield@thewestgallery.com>
Date: 3 January, 13:12
Subject: WTF & Observer

Bea,

Firstly, happy new year to you too. I had a quiet one—just supper with a mate.

Yes, I did find the tent. Nothing to tell really. I was out for a walk on New Year's Day and came across it, and it looked abandoned, which felt weird, so I called a friend and then we called the police. Apart from that I know as much as you. Don't know how the bastard press got wind it was me.

As for the other thing, I get why you've asked me, but also, we've known each other a long time now and you must know what my answer is going to be. Photographing me by the site of the tent wouldn't only be in bad taste, it also would be a terrible idea—something you're going to have to trust me on, okay? The same as when I walked into your office fifteen years ago with a plastic bag full of drawings and a head full of ideas. I know what I owe you because no one else would have taken a chance on a scabby upstart who knew literally nothing about art or artists or galleries. But what you have to remember is that, deep down, I'm still that scabby upstart.

If Nate asks why I won't talk to him tell him it's because when I started out, none of the critics took me seriously. They were like, "God, she's from a council estate, she didn't go to art college, she hasn't even got a GCSE, her mother was a loser who got herself murdered, her dad fucked off when she was a baby, she's a single mum herself, so don't take her too seriously." Now the same journalists are all falling over themselves to mention how those things make me so authentic and relevant. So no visits to the cottage, no moody photos of me at a crime scene, no bad headline, no sob story that will ever come close to anything resembling my actual life.

LB

TWITTER

THE WEST GALLERY @thewestgallery

We are very proud and excited to announce that we will be hosting a new exhibition by internationally acclaimed artist Lennie B @LBart in June this year. Watch this space for upcoming details. It promises to be the most talked about show of the summer.

(comments 134)   (retweets 51)   (likes 622)

AMANDA SHAW @colourshapes

Replying to @thewestgallery

Looking forward to this. Love her work.

PAUL @Pauldrawsstuff

Replying to @colourshapes and @thewestgallery

You only think you love her work because you've been told it's good. My 5 yo nephew could do better.

AMANDA SHAW @colourshapes

Replying to @Pauldrawsstuff and @thewestgallery

Thanks for telling me what I think @Pauldrawsstuff!! I do love her work actually. And I bet it's a lot better than anything you could do.

ALANAF @lightfantastic

Replying to @thewestgallery

You should be promoting up-and-coming artists, not an overpaid celebrity whore like @LBart. This is what's wrong with the art community. It's all emperor's new clothes. Everyone's too scared to say she just makes shapes, that's it.

PAUL @Pauldrawsstuff

Replying to @lightfantastic and @thewestgallery and @LBart

Have you noticed that all the celebrities have one of her shapes hanging somewhere in their homes? They all have the same smiling Buddha and one of her shapes.

LUCY COBB @lucycobb

Replying to @thewestgallery

Ha ha! I've just googled her stuff. You've got to be having a laugh.

CHURCHY @churchillart

Replying to @lightfantastic and @Pauldrawsstuff and @thewestgallery and @LBart

I think you've hit the nail on the head. We're a bunch of sheep who need to be told what we like. This is obviously a massive practical joke.

CHURCHY @churchillart

Replying to @lightfantastic and @Pauldrawsstuff and @thewestgallery and @LBart

Mustn't criticize anyone who comes from an "underprivileged" background.

TOM BRUSH @brushworks

Replying to @churchillart and @lightfantastic and @Pauldrawsstuff and @thewestgallery and @LBart

Are you joking, mate? You straight white guys have had the whole of history to play with but you still won't let other people have a turn?

ELLA @ellaella

Replying to @thewestgallery

So looking forward to this. Her Visionary show saved me when I was a depressed student with no money. I've had a postcard from that show stuck on my bedroom wall for about 5 years. #walkforwomen

---

MR. ART SUCKS @artsucks

Replying to @thewestgallery

Cannot believe you're showing her work. Her shapes are intrinsically heteronormative and establishment centered. They ask us to simplify and conform.

CATHY FISHER @paintthroughsadness

Replying to @thewestgallery

Her work is derivative and an insult to our intelligence. Please use your platform to showcase the work of talented artists without representation. Check out my stuff www.paintthroughsadness.com.

ASHLEY BOWLER @ashsays

Replying to @churchillart and @thewestgallery

She's a complete mess of a person as well—have you seen this piece in Art Scene from a few years back www.artscence.com/thetroubledartofLennieB @LBart. And now all the stuff with those girls who just happened to go missing right outside her door.

CHURCHY @churchillart

Replying to @ashsays and @thewestgallery and @LBart

There's this one as well www.artmatters.com/shapedbytrauma. And did you see that photo of her today singing with those women holding a vigil for Molly & Phoebe? She's a publicity whore. Always had such a hard face.

ASHLEY BOWER @ashsays

Replying to @churchillart and @thewestgallery and @LBart

I feel sorry for her daughter. Don't know why people like that are allowed to have children.

ASHLEY BOWER @ashsays

Woohoo finally!

@LBart has blocked you

THE WEST GALLERY

Thank you for visiting "One of the Good Guys" by Lennie B.
We understand that it might have been a challenging experience, not only because of the nature of the exhibition, but also
because of the controversy surrounding the events depicted in
the show. We stand by our commitment to this exhibition.
Please read Lennie B's following artist statement, which, we
hope, will explain the decisions she made.

—BEATRICE WESTERFIELD,
Gallerist, the West Gallery, June 5

Let me start by saying that I know most of you hate Mel and me for
what we did to Cole. But we did—we do—have good reasons.

We knew Cole was dangerous when we went into this, I hold my
hands up to that. But let me tell you, he was also very charming.
And I wasn't prepared for how invested he was in being that person. You know, it's not an act with him. He truly believes himself to
be kind and thoughtful, a good partner. Which was disconcerting
because I'd almost expected this sort of pantomime villain. But, of
course, people are more complicated than that. Even villains have
humanity, which is extremely confusing.

It was pretty easy to get Cole to notice me. I mean, there were
hardly any people on the cliff. I could have simply sat on the edge
like a lighthouse and still Cole would have come to me.

For the record, I want to say how much I hated that landscape. I know some people will say that makes me a philistine, but when I looked across the wide-open seas and high cliffs, I didn't see beauty. I saw steep drops made for falling and jagged rocks that could be used to crush fragile skulls. I saw deep waters good for drowning. I saw huge expanses that would absorb any screams. I saw miles of damp grassland between myself and help. That land-scape isolated me, got inside me, and it still haunts my nightmares. Give me a city any day, with all its mess and confusion, because at least it has all its people, its accountability.

At first, I thought Cole was so easy to read, it was almost boring. It was annoying to play the part of a simpering woman who didn't bloody mind anything, but it wasn't hard. Except I must have got-ten complacent, because I wasn't expecting it when he left rabbit guts on my back doorstep.

The night after Molly and Phoebe went missing, I noticed him in my garden when I went up to bed. He was carrying a plastic bag and looked very agitated. For a moment, I thought I'd lost control of the whole thing and totally misjudged him. I shut the curtains and turned off the lights so I could watch him through a slit in the curtains, my mobile in hand in case I needed to call someone. But after a few minutes he walked over to my back step and emp-tied the contents of the bag onto it. He looked totally panicked after he'd done it and left quickly, running off down the path to the beach. I forced myself to go downstairs and look at the back step, where I saw a mass of slimy guts, dripping like a scene from a slasher movie.

At first, I couldn't work out why he'd done something so obvi-ously attributable to himself, or even what he hoped to get out of it. It was clear that he must have forgotten that he'd told me all about his traps and how he skins and guts the rabbits he catches. And how you have to dispose of those guts or you'll attract foxes into your garden. Not that it was surprising that he'd forgotten he'd told me that because men like Cole often slip up on their innate arrogance. But I still couldn't work out what he was hoping to achieve. I went back upstairs and made myself get into bed. And then the foxes started screeching and I understood. The noise that fighting, hungry foxes make is how I'd imagine a zombie apocalypse and is otherworldly scary. And the woman he thought I was would have been terrified.

In fact, the woman I am wasn't immune because the whole situation with Molly and Phoebe had really gotten into my head by then. I think it was their tent that did it. That image haunted my brain and transported me back to my childhood home, a white tent in my lounge covering the body of my dead, battered mum.

The truth is, my life has been filled with fear, but I'd worked hard to make sure it wasn't fearful. But something about being right in the middle of that investigation brought a lot of things flooding back. Which really shouldn't have been a surprise. Of course it was always going to be girls, as Cole and the media insisted on calling them, that brought real fear hustling back to my door. It reminded me that no one had noticed me when I was genuinely just a girl sitting in the back of a police car as my mother lay murdered in our lounge and considered what that experience might turn me into.

Life is very fragile, but it doesn't do you any favors thinking that way. When Mum died, I had a hard time deciphering reality. God knows she was hardly a grounding force, but without her it felt as if I had no tether to the world at all. Sometimes I used to have to lie on the floor because it was the only place that felt safe. But then a teacher or another adult would shout at me, and I found I didn't have the words to explain what I was doing. The point is that I have always known the ground is unstable, as Cole was so keen to remind us over and over during those strange weeks. One day it's right there and the next it isn't. It makes you feel insubstantial, shit like that.

Fear is always biding its time, waiting for an opportunity to assure us of its dominance. And, of course, I'd tempted it back, making it the star of my show and kidding myself that doing so would somehow tame and contain it, control it. But that made me an idiot, which the fear clearly already knew. *However strong you get*, it still whispers to me in the wind of the night, *I will always be stronger*. Sometimes I wonder if that's all life is, especially when you're a woman, continuously running from fear until it finally overtakes you.

What you have to remember when you're judging me is that Cole loved my fear. So many of the things he did, like putting rabbit guts outside my door, were to make me scared, even if he didn't work that out about himself. And remember also, if I wasn't the person I am, I wouldn't have lit a cigarette and gritted my teeth when the foxes started to screech. I would have cowered under my covers and called the nearest man. A man who prided himself on being kind and gentle. I would have begged him to come round if I had to. I'd have let him hold me and fuck me and I'd have felt grateful for him. Over time, I'd have started to believe that I needed him to feel safe and done anything to keep him by my side.

The day after the rabbit guts/fox incident, I doubled down on playing the scared, vulnerable woman, because Cole had presented me with irrefutable proof that that was what he wanted from me. I had him round for dinner. I listened to his stories. I asked about Mel and got him to open up about his marriage and the IVF. He was always very respectful when he spoke about her, but I could hear the underlying criticism in everything he said. He used all the words of the patriarchy, calling her overemotional and highly strung, and he'd stick out his bottom lip as he spoke, like a sad schoolboy reluctantly telling on the class bully.

He also loved to tell me about his shitty life philosophy—how he didn't believe in materialism and preferred emotional experiences, always with a side comment about how Mel liked the high life. And, of course, he reveled in talking about how much he wanted children. At every opportunity, he brought up how callous Mel was being for wanting to destroy their embryos.

I do, by the way, understand why you might feel sorry for Cole with everything you've heard. Because we do so love to give men the benefit of the doubt, don't we? And it's so cute when they care about babies. There were even times while I was chatting to him that I softened a little, comparing him to my own biological father, and Jasmine's when he'd first learned about the pregnancy. But then I'd think about how Cole wanted to implant those embryos into Mel, despite her vehement protests, and the sympathy would drain away.

Not that he would have ever known. He never questioned how I was feeling at all. When he put his arm around me as we sat chatting in front of the fire, I knew that he was looking down at me tucked into him, acting the big man. My stepdad, Graham, would occasionally catch us all off guard and do that to Mum, make her feel safe and small, and I always saw in her face how much she loved it. But the truth is, men who want to protect women should never be trusted because we only feel the impulse to protect the things we think of as weaker than ourselves.

As you read this document, please keep all of this in mind. Please remember how men employ lots of different tactics to make and keep women scared. Think of all the times you've been made to feel, or have made someone feel, physically or emotionally vulnerable. Has anyone ever told you that they're protecting you, or that they know you better than you know yourself, or that no one will ever love you like they do? Have you ever said those words? Consider what those sentiments mean.

It's all violence, when you think about it.

MATTER OF FACT
WITH ALICE FOWLER AND TOBY ROSS

Because facts matter, we'll make sense of them.
Breaking down news stories to get to the truth.

ALICE: So, guess we couldn't ignore it any longer.

TOBY: No, it's the story that keeps on giving and so many of you have tweeted and commented and whatever, asking that we cover it.

ALICE: I mean, I do feel a bit weird talking about it when Molly and Phoebe are still missing, but also it's all I talk about with my friends, so I'm presuming it's all anyone out there is talking about.

TOBY: I overheard two women discussing it on the bus the other day.

ALICE: And?

TOBY: They reckoned the girls fell off the cliff while filming that last video on New Year's Eve.

ALICE: You know, I've got a couple of mates who agree with that theory. But, surely, they'd have found a body by now? Or something they were wearing?

TOBY: Well, geek that I love to be, I did check out the tide times and it was high at midnight on New Year's Eve so, if they had fallen, it would have been into the sea. But the coast guard confirmed that the currents that night mean it's most likely they'd have ended up on a beach only a few miles away. Not, of course, that it's an exact science.

ALICE: Oooh, get you, teacher's pet.

TOBY: I aim to please. Obviously, though, the majority of our listeners think some sort of foul play was involved.

ALICE: I mean, it's hard not to. So, shall we go through what we know to date, Tobe? Because, this morning, there's been a big development in the case.

TOBY: That's right, Alice, there sure was. But let's start at the beginning, for anyone who's been living in a cave. So, Molly Patterson and Phoebe Canton, both aged twenty-three, disappeared in the middle of their 365-mile coastal walk to raise money for a domestic violence charity, Safe Space UK. We know this happened sometime between midnight on December thirty-first when they posted a final video, and two p.m. on January first, when their abandoned tent was found by a local resident.

ALICE: But not just any local. That person happened to be one of the enfants terribles (did I say that right?) of the art world, Lennie B.

TOBY: Side note, do you like her stuff?

ALICE: I mean, sort of. If I'm honest, I don't really get it. All those massive shapes. I never know exactly what I'm meant to be seeing when I look at them, if you know what I mean.

TOBY: Yeah, they're definitely confusing.

ALICE: Anyway, Lennie B, has been living in a rented cottage right on the edge of a cliff to prepare for her latest show. It's in this very remote place on the South Coast, about forty minutes outside Brighton. One of those places you sort of have to see to believe. I mean, it's wild. Rough seas, really sharp drops—

TOBY: And the cliffs are totally eroding. You're not meant to get anywhere near the edge as they can literally collapse at any moment.

ALICE: Supporting bus ladies' theory.

TOBY: Except there wasn't any collapse that night. They could have fallen, considering it was dark and they'd been drinking, but it still seems unlikely since they've found no trace of them below or in the sea.

ALICE: So, this cottage Lennie B has been living in, is like the creepiest thing you've ever seen. When we say it's right on the edge, it is literally meters away from a fifty-foot drop. And it's so rickety. I mean, it looks like a strong gust of wind would bring it down. I doubt any of the locks work, but even if they do, I bet you'd only have to lean on the front door for it to open. And it's so remote, there's no road leading to it, just a track across these totally windswept fields.

TOBY: I have no idea how she stayed there alone even for one night. It would have totally freaked me out.

ALICE: There is no way I'd have slept a wink.

TOBY: But, anyway, the point is this cottage is on the South Downs Way, which was part of Molly and Phoebe's route.

ALICE: Yes. And on New Year's Eve they set up camp about fifteen minutes from her. Which was also about fifteen minutes from the cottage Cole Simmonds was living in.

TOBY: So, we get to Cole. Now, Cole Simmonds had also recently moved to the area. In October, about a month after Lennie B. I've managed to track down a few of his colleagues at the PR firm where he used to work, and they told me he'd recently separated from his wife and wanted a new start. But they were perfectly happy to talk about him, and the general consensus wasn't particularly favorable. They described him as sullen and unfriendly, like he was always looking down his nose at them.

ALICE: Interesting. And it was Cole who Lennie called when she first found Molly and Phoebe's tent on New Year's Day. Were they in a relationship?

TOBY: Not necessarily. But they must at least be friendly if she called him. Which isn't that odd. There really aren't many people around there.

ALICE: Except they also spent New Year's Eve together.

TOBY: Yes, that would suggest a relationship. But I spoke to someone from there—they want to remain anonymous—who has a relative in the local police force. They heard that Cole left Lennie's shortly after midnight on New Year's Eve. Which suggests to me that they weren't in a relationship, as surely you'd stay the night?

ALICE: I'd have thought so.

TOBY: But, more importantly, if he did leave at that time, that means they were both alone and without an alibi when the girls went missing.

ALICE: Precisely.

TOBY: That same person said that Cole could have easily walked past where Molly and Phoebe were camping to get home. And, interestingly, they also described him as a bit of a loner, in almost the exact same way as his coworkers in London did.

ALICE: And then, last night, Cole was taken in by the police for questioning.

TOBY: Yup. And why don't you tell our listeners exactly what for.

ALICE: He's been accused of a rape by an old girlfriend from twenty-odd years ago, a woman called Laura Perkins.

DAILY MAIL

When Will We Start Admitting That Women Are at Fault as Well?

BY FIONA TYLER-JONES
@fi-ty-jo

There's a certain brand of feminism I'm pretty exasperated by, one in which we're all meant to be victims. Poor us, these women cry, wringing their hands because Clive in accounts happened to brush their fingers while passing over a coffee. How dare you, they shout at any hapless man who holds open the door for them or offers to pay for dinner. They scowl at jokes, they correct your speech, they take offense at everything. In fact, taking offense is their super-power. I imagine them with their lips constantly pursed, hands on their hips and anger in their eyes. They are completely joyless.

But the thing I hate most about these women is how pathetic they make the rest of us seem. Because I'm perfectly strong and capable and intelligent, thank you very much. If Clive from accounts annoys me, I'll deal with it. And though I can open my own doors and pay for my own dinners, that doesn't mean I don't appreciate a bit of chivalry in this bleak world. And, yes, I do find jokes funny even when women are the butt of them and sometimes I get people's pronouns muddled—so shoot me.

I have a nasty feeling that Laura Perkins is one of these women. She certainly looks like one. And, really, why would anyone wait twenty-four years to accuse someone of rape? It sounds ridiculous, doesn't it? They were in a relationship. And when he apparently broke into her room, she didn't scream? Methinks the lady doth protest too much, or rather, not enough.

It also strikes me as a little too much of a coincidence that Laura is choosing to do this now, when Cole Simmonds is already in the news for finding Molly and Phoebe's tent. Could Laura be looking for her own moment in the spotlight? Amazingly, the desperate-to-be-woke Crown Prosecution Service appears to agree with me, considering they've granted bail to Cole Simmonds.

But we can't question Laura's motives because she is, wait for it, a woman. In the same way, we can't question the basic common sense of Molly and Phoebe walking the South Coast of England in the middle of winter. Now, I'm not saying what happened to them, whatever that might be, is their fault. But, at the same time, I don't think we should willingly put ourselves in obviously dangerous situations. Because, seriously, who would think it a good idea for two slight, twenty-something girls, to go "wild camping," as they put it, in the totally deserted countryside during the time of year when it's darker for more hours a day than it is light?

Molly and Phoebe were walking to raise money for a domestic abuse charity and to bring awareness to male violence. I mean, really? Doesn't it all seem a bit well, performative, considering the thousands of women who have no choice but to put themselves in dangerous situations to earn a living? I'm talking about all those shift workers coming home in the middle of the night or cleaners in deserted offices or policewomen on the beat. I hope to God that Molly and Phoebe haven't become victims themselves, but also part of me feels angry every time their faces pop up on my screens. Because, surely, they could have directed their energies in a more safe and sensible way.

The feminists will probably rail against me for saying this, but I think it's time we expect more from our women. Let's be sensible. Let's toughen up a bit and roll with the punches. Let's learn to bat Clive away instead of shouting for a tribunal. And let's stop wasting everyone's time by pretending we're going to achieve anything as whimsical as ending male violence. Instead, let's teach girls how to defend themselves.

Mainly, let's not cry rape twenty-odd years after an event that hardly falls into the category or put ourselves needlessly in the path of danger in the hopes of gaining a few column inches or social media followers. Let's make good decisions.

TWITTER

KAYLEIGH ADAMS @kaybae

I work at the local pub where those girls went missing & Lennie & Cole were 100% an item. They were in here a couple of days before it happened—all over each other. And mates saw them on the cliffs together holding hands #findmollyandphoebe

(comments 1,238)   (retweets 7,389)   (likes 12,449)

SARAH @sazzys

Replying to @kaybae

That's vile. Do you think she knew he was a rapist?

VICKY HOLMAN @vickyH

Replying to @sazzys @kaybae

Alleged

HELEN GROSE @potsandsmiles

Replying to @kaybae

Did you speak to either of them?

KAYLEIGH ADAMS @kaybae

Replying to @potsandsmiles

Her a couple of times. She seemed sound. He only came in once—when they met for a drink.

HELEN GROSE @potsandsmiles

Replying to @kaybae

How do you know they were a couple?

KAYLEIGH ADAMS @kaybae

Replying to @potsandsmiles

Just obvious. They left together. People saw them together a lot. It's a small place so we notice things.

PETER STEIN @peterswims

Replying to @potsandsmiles @kaybae

I wonder if they could both be involved somehow? #walkforwomen

---

CATFISH67 @truthteller

Replying to @sazzys @kaybae

There's no way that rape claim is real. I smell a conspiracy here. More anti-man crap. If you ask me we should be looking @LBart

---

YATESY71 @yatesy71

Replying to @sazzys @truthteller @kaybae

She's an odd person with an odd past. But it's quite a leap to suggest she's hurt two young girls?

GEORGIA ROSE @georgieporgie

Replying to @kaybae

Wasn't I just saying this last night @katiecross1??

KATIE CROSS @katiecross1

Replying to @georgieporgie @kaybae

They were obviously sleeping together! Why else was he the first person she called? There's more to this than meets the eye, I'm telling you! #findmollyandphoebe

---

ED WHEETON @reporterEd

Replying to @kaybae

Hi, Kayleigh, would you be interested in talking to me for an article I'm working on? If you follow me I can DM you.

DAILY EXPRESS

Detectives investigating the rape claim brought by Laura Perkins, 43, against Cole Simmonds, 43, are looking into her and her husband's finances. James Perkins, 45, served as the director of two companies that went into liquidation, in 2016 and 2018. He now works as a marketing manager at a local haulage firm. Mrs. Perkins works as a bank teller. The couple were married in 2012 and live in Bristol with their two children.

A friend of the couple said they had to move a few years ago, downsizing to a much smaller house, after the failure of Mr. Perkins's second company. The friend, who did not wish to be named, said both had seemed low since then.

Cole Simmonds, who lives close to the spot where Molly Patterson and Phoebe Canton disappeared four days ago in the middle of their charity coastal walk, has been released on bail pending an investigation. Police have said that he is not a suspect in the disappearance of Molly and Phoebe.

THE WEST GALLERY

I always say no when people ask if I'm surprised by the media's coverage of the last few months. But I've been on the receiving end of the press for over a decade now, so nothing really surprises me. We wonder why male violence rises, the bodies of women littering our collective consciousness, but we never look at the diet we're fed day after day. There's no letup when you're a woman, whether that's in the public eye or waiting at the school gates. You can never do anything right. You're judged for what you say, and even what you don't say, but never actually heard. So, in the end, you either break or you think, *Fuck it, I might as well just be the person I want to be.*

Cole told me early on that he wasn't going to read about the investigation in the media, which was easier for him than most considering he didn't have any social accounts. But the story was everywhere, so he still found out who I am. He acted a bit hurt that I hadn't told him I was Lennie B, but I just made up some crap about not wanting to be her anymore, which he seemed to get off on. Ten minutes on Google would have told him all he needed to know when we first met, but he obviously wasn't interested enough. Still, it worked in our favor, as his lack of interest also meant a lack of imagination.

So much of the speculation in that time was about whether Cole and I were sleeping together, which had zero relevance to the case. I saw a tweet in those febrile days that said: "If it looks like a duck and quacks like a duck, then chances are it is a duck. Except in this case let's replace the first letter with an *F*."

For the record, Cole never pressured me to sleep with him. In fact, he always seemed grateful when I told him I wasn't in the mood, which Mel had told me would be the case until he worked out if I was going to be receptive to the particulars of his desire. But also, for the record, I had no intention of sleeping with him. I'm a professional and I know better than to confuse the lines of consent.

He did however stay over quite a few nights, sharing my iron bed in a room that looked out across the deep, dark sea. I found it very hard to sleep when he was there. His body made mine feel weaker than normal, and I couldn't always catch my breath. A familiar threat of violence dangled in the air when he shared my space, in the same way as when Mum and I lived with Graham, his physicality shining off him, so I knew we were at his mercy.

When I did finally fall asleep during the nights Cole stayed over, my dreams were filled with my mother's weary face, and I'd wake with my heart pounding. Then I'd lie in the dark wondering how long it took her to realize she was going to die, if she raised her arms to stop the blows, if her bones cracked when they broke, if she bled a lot. And then I'd think about how many more women are going to have to disappear or end up broken and bloodied before something changes.

Plenty of people have called me a witch since everything came out. They've even made memes of me in my rickety cottage, incanting fear. Only a few hundred years ago, Cole could have had me put to death for bewitching him. He was scared of bloody mermaids, for god's sake. Often Graham would tell my mother that he couldn't be held responsible for his actions because of how she behaved. You almost have to feel sorry for all these men, so weak and pathetic that they're not in control of their own emotions.

As I lay awake next to Cole on those nights, I'd mostly think about how I want so much more for Jasmine, and how frightened I am that she won't get it. It makes my heart ache to think of all the ways she could be hurt, all the ways she could be made to feel less than she is. In those dark, small hours, I wanted to rush to her so I could forever put myself in between my daughter and the world of men. But I knew that I had to keep quiet and keep still like so many women before me have done. Except, I kept reminding myself, unlike all the women who had come before me, I wasn't waiting for something to happen to me. I was waiting to be the something happening.

WHATSAPP

Tequila Fridays

anyone know where to find that video of cole shouting at molly & phoebe Dais

wait what? they found their phones??? catty

nah but they got a warrant to access the data and apparently there's a video of Cole shouting at them on the cliff the day they went missing Dais

found it youtube.com/colemollyphoebe pookie

It's really not that bad. Don't think it proves anything. They're the ones being rude. catty yeah hardly damning   pookie

agree not damning, but odd that he spoke to them the day they went missing but never said he did   Min

true that   pookie

he said he panicked/knew he wouldn't be believed   catty

whole thing is so fucked-up. And the rape shit?   Dais

*alleged   catty

yeah right but like how much smoke do you need to know there's a fire??   Dais

police seem to be dragging their heels - keep saying he's not a suspect. surely he must be??   pookie

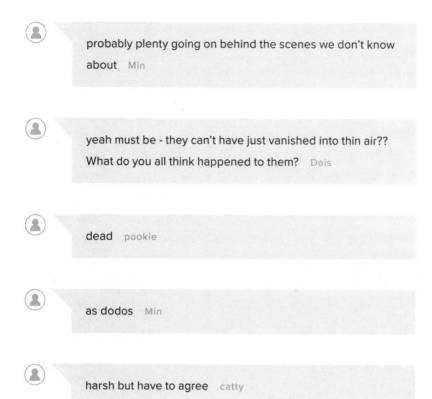

probably plenty going on behind the scenes we don't know about   Min

yeah must be - they can't have just vanished into thin air?? What do you all think happened to them?   Dais

dead   pookie

as dodos   Min

harsh but have to agree   catty

NEWSNIGHT

ANDREA: And now we're going to turn our attention to the case that is gripping the nation. The disappearance of Molly Patterson and Phoebe Canton. All we know so far about this baffling case is that the two women, both aged twenty-three, disappeared sometime between midnight on December thirty-first and 2:00 p.m. on January first. They had been taking part in a coastal walk to highlight the effects of male violence on women. Despite extensive police and forensic searches of the area not one trace of them has been found. I'm joined by Kelly Lester, who runs the charity Safe Space UK, which Molly and Phoebe were raising money for on their walk. Kelly, I know there's so much discussion about what might have happened to Molly and Phoebe, but what I'd like to talk to you about is the reason they were walking.

KELLY: Yes, Andrea, I think that has gotten somewhat lost among the constant speculation. And, apart from the fact that two young women are missing, that is the important part of all of this.

ANDREA: I mean, there's a terrible irony, isn't there—they were walking to highlight male violence and they could have fallen victim of that same type of violence.

KELLY: It's totally tragic. Of course, I hope that isn't the case, but also we can't ignore the fact that women fall victim to male violence each and every day. You know, I've heard lots of people saying that people can't just vanish, but this happens all the time, especially to women. In fact, in the time we've been looking for Molly and Phoebe, six other women in the UK have disappeared without a trace. And, of course, a few of them will turn up, but some will never be found.

ANDREA: What do you think it is about Molly and Phoebe that has made their case so interesting to the public?

KELLY: Well, it ticks a lot of boxes—they're young, pretty, and, let's be honest, middle-class white women. Those types of women always get way more coverage than poorer women or women of color, which is a subject we absolutely have to address in our society. We don't expect bad things to happen to women like Molly and Phoebe and, when they do, there's a certain element of thrill. We almost forget that real people are involved.

ANDREA: That's certainly a sense I've had from following the coverage— almost like watching a Netflix series play out.

KELLY: Exactly. We've totally normalized violence against women in our culture, which of course not only makes the violence easier to commit but also to witness.

ANDREA: And where do you think this all starts?

KELLY: Well, from all our research, I can give you a very simple answer: pornography.

ANDREA: There are lots of women who would very much disagree with you about that. Lots of feminists see sex work as a way of taking back control.

KELLY: Well, that's probably true for about five percent of women involved in sex work. Most are horrifically exploited and abused. And, more than that, the images that they're often forced to create, which are then fed to our children, are overwhelmingly degrading to women. And often very violent. Our young men are growing up with these images and, however well-educated they are, it is often a formative experience in their understanding of how to treat women.

ANDREA: And you're saying this leads to violence.

KELLY: Absolutely. All the research shows a direct correlation. And not just violence but also control, disrespect, and subjugation.

ANDREA: But pornography is so prevalent, how do you propose stopping this?

KELLY: I mean, in an ideal world I'd like it banned. But I know that's impossible right now. So, for a start, I want to see government legislation putting all pornography behind filters. We're also calling for an outright ban on anything hard-core. I know this wouldn't stop people from accessing it, but it would make people think. If something is illegal, we're saying we don't condone it as a society and that sends a powerful message to young kids. Even if they see it, they'll be left with a sense that it was wrong.

ANDREA: Kelly Lester, thank you so much for coming in.

TWITTER

FEMALE SOUND @femalesound

Sussex police = Keystone Cops. What exactly are they doing? Still searching fields and the sea? Still saying M&P might have had an accident? How is Cole not under arrest yet? Is a rape accusation and that video not enough #findmollyandphoebe

(comments 203)   (retweets 178)   (likes 604)

ALICE LASSCLES @alicemay22

Replying to @femalesound

It's a total disgrace. The whole investigation has been completely bungled. They concentrated on the immediate surrounding area for way too long when it's obvious they must have been moved. Have they even searched Cole's house?

LUCY @juicylucy

Replying to @femalesound

Women shouldn't trust the police anyway. Institutional sexism means nothing's ever taken seriously until it's too late #findmollyandphoebe #walkforwomen

---

SALLY @toofondofbooks

Replying to @femalesound

Cole had contact with Molly & Phoebe the day they went missing. He could have been the last person to see them. Yet he's walking around like nothing's going on!

YATESY71 @yatesy71

Replying to @femalesound

Very hard to prove a rape after a certain amount of time has passed, so doubt that will go anywhere. And all the video shows is a man trying to do his job, nothing more. Plus the police have questioned him and he's not been arrested. Lay off the speculation. #armchairsleuths #letthepolicedotheirjob

---

GINA GREGORY @GGdance

Replying to @femalesound

So odd that he didn't say he'd spoken to them that day. And being accused of rape. TBH wouldn't be surprised if Lennie B is involved as well—she's always struck me as being hard & they were together. And those shapes are weird.

GREG HANDS @handson

Replying to @femalesound

So many more men than women die from violence each year. Cannot understand why this case is getting so much attention. You'll all look pretty stupid when their bodies wash ashore & it turns out they got pissed and fell.

KAYLEIGH ADAMS @kaybae

Replying to @femalesound

Just to say there's lots of police activity here still. They're all over the cliffs and beach. Things are still happening!

JANE POWER @powertothejane

Replying to @yatesy71 @femalesound

Also, their parents made that appeal last night, so they're obviously working with the police. And if they accessed their data they must be looking into lots of other things too. #letthepolicedotheirjob

---

MANINTHEWILD @ManintheWild

Replying to @femalesound

Stupid bitches. Hope they're suffering now. Deserve everything they got.

THE SUN

Tin-don't: Missing Girls Molly and
Phoebe's Racy Tinder Profiles

Missing cliff girls Molly and Phoebe both set up racy profiles on the hookup site Tinder. Dark-haired Phoebe and blond Molly were happy to show off their toned bodies in bikinis and document their wild nights out. A friend of the girls commented that they were both really good fun and very liberated. Neither was in a relationship at the time they went missing. Keep scrolling for exclusive access to the recently deleted photos.

THE WEST GALLERY

Cole was a suspect from the beginning. Of course, the police didn't tell me that, but it was obvious by the tone of their questioning. I never lied about Cole. I told them the truth, that he'd left my house on New Year's Eve shortly after midnight, after we watched Molly and Phoebe's vlog on the cliff top, and that the video had annoyed him because people aren't meant to sit on the edge. I also mentioned that he had a headache and seemed distracted.

The police didn't have any actual evidence against him until they managed to access Molly and Phoebe's data and saw the video they'd filmed of their encounter with him on the day they disappeared. Not that Cole had said anything particularly bad, but what concerned the police was that he hadn't admitted to meeting them. He came straight to mine from the police station after they questioned him about it, extremely stressed and upset. He said he'd been a total idiot not to tell the police about his encounter with them, but he'd been worried about it being turned around to implicate him and then too much time had passed for him to say anything. I rubbed his back and told him I believed everything he said, which made him fall for me harder because men like Cole hate to be doubted.

And, yes, despite everything I knew about him, I did feel bad. That time was so confusing because I was also scared. And fear clouds your judgment, it makes you cling to ideas and people who you'd normally walk away from. But the problem with fear is that once you start letting it in, it's hard to stop.

Even before Graham came into my life, I felt scared quite a lot of the time. But I got good at creating stories, mainly about Mum, because I knew she was different from the other mothers who hung out easily in groups outside our flat or at the concrete playground nearby. I'd lie on my stomach in my bedroom drawing happy families, and that felt like a solid creation. But after Graham arrived, these stories became urgent, and I felt tasked with creating hundreds of scenarios that might save us.

I was twelve the first time he told me I was pretty. Mum was at the shops and when I thanked him, he laughed. After that, he'd say it every time Mum went out, which wasn't very often, so I could pretend it wasn't happening. He'd comment on my "development" as he called it, looking straight at my tits. Occasionally, he'd touch me as I walked past him, a hand run up my calf or a strong arm around my shoulder. He eventually stopped waiting for Mum to leave, but I'm not sure she noticed. At least she pretended she didn't. By the time I turned thirteen, I only showered when I knew for certain that he wasn't home, and I avoided eye contact unless he shouted at me to look at him.

The night I got home to find police tape strapped across our front door, I realized all my efforts to create a different story had been pointless. I was going to have to create a whole new life for myself without any help.

I didn't mean to create Jasmine and, although I love her with a ferocity I hadn't known possible, she brought with her an onslaught of terrifyingly foreign emotions. She was why I started creating art, at first to stop the itching in my blood and then because the work sold enough to allow me to realize the type of life I hadn't even been able to imagine. But these past few months

I've wondered if I'm all out of creation, if I have used myself up. Molly and Phoebe made me wonder if there's a fine line between a good and bad creation.

There were times after they went missing when I longed for the simplicity of only attempting another series of shapes. I could have followed my well-trodden formula, sculpting something huge and bold that I could reproduce smaller and smaller, eventually sending thousands of prints of it out into the world. It was what everyone was expecting of me, and I couldn't remember why that process had seemed so stale. It worried me that I'd bought into the myth that if something is popular it can't also be good. But it's also true that at the end of my last show, I felt hollow.

All throughout my career people have asked me what the shapes represent, and I've cobbled together answers, none of which sound particularly true, all the answers essentially boiling down to my desire to take up space. But, at the end of my last show, as I watched the big central sculpture being dismantled so it could be shipped to a bank in Beijing, I realized I'd achieved that goal many shows ago. The space was mine, so surely I needed to fill it with something meaningful. At least that's what I said to Mel the first time we met at that god-awful awards ceremony.

I once was as brave as Molly and Phoebe, carrying my possessions on my back and shouting my rage at the world. But time, or maybe money and success, has softened me, so now I stand slightly removed from the women on the front line. And I don't know if it's a good thing that I've penetrated the barriers and gotten so close to the general's tent or if it makes me a sellout. I still don't know if I've used my voice wisely, I don't even know if sticking pictures onto walls means anything when there are women out there, every day, still living dystopian realities that we all blindly accept.

A few years ago, I got into a Twitter row with someone who called me privileged. I don't think I won because I couldn't work out the argument. It is a simple fact that I bought myself a flat without a mortgage, that I eat in fine restaurants and take exotic holidays, that I can pay for Jazz to study without getting into debt, that my bank account is cushioned in security, that I never worry about bills or food prices, that my clothes are comfy and my home is warm, all of which is surely the height of privilege. And yet, how do you reconcile that privilege with a childhood spent in poverty, both emotionally and physically? There doesn't seem to be an adequate answer beyond the fact that none of us is just one thing. Especially not women, who so often contain the burden of multitudes.

BAD TO THE BONER

(41.5k followers)

I've been thinking about all the things I would have done to Molly and Phoebe if I'd come across them all alone in their tiny tent, on top of a hill, with no witnesses. To hear my very X-rated account you know where to find me, dudes.

Subscribe to my channel for foolproof tips on how to get any woman you want to sleep with you. No is never an option.

(likes 17.1k)

THE SUNDAY TIMES

When Fantasy Meets Reality

BY LUCY SCHOLES

Melanie Connelly is clearly uneasy being the center of attention. As she says to me almost as soon as we sit down, she's much more used to operating behind the scenes, guiding what people like me write about her clients. She runs a very successful company, Melanie A. Connelly PR Agency, which holds large contracts with lots of household name brands, as well as quite a few celebrities who often end up on the front pages.

"I've always been fascinated by the power of stories," she says, playing with the froth on top of an oat milk cappuccino in the lobby of the smart hotel she's arranged for us to meet in. "But I've never been interested in being part of the story. I think it's much more interesting to control things from the background." When I ask her what she means by that she looks a little annoyed that I haven't gotten her meaning the first time, but smiles pleasantly enough as she fills me in. "I guess, I've learned over the years that if you just shout about something, people stop listening. You have to find inventive ways of getting your point across."

"Almost like subliminal messaging," I say, which makes her laugh. And it's nice to see Melanie laugh, because her whole face changes and you can see that a fun person lies behind her hard exterior.

But laughing isn't something Melanie's been doing much of lately. She's had a difficult couple of years, which she'd hoped to put behind her until Molly Patterson and Phoebe Canton disappeared, and her estranged husband Cole Simmonds was not only questioned about them but also accused of rape by another woman, Laura Perkins.

Melanie and Cole met about eight years ago on a dating site. They were both in their mid-thirties and Melanie says it was a pretty instant attraction. "Cole was very different to the type of men I'd been used to dating," she says, and I can see the weariness in her sharp blue eyes that every woman must feel at some point. "I was really bored of all these men who saw life as a sort of weird competition. You know, lying or playing around or drinking too much or whatever. And Cole really genuinely isn't like that. He was so attentive and kind and funny, and he always was where he said he was and totally committed to our life and future. It was really easy to fall for him and I did pretty quickly."

I ask what went wrong then, because they separated nearly a year before any of this happened. Some of it, she admits, had to do with the IVF that took over their lives. They started trying for a baby a couple of years after meeting and the process was "total absolute hell." Melanie calls it grueling, trying to run a business and get pregnant. She said that Cole was far more eager to plow through the heartache of all her miscarriages, and then the cracks really began to show in their relationship.

"But," she says, taking a deep breath, "it wasn't only the IVF." I give her a minute because a steeliness has entered the air and she starts to fidget, tucking her sleek hair behind her ears and picking at a manicured nail. "The truth is I had been feeling like Cole wasn't listening to me for a while. It's like . . ." She lets her gaze rest behind me and I can see the worry like a force field around her. "It sounds silly, but because Cole was so 'good,' for want of a better word, he felt he was owed everything he wanted, if that makes sense. I'm not saying he was pretending to be nice to me or anything like that. What I mean is the way he acted made it hard to question anything I found uncomfortable. In fact, I think it made it hard for him to question himself."

I tell her that her description fits a lot of the men I know. Men who carry tote bags and visit galleries and read novels and talk about their feelings, but then hate it if you challenge them—as if we should let them get away with everything because they're so evolved. Twenty years ago they'd have told us to stop nagging. Melanie leans forward when I say this, her eyes shining as she finally meets my gaze.

"And the sick thing is we are grateful. We do let them get away with things."

She's right of course, but I also feel the need to push her because the men I know might dig in their heels during fundamentally irritating arguments, but I don't think they'd ever actually hurt a woman. So I ask her outright if she believes Cole is capable of rape, or if he could be involved in Molly and Phoebe's disappearance.

She physically shivers at my words, but then pulls herself together. "If you'd asked me that five years ago, I'd have said categorically no, but also I think I'd have been lying to myself on some basic level." She takes a very deep breath, as if she's been preparing for this moment for a long time. "Cole has this thing," she says, "he can only have sex in a very specific way. Basically, he liked to stage a break-in and then tie me up. You know, we wouldn't speak or anything, it was like . . ." She pauses and her eyes fill with tears.

"A rape fantasy?" I offer.

She nods tightly. "Yes, that never crossed my mind when I was with him. But yes, I've come to realize that's exactly what it was." She looks across at me again. "You must think I'm pathetic to have let that happen, but it wasn't violent. And, I mean, I did agree to it. He has this very strong belief that sex is just a series of conventions that we've all sort of blindly agreed to as a society and that experimentation within a loving relationship was fine. Which, of course, is true. But when it's the only thing you do and when you're made to feel bad for questioning it, that can start to feel strange."

As we continue to talk Melanie makes it very clear that she's not going to go any further. "I would never have said anything if it hadn't been for Laura Perkins," she says. "But I see how the media is treating her and I know how it's going to play out. I mean, I've worked in this business long enough to see when a narrative's building. And this one is all about questioning her, rather than Cole. And that seems so unfair, when I know what he's like."

I tell Melanie that I think she's being very brave, but she just shrugs and, as she's getting ready to go, says, "You know I thought a lot about who to approach with this story. After this, I'm not going to speak about it ever again, apart from at the trial."

I tell her that's understandable and then ask her who she'll be a witness for.

She fixes me with those eyes and says, very clearly, "The prosecution."

REDDIT

MEN'SJUSTICELEAGUE

Anyone else read that fucked-up interview with Cole Simmonds's ex-wife? Isn't there some sort of law against basically damning someone without any evidence? I mean, I know women are the superior species, but I didn't know they'd now developed superpowers and can look into the future. I think this might be a reason for the case to be thrown out? Because as far as I can tell Cole Simmonds hasn't done anything wrong. He's not been charged with anything. He was questioned about Molly and Phoebe's disappearance but nothing since. And he hasn't been found guilty of the rape. In fact, it seems very unlikely that he will be because none of it adds up—it was twenty-four years ago and they were going out! I can't even understand what his wife's gripe is? He liked weird sex but, as she herself said, she agreed to it? I mean, am I going mad here? What am I missing? Are we now saying that even when women give their consent it's not enough? Are they going to be demanding a written document going forward?

DADSRIGHTS

Men don't have rights anymore. Simple as.

PAULCOLLINS68

It's all bullshit. He was clearly in the wrong place at the wrong time. He seems like a decent guy who's gotten caught up in a load of crap. Terrible choice in women though.

TOM7230

Cannot stand women who cry rape years after the event. You either were raped or you weren't, love. It's not a good way to get out of an embarrassing shag.

MANINTHEWILD

Women are cunts. They think they're so special, parading themselves around and making us want them, but then never putting out. Molly and Phoebe were stupid bitches who got what was coming to them. Good on Cole if he did those things. Men need sex, it's a basic human right and all these bitches have to start understanding that. Things get ugly when men are denied their rights.

MEN'SJUSTICELEAGUE

Reply to ManintheWild

we do not support these views. Men's Justice League wants a fair society in which men's rights are recognized. Incel crap is not encouraged.

PROFBLUE

Reply to Men'sJusticeLeague

take the red pill and open your eyes.

Boohoo. I participated in something for seven years, but now I've decided I didn't like it and I want my money back. This is liberalism gone mad. What do women actually want from us? Nothing is ever enough. I honestly don't think they'll be happy until they're in control of everything and we're slaves locked in the house.

SIMONSHAND

Sexual relations are so hard now and men have no idea where they stand. Women want to be desired, but if our desire is "wrong" or too strong, they pretend to get scared and shout abuse. We're all walking a bloody tightrope every day. And we should all be very scared by what's happened to Cole Simmonds. Honestly, it could be any of us up there.

YATESY71

I think the truth is women don't know what they want. They're very driven by their hormones and it makes them deeply irrational. There's a reason why men were put in charge of making laws and everything. I'm not saying women shouldn't have rights, but things have gotten so much worse in the past fifty or so years. We need level heads governing us. If people accepted what they were good at, it would make things so much easier. Women are wonderful nurturers, surely we should all applaud and encourage that.

LIGHTSABRE5

When's International Men's Day again? Oh, yes, it doesn't exist.

WHATSAPP

Tequila Fridays

this is insane how has cole not been arrested??   Dais

it's not a crime to like kinky sex   Min

yeah but on top of everything else   Dais

police must be looking into it   pookie

been refreshing news all morning and he's not been taken in

Dais

you are well invested   pookie

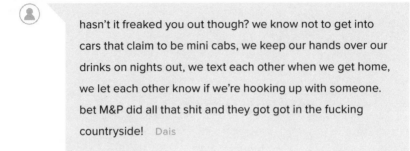

hasn't it freaked you out though? we know not to get into cars that claim to be mini cabs, we keep our hands over our drinks on nights out, we text each other when we get home, we let each other know if we're hooking up with someone. bet M&P did all that shit and they got got in the fucking countryside!   Dais

i know man it's all kinds of fucked-up   pookie

do you all remember desperate dan?   catty

how could we forget that charmer   Min

never told you guys but he was into that shit cole liked. that's why he dumped me in the end—said I was frigid   catty

starts researching women-only communes   Dais

THE WEST GALLERY

Two things happened during my time with Cole that I think are worth mentioning. One evening when he came for dinner, a rat ran over my feet as I was getting a chicken out of the oven. I dropped the pan and hot fat spewed up my leg—I still have a scar on my ankle. Now, I don't think Cole wanted to see me hurt, but also I can't help thinking that he somehow planted that rat. I'd never seen any evidence of a rat in the cottage before and he'd told me how rats always ended up in his rabbit trap. Plus there was something so Cole about the whole incident and the girlish terror it inspired in me.

The other thing was that my birth control pills kept going missing. It took me a while to notice, but on nights he stayed there were less in the pack when I went to take one the next morning until, one day, there were only empty foil strips left. And that same day, I swear I saw a pill sitting at the bottom of my toilet. It sent a chill through me, especially after hearing about his desperate desire to impregnate. Mel said that when they were doing IVF it sometimes felt as if she'd lost control of her body. Like Cole thought he had as much right to it as she did.

It was hard to keep my cool during those weeks. I became more acutely aware of my surroundings, so anything could make me jump: a blast of wind knocking against the side of the cottage, branches scratching against windows, turning off the lights at night when I went upstairs. My heart wouldn't settle and my movements were skittery, so I was often clumsy and unfocused.

And it wasn't just my present that was closing in on me during those feverish weeks, my past was creeping up too. I've accepted now that I have a stock of memories that will never leave me, but I can usually keep them at bay. Except the longer I spent in that weird liminal state with Cole, the more my mind fixated on my worst memories.

One seemed to play on a loop inside my head. I was getting ready for a party when I heard the front door bang shut and then Graham's heavy tread on the stairs. I felt immediately nervous because Mum hadn't gone out in the evening for ages because Graham didn't approve of her friends. I quickly pulled on a T-shirt and tugged at my skirt, wishing I could make it longer. He came in without knocking.

I tried to dodge past him, but he grabbed my arm so tight the skin twisted under his fat fingers. He pulled me close so I could smell his stale breath, tobacco and belched beer and the shepherd's pie Mum had cooked for tea. He'd thrown it across the room because it was too dry and stood over her as she'd cleared up the mess, his eyes never leaving what she was doing. He told me not to be a stupid little prick tease like my mum, that men hate that, while his eyes traveled the length of my body, resting on my visible bra strap.

He yanked me over toward my bed, the same one I'd had since I was little, so my feet stuck out the end if I lay completely straight. He threw me onto it and started fumbling with his belt. My insides were liquid and my vision was dimming, as if someone had turned down the lights. Little spots forming at the corners of my sight. Graham was a big man, and I knew what happened when Mum made him angry. I'd heard the whimpers through the wall enough times. He could, I was sure, break me along with the bed.

If he had held me down, I'm not sure that I'd have struggled, but instead he casually told me to get undressed, as if it was something we'd already agreed to. And that was too much. I felt anger in a way I never had before, like a seam of searing heat. It was the first time I understood the power of that emotion.

I ran at the door, but Graham was surprisingly quick, catching me just before I reached the stairs. He slammed me against the wall, pinning me back with one arm on my chest so I could barely breathe. But his belt was still giving him trouble, so he looked down for a second, and that was all I needed. I summoned my whole strength and rammed my knee right between his legs. He screeched in pain and then collapsed on the floor. I didn't hesitate, jumping over him and down the stairs so fast I thought I might fall.

The night was dark and cold, and my T-shirt was thin and my skirt short and I knew the world seethed with bad men. But a very bad man was already inside my house, so I ran, gasping at the cold air, all the way to my mate's house, where I put on a good front of being fine. We smoked a joint and went to the party like nothing had happened. I know now I should have said something to my friend's parents, who were decent people and probably would have called the police, but then I didn't have the words. I didn't know you could complain. I didn't know anyone would listen.

I'm still woken up on too many nights by the words Graham screamed after me as I ran out of my house, "Leo-fucking-nora. You're going to pay for this, girl."

MATTER OF FACT
WITH ALICE FOWLER AND TOBY ROSS

Because facts matter, we'll make sense of them.
Breaking down news stories to get to the truth.

ALICE: Hello, we're bringing you a hastily put together special today to address the breaking news from last night.

TOBY: So, as I'm sure most of you are aware, the police were all over Cole Simmonds's house yesterday afternoon. Forensics vans, the lot.

ALICE: Some of our sources say there were at least twenty police inside his property and garden.

TOBY: And, most importantly, they were all over the outhouse at the bottom of his garden.

ALICE: Yes, a lot of you have been very interested in the outhouse. There's been a lot of people studying Google Maps and aerial shots of the area and questioning why it hadn't been searched earlier.

TOBY: But to search someone's private property you need a warrant. And there has to be sufficient evidence for a warrant to be granted.

ALICE: We don't know for sure what new evidence secured the warrant, but we're pretty sure it has something to do with Cole's ex-wife, Melanie Connelly, visiting her local police station yesterday.

TOBY: There's no suggestion that Melanie is under any sort of suspicion. She wasn't arrested, she went to the police station voluntarily, although it seems likely that she would have been asked to come in.

ALICE: And we're presuming this must be because of the interview she gave to *The Sunday Times* about Cole's sexual predilections.

TOBY: Weird shit.

ALICE: Right. But anyway, what she said must have worried the police as much as the rest of us.

TOBY: And then whatever she told them must have made them feel justified in applying for a warrant, which was obviously granted.

ALICE: I mean, I don't see how it could have been refused, when you take into account that he's also been accused of rape by Laura Perkins and that he failed to tell the police he'd spoken to Molly and Phoebe on the day they disappeared.

TOBY: It's really not looking good for him.

ALICE: Well, in fact, it's looking worse than not good. Considering you've managed to find out what the police found in their search of his property.

TOBY: That's right, Alice, I have. The police are remaining tight-lipped, but I have it on good information that they recovered a blond hair from the outhouse.

ALICE: And, as we all know, Molly has blond hair.

TOBY: Now, I know lots of you will be calling for Cole to be immediately arrested, but the police have to follow the correct protocol. They'll have to do DNA tests on that hair to establish if it is Molly's before they can think about any arrests.

ALICE: But if it is Molly's, I think we can assume the arrest will happen very quickly.

TOBY: Oh yes, I can't see him getting out of that. And also, it's worth saying Lennie B arrived at Cole's cottage soon after the police did.

ALICE: Again, no suggestion that she's a suspect. But do we know if she was asked to go there by the police, or what?

TOBY: We don't know for sure, but I don't think the police would have asked her to be there. More likely Cole did.

ALICE: Can we take that as final confirmation that they're in a relationship, then?

TOBY: That would be my reading of it.

ALICE: And, you know, she must think he's not guilty, because there's no way anybody would stand by him if they thought he'd done anything to Molly and Phoebe.

TOBY: I mean, you'd hope not. And she must know about the ex-wife's claims? So, if she's still supporting him, it means she either doesn't think it's a big deal or doesn't believe it's true.

ALICE: And what are we thinking on the DNA results? Twenty-four hours?

TOBY: Yeah, I'd think so.

ALICE: I just hope if it is Molly's hair there can be some sort of resolution. You know, I can't bear it if they never find their bodies, if that's where we are now.

TOBY: I think that is where we are now. I mean, there have only ever been three possibilities: they fell in the sea by accident, they took their own lives, or they've been taken.

ALICE: And the coast guard say it's very unlikely there'd be no trace if they fell in the sea. And from everything their family and friends have said, suicide seems totally unlikely, which just leaves us with one awful option.

TOBY: I'm afraid it does. And tragically, from all we know about abduction cases like this, it is very rare for the victims to be kept alive past twenty-four hours.

TWITTER

KATY JONES @whatkatysaid

Anyone with a camera get down to Clapham Common now. Serious police brutality going on. Women are on the floor and tear gas has been fired #reclaimthestreets #marchformollyandphoebe #walkforwomen

(comments 65)   (retweets 89)   (likes 308)

JANE STANLEY @janedoe1

Replying to @whatkatysaid

It's madness there. Saw one woman with a huge gash on her head and quite a few in handcuffs. We weren't doing anything, just marching peacefully. #reclaimthestreets #walkforwomen

---

ANNA @amac42

Replying to @whatkatysaid and @janedoe1

My friend has broken her foot. We need to sue @metpoliceuk over this ridiculous overreaction. #reclaimthestreets

---

YATES @yatesy71

Replying to @whatkatysaid

It's not police brutality. They're controlling a difficult situation and suffering horrendous abuse. What are these people even marching for?

MEDUSA @angryandproud

Replying to @yatesy71 and @whatkatysaid

Fuck off, mate, and get back under your rock. We're marching for the right to
be safe on the streets where we live. #reclaimthestreets

SUNSET PHOTOGRAPHY @sunsetphotography

Replying to @whatkatysaid

I'm here now, will post shots later. Shocking overreaction by police. Women
being restrained in totally unnecessary ways. Lots of injuries.

METROPOLITAN POLICE @metpoliceuk

We would ask all the people on the #reclaimthestreets march on Clapham
Common to please remain calm and make their way home. Do not head to
the area. There has been some disturbance, which is being dealt with.
Unlawful behavior will not be tolerated.

KATY JONES @whatkatysaid

Replying to @metpoliceuk

when did it become unlawful to protest peacefully? Your officers are
behaving violently. Call them off now.

MISUNDERSTOOD @nohope

Replying to @whatkatysaid and @metpoliceuk

Male violence against women is endemic. We have to find a solution to this
that doesn't involve more violence. Justice for Molly and Phoebe.
#marchformollyandphoebe #walkforwomen #reclaimthestreets

THE WEST GALLERY

Cole rang me in a terrible state when the police turned up unannounced at his cottage with a search warrant. I went straight over, so I was there when a policeman in a white boiler suit came into the kitchen carrying a small plastic evidence bag. It looked empty, but when DS Croxley held it up we could all see the blond hair inside. Cole was perplexed, but the explanation that he came up with was very plausible. He said that Mel, who has blond hair, had been to see him a few days before and one of her hairs must have transferred itself to him, which he could have then shed in the outhouse. He laughed at the specks of blood they also found, saying it was from the rabbits he caught. After they'd gone, I told him I believed him, as I had when the footage of him with Molly and Phoebe emerged, but it was harder, the fear by then like a hard lump in my stomach.

Cole cried when I comforted him, nestling into my shoulder and saying that he hadn't ever met anyone as genuine as me before. I made myself cry with him, I said I was so sorry for how he was being treated. I ladled it on like cream. My whole body itched with the desire to push him from me, but I held on tight because I knew we were working on borrowed time—probably only about twenty-four hours until the DNA results came back, which meant I had to act fast.

I told him that I wanted us to take the next step.

He looked up at me and I saw that something had shifted in his eyes. He told me that he had to tell me something. And I knew I'd got him.

My phone was in my pocket, and I had taught myself how to start recording without looking at the screen because I always knew that I'd need to be very careful in how I quoted him later. So, to be clear, what follows is a written transcript of a recorded conversation:

"It normally takes me a bit longer to trust people. But things feel so different with you, Leonora. What you said about wanting to take things to the next step. I want that as well. And then your reaction now about that ridiculous hair. You didn't doubt me for a second, you knew I couldn't be part of what they're implying."

"Of course I couldn't think that; it's total madness."

"I want to be totally honest with you."

"Go on."

"It's nothing to worry about. It's just, I like you too, a lot. So I want to be completely up front about everything. I mean, I think we've made a real connection and I don't want to lose that. I want to really be in your life. And I could give you such a good life, Leonora. I want to love you and protect you and make sure you always feel special."

[Brief pause]

"Okay, so, sometimes sex is hard for me. I overthink things. It's like I feel too much, or I care too deeply. I don't know, it's difficult to explain. But, you know, this whole area is difficult for men. Or, at least, men like me. I mean, if you're just in it for the conquest or whatever, I guess it's not that hard. But I need to feel an emotional connection to have sex. And when I feel that connection, well, then I get intimidated by what's expected of me. You know, that stupid image of the all-conquering man."

"You never have to feel intimidated by me."

"I know. That's why I'm telling you this now. I want to open up my whole self to you, make myself completely vulnerable."

"Cole, it's okay. You can tell me anything."

"I had a pretty loveless upbringing and it's made me very insecure. I can't really, I mean, the thing that makes sex so much better for me, is if I feel in control."

"In what way?"

"Honestly, it's nothing to be scared of. I have this, thing. This sort of fantasy, I suppose you'd call it. It's not even strange. Sex is such a convention, when you think about it, and there's a real freedom in not letting yourself be dictated by all the things you've been told are right or wrong."

"I totally agree, Cole. You can tell me anything."

"My ultimate fantasy is breaking into a woman's house to have sex with her."

[Longer pause. (I had known what he was going to say, but it sounded so shocking out in the open, it must have shown on my face.)]

"Shit, sorry, that sounded wrong. I don't mean a woman I don't know. I mean, a woman I'm in a relationship with. And not for real. Not in a creepy way. I don't want to actually hurt anyone or make them do something they don't want to. Christ, of course not. I mean as a totally mutual act in a committed relationship."

"Okay, right."

"Listen, Leonora, I'm trying to show you my whole self because, well, if we're going to really do this, I don't want to hide anything. I'm not the sort of man to keep secrets or anything like that. And this, this is a big part of me, an important part."

"Of course, I want to know everything about you."

"I hate it when people try to stop their partners from being their best selves. Too many women have done that to me in the past and

I don't think I could go through it again. It's better if we lay our cards on the table from the start, so we don't get in too deep if the other one isn't into it."

"No, I'd rather we were honest with each other as well. Listen, I read that interview Mel gave yesterday."

"I thought you would have. But that's not why I'm saying any of this. I was going to talk to you anyway. That interview was such bullshit. She made it sound like I forced her into something. And, I mean, calling it a rape fantasy is insane. Rape is having sex with someone against their will, but, if anything, she encouraged me. And she never, ever said she wasn't into it."

"It's hard. I mean, to know you've done that with Mel and now you want to do the exact same with me. Have you done it with other women as well?"

"No, I really haven't. And I totally get how everything Mel said in that stupid article would make you feel strange. But it really wasn't how she made it out to be. I genuinely don't know why she's doing all this. Sometimes it feels like she's gone mad. And I absolutely know it would be different with you. Mel was never honest about how she felt, I can see that now. We can work through everything together, Leonora. We'll wait until you're completely, one hundred percent comfortable with it. And it will be a wonderfully loving experience that builds so much trust between us."

"And if I say no?"

"I would totally respect your decision, of course. There'd be no hard feelings, but also, I don't think we could be together."

"Look, I'm going to need a little bit of time to think it through."

"Of course. There's no pressure on this."

"Why don't you let me sleep on it. Could we meet tomorrow?"

"And it's totally fine if you need more time than that. Shit, Leonora, you're so special. I don't think I've felt like this before, not even with Mel."

"Listen, I really do appreciate your honesty. It's such a rare quality to find in a man."

"I would hate to be anything other than totally honest with you. You'll always know what you're getting with me. I'd never do anything to hurt you."

BEAUMONT COMPANY

Following is a statement from our chairman, Felix Beaumont. This statement will be posted on all our social media channels shortly.

Over the last few days, I have become increasingly aware of rumors circulating regarding my involvement with Melanie Connelly. Ms. Connelly's company, Melanie A. Connelly, acted as our PR agency for three years, a partnership that ended last March. For the record, I want to state that Ms. Connelly was a pleasure to do business with and her work was always of the highest standard. We, however, were forced to part ways when Melanie's husband, Cole Simmonds, began insinuating that her and I were involved in a romantic relationship. This was entirely untrue and had no foundation in fact.

Mr. Simmonds, however, began a campaign of harassment against me. I did have an initial conversation with him, in which I assured him that nothing was going on, pointing out that I am happily married and that his wife had never showed any interest in me.

Over the course of the following month, he sent me increasingly deranged and abusive texts. By the end of four weeks, I had over one hundred of them. I stopped replying, which seemed to enrage him further. Then one night he turned up on my doorstep and shouted at me. My wife and two children were at home, and it was deeply upsetting for all of us. The next morning, I woke to find dog feces smeared across my car, though I have no direct evidence that Mr. Simmonds did it.

I rang Ms. Connelly to tell her that her husband had come to my home. She was extremely embarrassed and begged me not to go to the police, which I agreed to because I felt sorry for her. We parted ways professionally and since then I have wished her nothing but luck and happiness.

My girlfriend is threatening to split up with me if I go on defending Cole Simmonds

AITA? So my girlfriend (F26) and I (M32) got in a big fight last night because I made an off the cuff comment that we should give Cole the benefit of the doubt. I pointed out that there might be a reasonable explanation for the hair in the outhouse and she got in a massive mood and stormed off upstairs, but when she came down she still wasn't over it and kept on bringing it up and asking why I never just believe women and always take the man's side. So I said that I wasn't taking sides and obviously if he's done something to those girls then I won't be defending him, but there are other plausible explanations as to why the hair might be there. Innocent until proven guilty and all that. She freaked out and was like, what you think Molly planted her hair in Cole's outhouse or something? I told her to stop overreacting and she wasn't making any sense as they don't even know whose hair it is but she was so mad by then she started bringing up this ongoing argument we've had since the beginning of our relationship. She runs along our local canal to keep fit, but in the winter she hardly ever goes because it's dark when she gets home from work. And as a result she always puts on a bit of weight. I don't really mind, but she spends hours moaning about what she looks like and how she can't fit into her clothes and basically trying to get reassurance from me, which is totally exhausting. So once I asked her why she wasn't running if she was worried about getting fat and she freaked out and asked if I wanted her to get raped and murdered. I pointed out that statistically that was very unlikely to happen. And she was all like, right so if you knew there were man-eating lions in a huge jungle, would you still walk through it even though you're statistically very unlikely to get mauled to death. Anyway, in the end she stormed off to her mum's last night and sent a text saying she's not coming home until I stop defending Cole Simmonds and try to understand her viewpoint a bit more. It feels mad to me. I mean I wasn't really even defending him, and I do think she's ridiculous for not running in the dark—I mean nothing is going to happen to her. I don't know what to do because it feels like if I apologize now, it'll set some sort of precedent and she'll have me over a barrel. But maybe I should, to keep the peace?

MICKY88

No way, man. That's what women want—to turn us all into groveling wrecks who say sorry even for fucking breathing. What you said was a completely fair point even. And she's being totally overdramatic not running in the dark. Who wants a fat gf!

REDPILLDUDE1000000

Feminism is a giant plot. They want to create a whole new world order in which we are enslaved to them. They are inventing a world in which all men are wrong and all women are right and if enough men agree with them it's going to topple everything and they will become dominant. It's all an illusion. She is literally gaslighting you when she says that about being raped and murdered—making you believe in a reality that isn't true. Take the red pill, dude, and open your goddamn eyes.

STACEYQUEEN

Yes, you are the a-hole. I think about my safety every time I leave the house, especially in the dark. You need to be more compassionate to your gf.

FACEBOOK

 PSYCHIC SUZIE 3 hours ago

Mark my words, Molly and Phoebe will be found near water. I've spent the past two days walking the cliffs and beach where they disappeared, and I can categorically state they are still close. Their souls spoke to me and begged me to tell the police not to give up looking. They suffered in their final moments but are free from physical pain now. However, they won't be at peace until their bodies have been recovered. I got the strong sense of rocks, a confined space, and farm equipment. I also sensed a strong male presence. I have told the police all I know and urged them to search Cole Simmonds's property. I feel confident this will be resolved soon.

(84 likes)   (7 comments)   (1 reshare)

THE WEST GALLERY

On my walk back from Cole's cottage the afternoon he told me about his fantasy, I rang a company that installs security cameras. I'd told him that I needed time to think, but, really, I needed time to set everything up. I arranged for the cameras to be put in the next day, paying through the nose for an emergency service. Obviously, it would have been better to have installed them earlier, but we couldn't have risked Cole noticing them. The bloke who did the job said there wasn't much point in cameras without alarms. I nodded along, imagining what he'd say if I told him that safety was the last thing on my mind. That in fact, what I was planning was disastrously unsafe. I had one put in facing the back door, one going up the stairs, and one by the window in my bedroom.

I know the general consensus is that all this was super calculating, but that was sort of the whole point. Our plan had always been to try to get Cole to enact one of his rape fantasies on me. Which had meant getting him to a place where he trusted me and thought I'd fallen in love with him. I'm not going to apologize for that because it's what thousands of people, usually men, do every day in order to get other people, usually women, to have sex with them.

Mel was very worried when we got to that stage and almost wanted to back out. She warned me that however I thought it was going to feel, it would be worse. And of course there was a distinct possibility that I would be hurt because we knew what happened to Laura. But I'm a stubborn bastard and told her I was a big girl who'd been in worse situations, a story I'd been telling myself for so long I believed it.

But what I had forgotten is that, even though we kid ourselves that we're in control of our own stories, sometimes things happen that we haven't accounted for. Something this last year has taught me is that art is simply the telling of stories and stories can only ever be as perfect as the person telling them. You can hate me for all the choices I've made for this story, but one thing I'm sure of is that how I chose to tell it is just as valid as how anyone else would.

On the night my mother was murdered, she'd warmed up a pizza for us to share as we sat curled under a blanket together because Graham often got cross about the cost of electricity. She kissed me when I got up to leave and I was engulfed by the sweet vanilla scent she always wore. The police told me that the reason she went out shortly after I'd gone upstairs was because Graham had sent her out to buy his cigarettes. He said that I'd been leading him on for months, that I was a filthy lying whore.

I know what it is to be scared right down to the bone and I'm sorry if what I did has added to your fear. Maybe you're right to hate me? But also, let's be honest, it's not as if you weren't already frightened anyway.

The cameras were fitted first thing the next day so, after that, I texted Cole and asked him to meet me on the beach. The sea was that strange silver color it picks up when there's light behind the clouds, making it look like a pool of poured mercury. A storm was brewing on the horizon, dark clouds hanging like a magnetic force was drawing them toward the water. From the beach my cottage looked top heavy and unsafe, the base of the rocks beneath it gouged out by the sea, so I wondered just how long it would be before it fell. And the wind was filled with a low murmur from the women who never left the cliff top, keeping a vigil for Molly and Phoebe.

Cole was annoyed by those women when he arrived. He was holding the bases of their silver tealights and ranting about how they were being totally irresponsible, leaving litter lying around when surely there are better ways of getting attention. Naturally, I had to agree with him, but I would have liked to scream in his face that we all know it's pathetic. That we don't want to rely on candles and vigils to shoehorn our way onto the agenda. That, if people listened to us, we wouldn't need to walk along cliff edges or leave silver candle holders anywhere.

Instead, I told Cole that I was so honored that he'd shared his fantasy with me, that I wanted to share one of mine in return. I told him I wanted to have another baby, but this time with a man who loved me and wasn't going to run away. I said it was still early days, but if things went on as they were, then I could see it happening with him. But I also told him that I couldn't stop thinking about those embryos he had on ice. I said that I didn't want to be abandoned again and couldn't stand the thought of him leaving me and our potential baby for them one day, especially if Mel wanted them gone as well. He offered to write to the clinic immediately.

I know this is one of the things that lots of people really hate Mel and me for. But why don't you stop for a minute and consider the possibility that a tiny nonsentient speck of yourself exists somewhere and that someone else wants to turn that speck into a person. A person you'll be bound to by love and responsibility forever. We've been called everything from unnatural women to unfit mothers to murderers. But maybe it's the other way around. Maybe what we did shows that we understand just how precious mothers and their children are. Maybe we are the ones who really value life.

I told Cole that I wanted our new life to start as soon as possible and would go to bed that night forgetting to lock the back door. He was shiny with excitement and ran after me as I left the beach. When he caught up, panting, he told me that he was a fool for thinking that he could've created the life he wanted with Mel. He went on and on about how his current excitement made him better understand why people say men supposedly think about sex every ten seconds. It's not because they're sex-crazed animals, he said, but because of this electric feeling of anticipation without fear of failure. It made him realize that he had never been the problem, he'd only ever needed to find the right woman. Me.

I barely made it off the beach and round the corner before I was sick, acrid half-digested lumps spewing out of me onto the dark grass. The wind pushed the smell back up my nose, making my tongue bitter. But I made myself straighten up and stumble to my cottage, forcing myself not to check over my shoulder, even though I could feel the fear at my back, tumbling out of the sky and across the ocean to find me.

Reaching this point had always been important for our project, but, when it came, I didn't feel any sense of achievement, just a stultifying dread. Because it was impossible to hide from the fact that what was coming next was dangerous.

In truth, every fiber of my being was screaming at me to stop, but I felt compelled to carry on. I owed it to all the missing girls and terrified women out there. Except I think also I had gotten too caught up in the idea of my bravery. It was almost how I defined myself. The cottage taught me that fear exists at the edge. But we don't always need to go right up to it, we can do all the things we want a few steps back.

I had to sit on the bottom of my stairs after I made it home that afternoon because I felt so weak and dizzy. My head was filled with Jasmine and all the ways I would do anything to make things better for her. Because the moment a baby tears out of your body, it releases an ultimate fear, dragged along in the blood and pain of birth, a fear so big it can't exist within your mind or you would go mad. Some women do go mad, unable to battle the anxiety. And really, they aren't mad, they're right, but we can't let ourselves think that way. My mother's life was hell, but at least she didn't have to lose me. I think the mothers of all the missing and dead girls would probably swap places with her if they could. I pinched the soft, inner part of my palm to remind myself that I remained, that I needed to do right by my mother and myself and Jasmine. But still I started to cry, for all the dead girls and their lost stories, all their mothers.

Seagulls were shrieking outside, and the wind had picked up again, rushing through the trees in the garden and rattling the windows, so it sounded like a million women screaming.

I fumbled my phone out of my pocket and sent Jasmine the text, I've been an idiot about your hair. Shave it all off if you like. You'll always be beautiful to me, whatever you do. And you'll always be mine, whilst also being your own person.

I forced myself to stand and go into the kitchen, where I tried to make myself believe that I was ready for what was about to happen. Although I also knew I would never be ready. Which will perhaps always be true. We can plan and plot, but in the end the narrative is never entirely ours.

When we first met, Cole asked me if I was frightened walking home alone from the Christmas party. Normally I would have laughed at the idea, but I'd said yes because it was the answer he wanted to hear. But it wasn't a complete lie either. Like every other woman I know, I carry my keys splayed between my fingers, I pretend to receive phone calls while walking deserted streets, I avoid empty parks and badly lit spaces, I hate parking garages, I flinch when I hear loud footsteps, I never wear headphones, I bolt my door and lock my windows, and my heart sinks during the winter because the sky darkens at four. Before this, I hid that person from myself. Which is another thing the cottage taught me—it is unkind, even unwise, to deny that woman.

From up above me I heard little feet skittering across the landing. It sounded like Cole's rat, or maybe an army of rats, although my mind jumped to an intruder. And then I laughed at myself because I'd invited Cole to be exactly that. I had placed myself teetering on the brink. I could taste my heartbeat and smell my fear as I moved. And I'm not going to lie, I wanted to rush to my car and drive away. I wanted to scream and tear and ravage. But I knew I couldn't. I had to face this creation of my own making. I stayed quiet because I knew that Cole would soon be creeping toward me across the darkened landscape and I needed to atone.

When Graham first pointed his finger in my mum's face, I should have known where their story was heading. When I ran into the night as he lay on the floor clutching his balls, I should have realized what role I occupied in their narrative. I should have known that he would break my mother's body in lieu of my own because he couldn't bear to see any of us free. And I should have known that the fear would never go away.

TWITTER

SAFE SPACE UK @safespaceuk

Thankfully no one was hurt in the fire at our headquarters last night. We refuse to be intimidated and will continue supporting the #reclaimthestreets and #walkformollyandphoebe marches going on across the country, along with the #womenonthecliff in their vigil for Molly and Phoebe. Please take the time to watch five minutes of this TED Talk by @jamesanderson, CEO of the charity @boysmind.

[ID: Video clip of speaker on stage. Audio: What we have to understand is that it starts with pornography. Everything does. You think you know what your fourteen-, fifteen-year-olds are up to, but the truth is once they shut their bedroom doors and open their laptops, it's the Wild West. Accessing hard-core porn only takes two clicks, and the images are way beyond what you can imagine. Eighty percent of contemporary pornography involves violence against women—including acts such as choking and spitting and much worse. And while your kid is watching this, they'll be fed continuous pop-ups leading them to influencers who preach about getting rich and getting women. It's all about control and degradation and a man's right to get what he wants. Most kids will eventually grow up to be decent humans. But, naturally, a few won't. And all of them will have absorbed something from the hours they spent in front of a screen watching and listening to this hate. We need to put pornography behind barriers. We need to stand up as a society and say we don't condone it; we don't support violence against women.]

(comments 540)   (retweets 223)   (likes 1,267)

WHATSAPP

omg @Dais have you seen they've finally arrested cole???

pookie

just catching up now—so the hair was molly's?   Dais

yeah they just made a statement   pookie

fucking knew it   Dais

let's not get too celebratory—still haven't found their bodies

Min

they must be on his property?   Dais

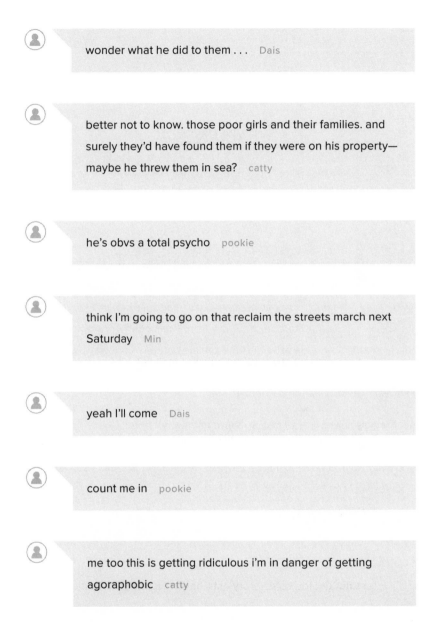

wonder what he did to them . . .   Dais

better not to know. those poor girls and their families. and surely they'd have found them if they were on his property— maybe he threw them in sea?   catty

he's obvs a total psycho   pookie

think I'm going to go on that reclaim the streets march next Saturday   Min

yeah I'll come   Dais

count me in   pookie

me too this is getting ridiculous i'm in danger of getting agoraphobic   catty

THE SUN

Missing cliff girls Molly and Phoebe were part of a group called Sisters for Survival. They attended meetings at the group's headquarters, a rundown community center in South London, a far cry from their posh upbringing in the suburbs, where both girls attended the private school Highfield at a cost of £8,000 a year. Little is known about the fringe feminist group, who claim to be in a state of war against the patriarchy.

A local resident who lives close to the community center said, "They meet about once a month. You can tell when it's happening because all these odd-looking women wearing mad clothes and rings through their noses appear. Sometimes you can hear singing from inside."

A meeting held a few nights ago called for direct action if the police fail to find Molly and Phoebe. *The Sun* tried to speak to members of the group but were met with hostility.

THE WEST GALLERY

I made myself turn off the lights as I went upstairs around eleven. The wind was whistling through the house and down the chimney like a horror film score; the radiators were ticking and there was a faint smell of burnt toast in the air, which had been all I could stomach. I brushed my teeth and then debated what to wear, settling for my customary tracksuit as the safest option. I climbed into bed and pulled the covers up to my chin and then there was nothing to do but wait. Except nothing was still. Even my body was a cacophony, my heart thumping, my breath hitching, and my muscles clenching. I thought of Mel and wondered if she ever got used to feeling that scared.

Something clicked in the kitchen below and my heart leaped like a startled fish. A chair scraped against the floor and a sickness nestled deep in my gut, which made me understand that I had been a fool. I can't describe the fear I felt in that moment in any way other than to say it made me want to disappear. If I could have, I would have sunk into the bed, dissolved into the mattress. Because the terror was too much, too visceral, too real.

I heard a low tread on the stairs, which meant it was too late to back out. My whole body strained to hear his movements, but he was so quiet and the sound of the sea was so insistent against the cliffs. I knew that he must be creeping, holding his weight into himself like a proper intruder.

He pushed open the door. A dark, hooded figure in my doorway. I understood then why women scream. My eyes were mostly shut, but in the low dancing moonlight I could still see him advancing through my thin strip of vision. I inched my hand up under my pillow, my fingers brushing the reassuring coldness of the metal there.

My breathing shallowed the closer he got, and my heart galloped against my ribs as all the pores on my body opened and sweat poured out. He stopped when he reached the bed, the air so alive with tension I was sure we would combust. And the fear. My god, it was expanding as big as one of my sculptures, taking up all the available space. And in that moment, something recalibrated in my head, and I realized what in fact my sculptures have always been. They're not about taking up space, but filling it, in an attempt to blot out the fear and misery of my mother's murder.

All the things I'd planned evaporated, my mind too full of Graham, my mother, Molly, Phoebe, and Jasmine. I had to bite down on my lip to stop myself from screaming because this was it, the moment we spend our lives avoiding as women, so I knew it would fill my nightmares forever. He reached forward, his hand heading for the duvet, which I knew he intended to peel from my shaking body. I darted my hand upward under my pillow, but my blood was running with anxiety, which made me clumsy, so I lost my grip and the can fell to the floor, a loud metallic ringing in the room. We both froze and I willed myself to say something, but every word I'd ever known vanished, so I was nothing more than a shivering, beating creature.

Cole bent down and picked up the can. Even from where I was lying, I could read the words: PEPPER SPRAY. He took a step back and I heard his breathing quicken as he looked between me and the can, trying to understand what it meant. My own breathing had become so shallow I was worried I was going to pass out, which at the time felt better than facing whatever was coming. He took off his glove and reached his hand forward, brushing it down my face as if he was scraping my skin from my bones. He pulled away sharply when he felt how wet my cheek was.

He raised his arm in a way that made me flinch, my own arm instinctively blocking my head. But then I heard the ricochet of the can hitting the wall, so I peeked between my arms and saw that his fists were clenching and unclenching by his side. I knew that the time to scream, or appeal to him, was past. All I could do was wait, as quietly and silently as possible. Time slowed. I imagined his fist connecting with my face and the snap my leg would make if he bent it against the metal of the bed. I imagined him lying on top of me and forcing himself inside, his seed traveling uninvited through my body and implanting itself in my womb. It would only take him minutes to kill me, which is maybe all it took Graham to kill my mum. I squeezed shut my eyes and thought of Jasmine, her life flashing before me in snapshots. And then I imagined the police knocking at her door to tell her that her mother had been murdered and it was too fucking ridiculous. History has got to stop repeating itself. For all women.

Cole made a strange sort of hitching noise, like something was stuck in his throat. Then he started to cry, in big heaving sobs. The darkness was howling in sympathy, the wind banging against the window, intent on breaking them. The atmosphere contracted around us, becoming fetid and swamp-like.

I don't know how long we stayed in that strange state, Cole and I, but in the end, he turned and ran, clattering down the stairs and slamming the front door. I let myself cry then, matching his big heaving sobs, which shook me so hard I wondered if I was going to break myself.

SKY NEWS

"Following up on our breaking news story, we're going to take you live to the Sussex coast and Lennie B's cottage, which has been the focus of so much attention over the past couple of weeks. Our reporter, Sara Graves, is at the scene. Sara can you tell us what's happening?"

"Hi, Justin. It's a pretty muddled scene, if I'm honest. As you can see, this usually quiet stretch of coast is completely packed with media. I've rarely seen this big a turnout outside of an official government announcement or the birth of a royal baby."

"And you were all summoned by a press release from Melanie A. Connelly PR Agency, run by Cole Simmonds's estranged wife?"

"That's right. At 10:00 a.m. this morning all the major newsrooms received an email from Melanie A. Connelly PR Agency informing us that Lennie B was going to make a statement concerning the disappearance of Molly Patterson and Phoebe Canton at 1:00 p.m. today outside her cottage."

"Any idea what she's going to say?"

"Absolutely none. The curtains have been drawn all morning and no one has heard anything."

"Well, we can't have long to wait as it's just turned one."

"Yes, we're expecting . . . hang on. Yes, Justin, the door's opening. Here she is. Oh, and Melanie Connelly is with her."

"Hello, thank you for coming all this way. Mel and I have called you here today to witness what we hope will be an ending, but also a beginning. An ending to a story, but the beginning of a long overdue and much-needed discussion. What we are about to show you will be deeply shocking. We ask you to please reserve your judgment. Please try to understand what we are saying and why we felt the need to do this. The power to shock is still a vital commodity and I would ask you to remember that over the course of history women have been forced to resort to extreme acts in order to make ourselves heard. This is a project that I and others have been planning for a long time, but that came together when I met Mel, by chance, last year. But that's what art is—the meeting of minds and the exchanging of ideas. Finally, I want to say that it was always our intention to end this as soon as Cole was arrested. He is nothing more than a manifestation, a symptom, if you like. But enough from me, it's time for me to ask the real stars of this show to come out. It's time for you all to listen to the women who you've been talking about so much over the past couple of weeks: Molly and Phoebe."

"Hello, please, no questions yet. Please, let us speak. Thank you. Okay, so, firstly, Phoebe and I are fine. We want to make it clear that we haven't been held against our will. Nor have we been coerced into doing anything. In fact, a lot of what's happened was our idea. And we're sorry for all the worry and distress we've caused, especially to people who love us. We're sorry for the wasted police time. But we believe fully in what we've done. We believe it was necessary. In a world where over a hundred women a day are murdered by someone they know, we knew we had to make a stand. And, you know what, walking along a coast was never going to cut it. We would have been lucky to be featured in the middle pages of a local newspaper. Alive, our words about male violence were meaningless. But as soon as we became potential victims of the violence, we were suddenly interesting. Only when everyone thought we had been permanently silenced did the networks give us airtime. Why is that? Why are female bodies so much more appealing when they're broken? You were expecting this story to end with them finding our bodies, right? We should have been dug up or fished out of the sea, mutilated and desecrated. But here we are, alive. Why does that feel so much more subversive? Lots of people are going to hate us for this. And you know why? Because in this society we enjoy seeing our women scared. Well, we're here to say we've had enough of fear."

"Goodness, Justin, that was . . . actually, I hardly know how to explain what we've just seen. But it appears that the missing women, Molly Patterson and Phoebe Canton, are safe and well. That, in fact, they've been safe and well all this time . . . Molly, Phoebe, I'm here with Sky News . . . no, sorry, as you can see they've all gone back inside now and don't appear to be taking questions."

"I've been doing this job for a long time, Sara, and I don't think I've ever witnessed anything close to what's just happened. What do we think is going on here?"

"Honestly, Justin, I . . . I really don't know. It appears to be some sort of stunt, orchestrated by Lennie B and Cole Simmonds's ex-wife, Melanie Connelly."

"And who was the other woman with Molly and Phoebe?"

"I believe it was Lennie B's daughter, Jasmine Baxter."

"Well, for now, I suppose all we can say is that at least Molly and Phoebe are safe."

TWITTER

FIONA TYLER-JONES @fi-ty-jo

If they were my daughters I would be so ashamed. Their poor parents. We've all been gaslit in the most despicable way.

(comments 3,752)   (retweets 865)   (likes 8,788)

SANDY @sweetdreams

Replying to @fi-ty-jo

If they were your daughters they'd be ashamed to have you as their mother. You've been gaslighting us all for years with your right-wing agenda.

MEN'S JUSTICE LEAGUE @mensleague

Replying to @fi-ty-jo

Shocking behavior. And they say men are the problem??

ANGEL @angelic55

Replying to @mensleague

You must have some sympathy for what they were trying to do. I worry every time my teenage daughter is out after dark. And they're right, no one would have listened to them without this stunt.

PAUL DUNCAN @pdunc88

Replying to @fi-ty-jo

They've ruined any credibility they or the women's movement had before. Reckon they've put it back 50 years. Surely this is an arrestable offense @metpolice?

ROBBIE @robbiecop

Replying to @pdunc88

As an ex-copper I can tell you they will have wasted so much money and resources. I hope they charge them.

MUMMYQUEEN @mmmmqqqqq

Replying to @fi-ty-jo

It's @LBart who should be most ashamed and that lying ex-wife. Grown women using young girls like that. And making up stories about an innocent man. Disgusting.

REDDIT

u/Jack-daw posted in r/AITA?

I don't understand what's going on. A few days ago my gf (F26) and I had a massive argument when I (M32) said we should give Cole Simmonds the benefit of the doubt after they found that hair in his outhouse. She stormed off to her mum's and hasn't come home yet. After what happened earlier I sent her a text saying she owes me an apology because I was right but she said I need to apologize to her?? When I asked her what the hell for, she said if I couldn't work it out myself then could I let her know when I'll be out next so she can come and get her stuff. I'm genuinely confused. Which one of us is the a-hole here?

TWITTER

SAFE SPACE UK @safespaceuk

While we don't condone the actions of Molly and Phoebe, we understand why they felt the need to take drastic action. Women's voices are not otherwise heard and the culture of violence is a disease in our society. All money raised by this walk will be returned.

(comments 271)   (retweets 98)   (likes 4,788)

SHARON WRIGHT @shazzaw

Replying to @safespaceuk

Please keep my money. Respect to Molly and Phoebe. End male violence #walkforwomen

---

MANINTHEWILD @ManintheWild

Replying to @safespaceuk

Hope you all die.

THE WEST GALLERY

We all went into this with our eyes open. We knew we'd be judged and no one was forced into anything. Mel was perhaps the only one of us who needed convincing, but she was very scared when we first met, very unsure of herself and what she thought. Cole had done a real job on her, so she doubted pretty much everything about herself. But when she understood what I was trying to achieve, she got fully on board.

We knew that for the plan to work we had to find a very specific location—somewhere that would totally isolate me while being near enough to Cole for us to meet in a seemingly organic way. And on top of that, it also had to be somewhere that Cole would actually want to move to—somewhere in line with his man-of-the-land dreams. Mel's job made things much easier as she knew all about scouting for locations. As soon as we saw the two cottages, we both knew it was the place. Let's just say there wasn't much breath-holding when she sent him the details.

I am happy to own my part in everything I did. But I think it's worth mentioning that Cole was following his own agenda the whole time as well. Yes, he hadn't planned and plotted, but I'd argue that he was playing me as much as I was him, although his game was much more subtle, much more internalized. He wouldn't have even seen it as a game. Cole's fundamental guiding principle is that he believes in himself entirely. He doesn't question or doubt himself. He is comfortable in his integrity. If you asked him, he'd definitely identify as a feminist. If you challenged Cole on his behavior, he'd be shocked; he wouldn't understand what you were talking about. But that's because the bar is low for men, so low most women can step over it with barely a raised leg, which means men like Cole appear to float high above.

People generally seem to feel sorry for Cole, whereas a word often used to describe Mel, Phoebe, Molly, and me is *scheming*. There appears to be a lot of outrage around the fact that we had it all planned. Although how any of it would have happened without planning is impossible to imagine. I personally think our planning was magnificent and we should be applauded for our ingenuity.

I think everyone would have preferred it if we had been victims of our circumstances. If my mother had managed to find a blunt object while Graham was punching the life out of her, and if she'd managed to connect that object with his head, public sympathy would have been on her side, even if he'd died. But if she'd poisoned him, say, before he had the chance to beat her to death, the public would have condemned her. I guess women aren't meant to be strategic or cunning. Which seems unfair considering that gangsters and cowboys and superheroes are not only allowed vendettas but applauded for them. Men are allowed to act, but women, it seems, should only react.

It isn't nice to be hated, but it's not the worst thing in the world. Molly and Phoebe were in a pretty bad way when they first came out of hiding, but over the past few months they've become surprisingly resilient to the abuse. I think it's because they've grown up in a culture that takes sides. Having a limited space to make your point means that people don't have nuanced discourse anymore. It feels safer to pick a side and stick. Mel and I definitely find the hate harder, but I think that's because we were brought up in a time when women were meant to please. However much I know what we did was right, somewhere deep inside me there's always the sense that I've let someone down, that I've behaved inappropriately, that I've been too loud. And that's never an easy space for a woman to occupy.

MATTER OF FACT
WITH ALICE FOWLER AND TOBY ROSS

Because facts matter, we'll make sense of them.
Breaking down news stories to get to the truth.

ALICE: So, welcome to what is going to be a wild ride.

TOBY: Yeah, sort of feels like we'll need about ten shows to actually get to the bottom of this.

ALICE: I know, right. Except, for a strange story, it's also one of the easiest I've ever had to investigate. Because the women behind it have released a statement that lays everything out. They're not trying to hide anything.

TOBY: And we're going to go through it now.

ALICE: We are. So, it all started last summer when Lennie B and Melanie Connelly met each other by chance. Melanie and Cole had recently split up and she was still very shaken by everything she said went on in their marriage.

TOBY: You mean, all the sex stuff?

ALICE: Mainly, yeah, but it sounds like it was quite a controlling relationship altogether. Then, not long after she'd left him, she found out about Laura, who she tracked down, and they met up.

TOBY: So, she pushed Laura into going to the police?

ALICE: Probably. The press release says they all worked together on their timings. But it was Lennie B who was the mastermind of the whole thing. Lennie had been working on a show about female fear and male violence for a while before she met Mel. But, in the press release, she says it was Mel's stories about Cole that brought all her ideas together. The more Mel and Lennie talked, the more they realized they could help each other, until finally they hatched a plan for Cole to unwittingly take part in Lennie's show.

TOBY: And, this is important, at no point did Cole know he was part of an art project.

ALICE: Right. Very *Truman Show*.

TOBY: And ethically dubious. But, getting back to the facts, how did they actually pull it off? I mean, how involved were Molly and Phoebe?

ALICE: Lennie and Molly and Phoebe were already talking before Lennie met Mel. The central idea of the show had always revolved around Molly and Phoebe going missing and then turning up alive after a period of intense media speculation.

TOBY: How did they know Lennie B?

ALICE: Lennie's daughter, Jasmine, was part of a radical women's group, where she met Molly and Phoebe. And when she heard about their idea she introduced them to her mother because she thought it was the sort of thing she'd be interested in.

TOBY: Which she was.

ALICE: Absolutely. Lennie says in the press release that she immediately saw how their idea for direct action, as they call it, could be turned into a sort of living art show. But she says it still felt like a piece was missing until she met Melanie.

TOBY: So, how did they actually make it happen?

ALICE: Well, Cole made them think bigger. They knew if they got Lennie and Cole to move to the same bit of coastline that Molly and Phoebe were going to walk along, then not only could they implicate him in their disappearance, but also Lennie could engineer a romantic relationship.

TOBY: And we know what that meant, right? Has anyone seen the video that she claims to have of Cole breaking into her cottage?

ALICE: No, apparently it's for her show.

TOBY: That's pretty sick. Don't you think that's a bit far to go for art?

ALICE: Totally. It's gross. And super devious. I mean, they basically lured him in by presenting him with a new life they knew he wanted. Then Lennie tricked him into a false relationship so he'd feel comfortable enough to tell her about his fantasy.

TOBY: And, like, whatever you feel about his fantasy, he wasn't trying to hurt anyone.

ALICE: Right. I mean, it's not my cup of tea, but we shouldn't judge what goes on behind closed doors between two consenting adults.

TOBY: And where were Molly and Phoebe hiding out when they were missing?

ALICE: On the actual night they filmed that final video, then left their tent looking like there could have been a struggle. In fact, they hid in Cole's out-house, which of course Mel and Lennie knew all about because they had found the cottage in the first place.

TOBY: Which accounts for why the police found Molly's hair there. How did they get in?

ALICE: They had bolt cutters with them. And they only had to wait until the morning because Mel drove down first thing on the pretense of picking up some papers to do with her and Cole's house sale. While she kept Cole occupied inside, the girls got into her car. And, get this, she even rented a van with blacked out windows to make it easier. She drove them back to London and after that they were holed up in Lennie B's flat.

TOBY: I still don't get what the point of it all was.

ALICE: Well, it's performance art. And the point they make about missing girls does hold—I mean, male violence against women is at an all-time high and this has certainly got people talking about it.

TOBY: Yeah, I get that and obviously totally agree. But, I don't know, involving an innocent man does seem unnecessarily cruel.

ALICE: Yeah. Although of course if he did rape Laura, he's not exactly innocent.

TOBY: Of course. Except I'm not sure I buy it. I mean, if they'd been going out, then why didn't she tell him to stop? And why did she wait so long to tell anyone what had happened?

ALICE: Look, I'm not saying it definitely happened, but if it did, she could have been scared or embarrassed. Women don't tend to win many rape cases.

TOBY: I hear you. I suppose I just mean that this whole thing feels a little bit like revenge for a shit marriage.

ALICE: I'll tell you what I find the hardest thing to swallow about all of this: the embryos.

TOBY: Yes, I'd forgotten about that part.

ALICE: Yeah, they got Cole to write a letter to the clinic storing Mel and Cole's embryos asking for them to be destroyed, which is what Mel had wanted since they split.

TOBY: That's really sick.

ALICE: I know.

TOBY: You know what, whoever is wrong or right in all of this, I don't think I'd like to go for a pint with any of them.

ALICE: It would be a hard no from me as well. ·

WHATSAPP

Tequila Fridays

mind blown   Dais

in a good way though   Min

v confusing   Dais

it's not. women live under the threat of male violence 24/7. lennie etc have highlighted this problem in the most brilliant way and got everyone talking. it's epic.   Min

solidarity to them . . . it's the funniest thing I've seen in a long time. all the politicians are falling over themselves tryna figure out which side to be on   pookie

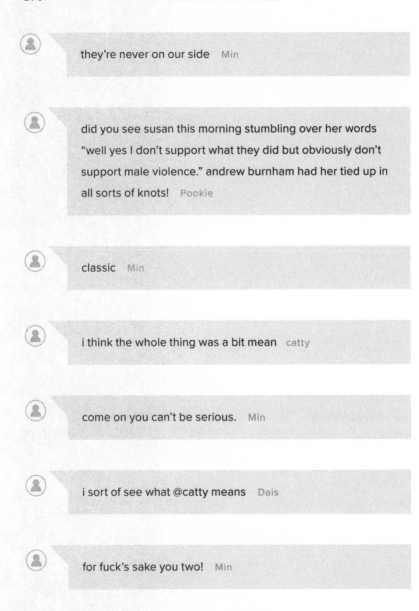

they're never on our side   Min

did you see susan this morning stumbling over her words "well yes I don't support what they did but obviously don't support male violence." andrew burnham had her tied up in all sorts of knots!   Pookie

classic   Min

i think the whole thing was a bit mean   catty

come on you can't be serious.   Min

i sort of see what @catty means   Dais

for fuck's sake you two!   Min

playing around with a man's life like that   Dais

our lives have been played around with since the beginning of time and they didn't let anything bad happen to him   Min

i'm still coming to the march on Saturday   Dais

yeah me too   Catty

heard a rumor Molly & Phoebe might make an appearance   Min

shit, no way. i saw they've both got nearly a million followers on insta now   Dais

their mission is complete   Min

APRIL 26

THE GUARDIAN

A Tale of Two Trials

BY SARAH SMITH

The trial of Leonora Baxter, 41, better known as the artist Lennie B; Melanie Connelly, 44; Molly Patterson, 24; and Phoebe Canton, 24, ended today. All four were charged with wasting police time and perverting the course of justice after a stunt that saw Ms. Patterson and Ms. Canton go into hiding in the middle of a 365-mile charity walk along the South Coast of England, that began in December last year.

Their disappearance sparked a massive police hunt and widespread media coverage, only for the two women to emerge unharmed in Lennie B's cottage on the South Coast on January 10 this year. During the course of the trial, it emerged that they had spent the time they were "missing" hiding out in Lennie B's London flat.

The whole thing had in fact been a piece of performance art, as Lennie B stated in her evidence. Their aim was to highlight the epidemic of violence against women, a point that has been somewhat muddied by the fact that they coerced Melanie Connelly's ex-husband, Cole Simmonds, into unwittingly participating in their scheme.

For a while Mr. Simmonds was the prime suspect in the girls' disappearance after a hair belonging to Molly was found in his outhouse. Ms. Baxter also entered into a false relationship with him and persuaded him to agree to the destruction of three embryos that he and Ms. Connelly had on ice. Neither point is part of the criminal investigation, but both were heavily referenced in the trial.

Prosecution barrister Charles Dunbar stated that the women appeared to be meting out a form of renegade justice against Mr. Simmonds. Although, in her testimony, Ms. Baxter refuted this description, saying instead that Mr. Simmonds was "a perfect representation of the type of man who believes that nothing is ever his responsibility. Men like Cole have not only made the world believe they're good, they believe themselves to be good. They are hiding in plain sight, and we all chose to look the other way."

Amazingly, the story doesn't end there. Another trial with many of the same protagonists has also been enthralling the nation, pouring more dirt into already very muddied waters. Just after Ms. Patterson and Ms. Canton went missing, Laura Perkins, 43, accused Mr. Simmonds of raping her in 2002, when they were both nineteen-year-old students. The charges were vigorously denied by Mr. Simmonds.

Ms. Perkins and Mr. Simmonds had been dating in the months leading up to the alleged attack. Ms. Perkins stated that when she ended the relationship Mr. Simmonds found it hard to accept. She said that he bombarded her with messages and presents and she often found him waiting outside her room. On the night in question, they had been to the same party but left separately and she woke to find him standing over her bed. Ms. Perkins's lawyer, Claire Bowers, did not challenge that Ms. Perkins did not actively say no, in fact no speech passed between them at all. She did however challenge Mr. Simmonds's assertation that Ms. Perkins was a willing participant in any sex game and stated that no speech equals no consent.

Ms. Connelly's testimony followed straight after Ms. Perkins's and proved to be damning. She claimed that she had been the victim of coercive control through-out her seven-year relationship with Mr. Simmonds. She also stated that Mr. Simmonds can only have sex while role-playing as an intruder and rapist, breaking into the couples' apartment, and often tying her up. In her evidence she claimed to have been so scared by this practice that her whole personality changed.

Judge Fairfax, however, said that the "he said, she said" nature of the case and total lack of forensic evidence made it almost impossible to try. The case was dismissed after a few days and all charges were dropped.

In the first case, all four women were found guilty. During their sentencing, Justice Penrose said that he saw no gain in sending the women to prison, but still enforced a fine of £10,000 each, saying that their stunt was ill-conceived and in poor taste. Feminist groups have reacted angrily, stating that they have an action planned in response to these verdicts. The police have warned against law breaking.

The women emerged from court together this afternoon, joined by Ms. Baxter's daughter, Jasmine, and Laura Perkins. Lennie B, dressed all in black and wear-ing sunglasses, refused to answer any questions. Instead, Melanie Connelly, who also acts as Ms. Baxter's PR, read a statement on behalf of all of them.

"Firstly, we want to say that this verdict, and the one for Laura's case, are exactly what we expected from our justice system. Secondly, we want to address our treatment of Cole. We would like to make it clear that we will not be apologizing for it today, or any other day. We remain convinced that our actions were completely justified, not only because they've made women aware of another rapist in their midst, but also because they've started a con-versation around the very serious subject of male violence. We still have a long way to go. We've had enough of the angry men."

Mr. Simmonds has refused to comment.

INSTAGRAM

SAFE SPACE UK @SafeSpaceUK

We're posting a pink box today in solidarity with the shocking verdicts handed down in the last few days. Until the law is on our side or there's a change in the law, we are not safe. As a society we have to stop supporting the routes to misogyny. Women's voices must be heard. End violence against women.

[ID: Image of pink square]

#thinkpink #walkforwomen #reclaimthestreets #endmaleviolence #endpornography

JODIEMARSH

feel totally hopeless today. What will a pink square do?

PED44

We have to keep shouting. What Lennie and her crew did was nothing compared to what happens to women on the daily #thinkpink

FETUSRIGHTS

They killed three innocent children. They should be in prison for life. Better still bring back the death penalty.

PRECIOUSLIFE

abortion is murder. We need a change in the law.

PED44

Replying to @PreciousLife

you do know that forcing something inside someone else's body is a crime, right?

MENSLEAGUE

You seem to have forgotten that Cole Simmonds has been found innocent. What he's had to endure is what's criminal. I wish he'd sue them all, but he's too dignified for that. All you do is support their lies and crimes—does the charity commission approve of your stand?

SSTOWELL5

Haven't been able to stop crying today. We're never going to be listened to or understood, are we? First they come for our bodies, next they'll come for our minds.

THERIGHTSOFMAN

women have disenfranchised us, socially, politically, economically, and sexually. A reckoning is coming. The stronger sex will rise.

JUICYLUCY

We've always scared them. And since they can't burn us as witches anymore, they have to legislate against us. Time for a revolution #thinkpink

HTTPS://THESHAMELESS.COM

The Problem with Condemning Cole Simmonds

BY LEILA CONSTANTINE

Society has had a problem with female sexuality since the dawn of time. The Virgin Mary set an impossible and biologically ridiculous standard that's been hanging over women ever since. We want our women pure or not at all. Unfortunately, fourth wave and even radical feminists buy into this myth, although they will tell you they don't.

In the forty or so years since Robin Morgan stated, "Pornography is the theory, rape is the practice," we've been policing sexuality. The argument—that all pornography is misogyny, and with it, kink—is fundamentally at odds with the feminist ideals of sex positivity and sexual liberation.

Never has this discourse been more relevant than in the last few months as we've watched the Cole Simmonds case unfold. Lennie B is an artist I've long admired. No one can argue against her stated mission to end the endemic problem of male violence in our society. However, publicly shaming a man for enjoying BDSM is neither cool nor clever. Lennie B and her supporters argue that women who participate in power play are suffering under oppression rooted in the patriarchy, contributing to the same rhetoric of sex shame and respectability politics they claim to reject.

The problem is that Cole's wife, Melanie Connelly, seemed to verbally consent to something she didn't want because of an extenuating power imbalance in their marriage. But the specific circumstances of Melanie and Cole's sexual and romantic relationship are no reason to condemn an entire community or practice, neither of which is inherently harmful. By demonizing Cole simply for his desire, instead of beginning a nuanced discussion about how established power dynamics—such as gender—can influence consent or the importance of establishing trust before exploring kink, we are toeing a dangerous line, and teetering ever closer to conservative, anti-feminist sexual moralizing.

THIS MORNING BREAKFAST SHOW

KAY: And now we're joined by Cole Simmonds, who is offering us an exclusive interview. Thanks so much for being here, Cole. You must be very relieved at the verdicts.

COLE: I am. But it's not a surprise. I mean, I knew I hadn't done what I was being accused of and I had faith in the justice system.

KAY: Absolutely. But how do you feel about everything now? How do you feel about your ex-wife?

COLE: Actually, she's still my wife, we're not divorced yet. And, mainly, I feel incredibly hurt and confused about the whole thing.

KAY: Understandably so. Have you spoken since?

COLE: Only through lawyers. I really feel like my whole marriage was a lie. Like I didn't know her at all.

KAY: I know this is a very hard question, but were the embryos destroyed?

COLE: Yes, they were. Which is, of course, the biggest tragedy in this whole mess. But I'm not going to blame myself for that. Looking back, I can see that I had been so gaslit by the time I agreed to it, I would have done almost anything they asked.

KAY: Are you planning on seeing Lennie B's show when it opens next month?

COLE: No. I have absolutely no interest in that. You know, she didn't even tell me who she was. She let me believe she was this little artist. I mean, if she'd have said she was Lennie B, I might have been a bit more wary.

KAY: Has this experience made you give up on love?

COLE: No, I remain an optimist. I still believe that there's someone out there for everyone. And I hope to meet my person one day.

KAY: Is there anything you'd say to Mel and Lennie, if you had the chance?

COLE: I guess I'd quite like to know why they hated me so much. I mean, I've thought about it and, basically, I don't think I've done anything wrong. They wanted to shame me in such a public way, but they're the ones who should feel ashamed, manipulating me and exploiting the public concern for two girls who were, what, playing some sort of trick? Eating takeaways and watching Netflix in a luxury flat while wasting precious police time and worrying their loved ones half to death?

KAY: Well, if our postbag is anything to go by, I don't think you're alone in those feelings.

COLE: But, you know, maybe we shouldn't be blaming anyone. Ironically, in lots of ways, I agree with what Lennie and Mel are trying to say. I mean, no one's going to argue that women have had a hard time historically. Perhaps it's no wonder some of them crack under the pressure of righting the wrongs committed against their sex. I truly hope both Lennie and Mel find peace and happiness one day.

KAY: Cole, can I just say how magnanimous that is of you. What are your plans going forward?

COLE: To go back to my cottage and work the land and get back to my life. I've had a few offers to write a book and, you know, I'm mulling that over, too.

Seeing as Lennie is still planning to put on her show, it would be a bit crazy for no one to hear my voice. I think it could be quite a cathartic ending to all of this. And, of course, hopefully one day I'll meet my person and we can have a good life together.

KAY: Well, again, if our postbag is anything to go by, you won't have any problems there either. Cole Simmonds, it's been an absolute pleasure.

SUNDAY TIMES CULTURE

"One of the Good Guys: A Study of Eroded Masculinity,"
by Lennie B, Now Showing at the West Gallery, London,
June 5 to September 23

BY THOMAS STERN

There aren't many artists who can inspire queues around the block, but I think Lennie B might have achieved this with her new show, "One of the Good Guys," even without the incessant media coverage of the past few months. Although it certainly helped. You would have to be living on the moon not to have heard about the trials or seen the social media fights in the comments section or listened to the debates on every culture show and news outlet.

One of the reasons for the queue is, of course, the nature of the experience. I hesitate to call it a show. It feels like an extension of what we've all been living through, every breaking news story, tabloid splash, and court case an essential part of it. Lennie B herself has said that it's a performance piece that will keep changing and evolving long past her involvement.

Visitors are only allowed in one at a time, for a maximum of twenty minutes, and only if you're over 18. Before I went, I thought this might be sensationalist affectation. I also remember thinking that since I'd seen so much coverage of these events already, there couldn't be anything more to be said about it. But, rest assured, twenty minutes is quite long enough; there is no way I'd let my children anywhere near the exhibit, and Lennie B has plenty more to show us.

When you get to the front of the queue, which took me just over three hours, you're let inside by a nice young person who tells you that the safe word is, incongruously, fear. If you shout it at any point someone will be with you in under a minute. You don't have long to prepare before the door is shut and you find yourself in total darkness. After a few seconds some lights come on that reveal you're standing on a set made to look like a street, tarmac below and high brick walls on either side. The heads of streetlamps each illuminate a single photograph. As soon as you start to walk, a soundtrack plays of echoing footsteps so it's hard not to feel as if you're being followed. The photographs vary between selfies of Lennie B on the cliffs, her mother, newspaper clippings covering the disappearance of Molly and Phoebe, group shots of the women who gathered on the cliff top to keep vigil, and close-ups of the coast-guard cottage. They are all bleak and desolate images that give the impression of lost lives and abandoned spaces.

At the end of the street, you emerge into a small, tight room, painted all black. A video is streaming on the wall in a loop, a video we must almost all know practically by heart. It is the footage of Molly and Phoebe revealing themselves outside Lennie B's cottage in East Sussex and making their now infamous speech.

From here you walk onto another street, similar to the first one, with the footsteps following you again. This time, though, the lights are pointed at what appear to be beautiful paintings capturing the magnificence of the South Downs landscape. Except as you get closer to each one you see that Lennie B has painted in lines of abuse that either she, Melanie Connelly, Laura Perkins, Molly Patterson, or Phoebe Canton have received online since the events unfolded. It is no exaggeration to say that I couldn't find one sentence that could be printed in a national newspaper. The abuse is shocking, filled with violence, threats, and misogyny. So bad, in fact, you feel sullied for having read them.

At the end of this street is a door. It's a wooden door, one you'd find in an old cottage and, sure enough, when you open it, you're met with a cozy scene. The off-white walls are slightly wonky and flowery curtains are drawn across a window in the corner. A black iron bed is covered by a cheery checked counterpane and banked with comfy-looking pillows. Wooden chairs on either side of the bed double as bedside tables, with small warm lights glowing on each. The soundtrack in this room is of a storm raging outside, wind whistling and rain battering against glass.

After about thirty seconds the lights flicker and then go out entirely, an eerie stream of moonlight cutting across the bed from the window. A rectangle of light suddenly appears on the opposite wall and then you realize you're looking at the same room, except from a different angle, as if a camera is filming you from the window. In the projection, there's a figure in the bed. The door opens and a hooded man walks in. The effect is so startling that I actually checked over my shoulder because it felt like I was in the bed and he was really in the room.

He approaches the bed, where he stands for a few minutes, before reaching forward. But, as he does, the figure in the bed moves and something drops to the floor with a metallic clang. The hooded man bends down, picks up a can and hurls it against the wall. The lights in the room then go crazy, as the soundtrack changes to women crying and screaming. I managed less than a minute of this before I stumbled toward the exit sign on the other side of the room and emerged into a big white room outfitted with a few chairs and more nice young people in West Gallery T-shirts.

The woman who had gone through before me was sitting in a chair, sipping on a glass of water, her skin the color of wax paper. The nice young assistants told me they'd had people faint or scream, and that almost everyone needs to sit for a few minutes after they get out. On average six people a day shout "fear."

I've thought a lot about what it means to be a good man over the past few days. I've always considered myself a fairly decent human. I checked with my wife, and she assured me I'd never done anything terrible to her. But then I thought about a boy I went to school with. He wasn't my best friend, but he was certainly in our group and we knocked about with him a fair deal. His name was Dominic, but we called him The Perv. He was loud and funny and much more daring than the rest of us, especially when it came to girls. He had a stash of his dad's *Penthouse* magazines under his bed and would regale us with tales of what he'd do to all the girls in our class. One girl in particular caught his attention and in the end she was the main feature of his quite frankly X-rated stories. Then he started to talk to her directly. He wrote her lewd poems, tried to walk her home from school. One time, he sat next to her on a couch and took out his penis. I know he made me and the rest of my friends uncomfortable, but we laughed along with him. I'd forgotten about The Perv over the years, but I've thought about him a lot since I saw Lennie B's show and how the girl in my class moved schools before we started sixth form. None of us ever spoke to Dominic about what he was doing and none of us flagged it to a teacher. It's about thirty years too late, but I feel deeply ashamed by that.

There is talk of re-creating this show around the country, and MoMA in New York has already expressed interest in an installation. I really hope this happens because I want as many people as possible to see it. Men especially should go.

As you leave the gallery you're given a small bound booklet, written by Lennie B, about the experience of making the show. I don't want to summarize it here because I think it's important you hear her voice. Please go and see what she's created and then please read her words. It seems to be time that we started listening to what women have to say.

THE WEST GALLERY

I'm going back to live in London, but I've decided to keep the cottage. Well, at least to keep renting it. The man who owns it says he doesn't want to sell, but he has raised the rent. Not that I blame him—he's done it for the same reason that I want to stay. The cottage has become a sort of strange shrine. There are always women walking the coastal path, leaving flowers and candles in the front garden, so it looks very beautiful when you crest the hill and see it shimmering in the distance. I'm probably going to have to get some security though, or maybe a caretaker. Some nasty graffiti appeared on the cliff the other day, BITCHES spray-painted in a lurid red, so it looks like blood dripping down the white rock. Eventually the sea will wash it away, but it could take years.

Sightseers and rubberneckers traipse past all day, every day, snapping selfies by the front gate or on the beach with the cottage looming over them. I've even seen a few people filming some weird dance routine that I can't be bothered to look up on TikTok, but Jasmine tells me it's trending. If I do get a caretaker, they should set up a café or print T-shirts or something. It makes me laugh to imagine what Cole must think about seeing his precious coastline so busy.

Mel has lost a few clients but gained others, me included. I thought it was better to ignore the press, but she made me understand that if they're going to write about me anyway, I can at least try to control the message. It made a strange kind of sense. Because what are we without our narratives? If we let others take control of this most important part of ourselves, I fear we'll end up like my mother, bloodied and broken.

And that's all Mel, Molly, Phoebe, and I were doing—reclaiming a narrative that has existed for too long. We did it for ourselves, but we did it for you, too.

Not that I'm claiming we got it all right. I often lie awake at night worrying about Laura. When I was lying in my bed with Cole panting over me, making a decision that could have changed everything, I thought a lot about Laura. Because Cole made a different decision when he stood over her. I guess he was younger then and less in control, but he learned something that night with her. He learned that he likes to wield power and, whatever he says, everything in his life has been about re-creating that moment, again and again, over and over.

Mel and I keep in contact with Laura and her husband. She has good and bad days. We didn't ask her to go to the police, that was her decision, but I also feel bad because I don't think there was any other decision she could have made. I said that to her a few weeks ago, that I was sorry for raking up the past, but she said not to be sorry because the past was so much a part of her that she couldn't have hidden from it for much longer. She told me one of the reasons she didn't go to the police when the rape initially happened was that she was sure she wouldn't be believed, to such an extent that she spent years telling herself it wasn't rape at all. She blamed herself for not being firmer with Cole, for maybe using the wrong language or giving off the wrong signals.

It is very important that Laura is believed now, despite the terrible verdict. I believe you, Laura. Lots of people believe you. Your words do matter, I promise. They matter so much more than Cole's, despite the fact that he is the one being listened to right now.

And before another person tweets me that they feel sorry for Cole, please understand that he wasn't in love with me. He was in love with his version of me. I never lied to him about who I was. I told him everything he needed to know, even my real name. But he didn't like that name, it didn't fit with his projection, so he insisted on calling me by another instead, which meant he never connected the dots. The truth is, he was only focused on what I meant in relation to him.

It was never our intention for Cole to be held accountable for something he didn't do. There is, anyway, quite enough that he has done. Cole is simply a representation, a symptom of our society. He's a manifestation of all the ways that we have to change, all the ways that we have to stop accepting outdated ideas of control and accountability. Violence against women will only stop when we address this issue, when we understand that a power dynamic exists that is damaging to everyone apart from a tiny percentage of men who have always held all the power.

I read an article the other day about how Cole has become an unlikely sex symbol. The woman who wrote it actually used that phrase, unironically. And then a few days later Mel sent me a poll on Instagram of what's hot and what's not. Cole was top of the hot list. I featured high on a list of "women most likely to get punched (if we hit women, which we obviously don't)."

I can't say I'm particularly surprised. Our stories have forever been filled with men battling the bad side of themselves but wanting to be good. And women have been only too happy to help them. When Bruce Banner becomes the Incredible Hulk, we tell ourselves that he doesn't mean to be violent. Men like that, they just feel too much, they're sensitive—amazing how different those words sound when applied to a man.

There's only one thing I'd like to say to Cole now: It's shit, isn't it? When someone does something to you without your permission.

I didn't mean for this statement to be so long, and I expect most people won't read it. But, if you've taken the time, then thank you.

I'm not going to end by pleading my case, which will no doubt annoy Bea, my gallerist. But I've just read it all back and I'm not sure I have to. I've given you my side of the story, which is all any of us can ever do. It's not a pretty story, but then again life is rarely pretty.

The final thing the cottage taught me was that there is so much to fear as a woman, but what people think of you shouldn't be one of those fears. It's okay if you still don't like me. I'm a woman, which means I have to expect to be seen as an unlikable character. Which, by the way, is different from accepting it. Because you are, of course, wrong if you think that. But I'm not unreasonable. I'll give you some time to catch up before I think up my next stunt.

ACKNOWLEDGMENTS

As ever, I have been surrounded by talented and inspiring women in the creation of this book. Without them all, it simply would not exist.

My agent, Lizzy Kremer, is always my biggest supporter, unafraid of asking the difficult questions. It is her incredible dedication to the process that always makes my books not just so much better, but actually saleable. Maddalena Cavaciuti is an exacting reader and offers invaluable advice. Nicky Lund, my film agent, is an amazing supporter and creator of dreams. And Margaux Vialleron and her translation team, who send my book out into the world and return it in languages I don't understand.

In the UK, I am incredibly lucky to be edited by Francesca Pathak at Macmillan, who is so brilliant at seeing the bigger picture in a novel and could not be more helpful and available, which, as all writers know, is basically the way to our hearts.

In the US, I have been entranced by the philosophy at Zando, and I am especially grateful to my editor, Sareena Kamath, who has edited with a keen eye for forensic detail. I'm also so honored by the fact that this book is part of Gillian Flynn's imprint. Gillian's passion for strange stories is a wonder and I could not be happier to be working with a writer I admire so intensely.

Thank you so much to Julianna Lee and Evan Gaffney for designing the fantastic cover. Covers are so important and this one exceeded all my expectations, so cleverly capturing the feel of the book.

On a personal note, thanks to my mum and dad, who I have always talked stories with and are both always very early readers of my books. And, finally, to Jamie, Oscar, Violet, and Edith, who make everything better.

ABOUT THE AUTHOR

ARAMINTA HALL is the author of *Everything and Nothing, Our Kind of Cruelty,* and *Imperfect Women.* She has an MA in creative writing and authorship from the University of Sussex and teaches creative writing in Brighton, where she lives with her husband and three children.